The Hermes Parchment

The Hermes Parchment

The umpteenth

Chronicles of Brother Hermitage

by

Howard of Warwick

From the Scriptorium of
The Funny Book Company

The Funny Book Company

Published by The Funny Book Company
Crown House 27 Old Gloucester Street
London WC1N 3AX
www.funnybookcompany.com

Copyright © 2021 Howard Matthews
All rights reserved. No part of this publication may be reproduced, copied, or distributed by any means whatsoever without the express permission of the copyright owner. The author's moral rights have been asserted.

Cover design by Double Dagger.

ISBN 978-1-913383-38-1

Also by Howard of Warwick.
The First Chronicles of Brother Hermitage
The Heretics of De'Ath
The Garderobe of Death
The Tapestry of Death
Continuing Chronicles of Brother Hermitage
Hermitage, Wat and Some Murder or Other
Hermitage, Wat and Some Druids
Hermitage, Wat and Some Nuns
Yet More Chronicles of Brother Hermitage
The Case of the Clerical Cadaver
The Case of the Curious Corpse
The Case of the Cantankerous Carcass
Interminable Chronicles of Brother Hermitage
A Murder for Mistress Cwen
A Murder for Master Wat
A Murder for Brother Hermitage
The Umpteenth Chronicles of Brother Hermitage
The Bayeux Embroidery
The Chester Chasuble
The Hermes Parchment
The Superfluous Chronicles of Brother Hermitage
The 1066 from Normandy
The 1066 to Hastings
The 1066 via Derby
The Unnecessary Chronicles of Brother Hermitage
The King's Investigator
The King's Investigator Part II
The Meandering Chronicles of Brother Hermitage
A Mayhem of Murderous Monks
A Murder of Convenience
Murder Most Murderous

Brother Hermitage Diversions
Brother Hermitage in Shorts (Free!)
Brother Hermitage's Christmas Gift

Audio
Hermitage and the Hostelry

Howard of Warwick's Middle Ages crisis: History-ish.
The Domesday Book (No, Not That One.)
The Domesday Book (Still Not That One.)
The Magna Carta (Or Is It?)

Explore the whole sorry business and join the mailing list at
Howardofwarwick.com

Another funny book from The Funny Book Company
Greedy by Ainsworth Pennington

The Hermes Parchment

Caput I	A Pleasant Invitation - For Once	1
Caput II	The Big Book of Big Books	12
Caput III	Murder in the Air	23
Caput IV	A Double Order of Colesvain	33
Caput V	Quiet in the Library	43
Caput VI	Beowulf Who?	54
Caput VII	You Just Can't Get the Staff	66
Caput VIII	Open the Box	78
Caput IX	Tapestry for the Pious at Heart	91
Caput X	It's All Greek to Everyone	103
Caput XI	One Book Short of a Library	114
Caput XII	Suspicious? Who Cares?	126
Caput XIII	Normal Service is Resumed	137
Caput XIV	Colesvain All Round	148
Caput XV	Devil of a Job	160
Caput XVI	Wisdom in the Woods	170
Caput XVII	Wisdom in the Dark	182
Caput XVIII	Wisdom in a Library?	193
Caput XIX	Blood and Curses	206
Caput XX	Over the Bridge and Far Away	217
Caput XXI	Witch Way?	229
Caput XXII	The Hermes Parchment	239
Caput XXIII	Help Arrives	248
Caput XXIV	Magic in the Air	258
Caput XXV	Kill Them, Kill Them All!	271
Caput XXVI	Cometh the Hour	279
Caput XXVII	Getting Away With It's Not What it Used to Be.	291
The 1066 From Normandy		301

Caput I: A Pleasant Invitation - For Once

Brother Hermitage, King William's own personal investigator, was at his happiest; he was in church, on his own, and no one was dead.

Of course, he couldn't guarantee things would stay this way. Being the King's Investigator seemed to attract death like the bottom of a cliff on a foggy night. And not the normal sort of death. Old people, nearing their time didn't simply drop at the sight of him, oh no. The perfectly healthy would find themselves suddenly murdered without a by-your-leave.

And then he would have to investigate it; frequently with King William or his awful man Le Pedvin, breathing down his neck. Why the two of them had to keep breathing when everyone else who came close stopped doing so, was not something he felt it proper to dwell upon.

But this was the Lord's day. Wat and Cwen, the weavers, were back in the workshop, having only stayed long enough in the church to be counted. Hermitage was planning to stay all day.

The priest of Derby was happy to accommodate Hermitage's devotions, although he was such a busy man he never had time to stay and debate the wide range of interesting questions that constituted Hermitage's head; mind you, it was a very wide range and the Lord's day only had the normal number of hours in it.

Once the rituals and ceremonies of the devotion were completed, Hermitage would sit in quiet contemplation until the next one began. He had even offered to assist the priest in any way that he could, but apparently, this would be unfair to all the other people of the town who might want to help; it wouldn't do to give Hermitage preferential treatment, just because of his habit.

Hermitage could see that, although he couldn't see anyone else actually helping at all. Like Wat and Cwen, most of the townsfolk made for the door as soon as they were able.

On this particular day, the rain was falling hard on the roof of the church, drumming the place into a noisy cave. Apparently, this meant that the townsfolk had to leave even earlier and more quickly than normal.

The priest was about his business somewhere beyond the back of the church, and Hermitage had the place to himself. An urge to get up and lock the doors so that no one else could come in was resisted as atrociously selfish.

He was in the middle of a fascinating consideration of why Enoch had only lived for three hundred and sixty-five years, while his son, Methuselah, lived for nine hundred and sixty-nine when a noise disturbed him.

He looked up and saw the priest coming down the church towards him, with a smile on his face. That was unusual. Even more peculiar was the fact that he had someone with him: another monk. This was not anyone Hermitage recognised, but the pair were clearly heading for him.

He briefly thought that it would be nice to engage with another brother, always assuming that brother was a reasonable fellow, and not like his old companions from the monastery of De'Ath's Dingle, where an approach in chapel was something to be very wary of.

Then he recalled his role as the King's Investigator and his heart sank. Surely not. Not in church of all places?

The priest and the monk drew near.

'Ah, Brother Hermitage,' the priest beamed his smile. 'I find you here, eh?'

That was a bit odd, the priest always found him here.

'I bring a visitor.'

'So I see,' Hermitage stood and gave a slight bow to the new arrival.

The compliment was returned, and the new monk threw back his cowl. He was a young fellow, having not many more years than Hermitage himself, with a bright and intelligent face that looked eager for their meeting.

'Brother Hermitage,' he beamed. 'I am Brother Martin and I must say it is a great honour to meet you.'

'Oh, dear,' Hermitage thought, but he extended his smile a little. 'I see,' he managed to say.

'I have travelled here from Lincoln specifically seeking you out.'

'Oh, I am sorry,' Hermitage couldn't help himself. At least he knew Lincoln reasonably well, not that his experiences of the place were altogether pleasant.

'Sorry?' Brother Martin looked a bit puzzled. 'Why would you be sorry?'

Hermitage had to admit that this Martin did look remarkably happy for someone who was bringing news of a murder.

'Well, you know,' Hermitage began. 'The reason people seek me out.'

'Indeed.' Martin was still bright and enthusiastic. Perhaps there was something wrong with him.

'Sit, Brother, sit.' Hermitage bade Brother Martin sit at his side. The priest was very happy with this and quickly skipped away back down the church to leave them to it.

'So, you seek me out?'

'I do,' Martin nodded happily.

'Even at the workshop of Wat the Weaver?' Hermitage knew that Wat's reputation was spread far wider than his own; it was spread far wider and it was a lot worse. He couldn't believe that a monk would come looking for some of Wat's old tapestries. The crude images were widely sought after by certain individuals; they were obviously very well made but were incredibly crude. No self-respecting individual would own up to any such interest.

'That did cause me some concern,' Martin admitted. 'But I am sure there is good reason.'

'Well, good circumstance, at least,' Hermitage said. 'And I have managed to move Wat away from his more disreputable images.'

'That is good to hear. But it is not for Master Wat that I came searching you out.'

'I can imagine.' Hermitage released a great sigh. He supposed that he'd better get on with it.

'So,' he turned slightly to face Brother Martin, solemn and serious. 'Who has died?'

Martin's happiness dropped from his face. It was such a shame to bring matters down to this level.

'Died?' Martin sounded lost.

'Yes. You've come to look for me, so who is dead?'

'Erm.' Martin looked as if he were being tested somehow, but that no one had warned him the test was coming. 'I don't know?' he made it sound like a question.

'Ah, I see.' Hermitage nodded to himself. He'd had a similar experience in Normandy when it wasn't clear who the victim actually was.[1] 'That'll be part of the problem then.'

'Will it?'

---

[1] Hermitage, Wat and Some Murder or Other; it becomes clear.

The Hermes Parchment

'It obviously makes things a little more difficult, but I'm sure that all will be revealed in the course of the investigation.'

'In the course of the what?' Martin now shuffled a few inches away from Hermitage.

'Investigation. From the Latin, vestigo, vestigare, to track.'

'To track,' Martin was now sounding very confused. 'Ah, I see,' he got it. 'Investigation. A fine word.'

'It is,' Hermitage nodded reluctantly. 'Appropriate, at least.'

'But, erm,' Martin was hesitant. 'Who is dead?'

'That's the question.'

'Yes, isn't it. Did you have anyone in mind?'

'Did I have anyone in mind?' Now Hermitage was getting confused.

'Has someone died?' Martin asked gently.

'I should think so,' Hermitage said. 'Otherwise what is there to do?'

'I wouldn't know.' Both monks were now frowning at one another.

It wasn't like Hermitage to want to get to the point, but they did seem to be dancing around one another. He could understand that Brother Martin might not want to talk about the gruesome details, but it had to be done.

'It is my curse,' he said. 'But also my duty. I sometimes wonder how it came to pass, but investigation of murder has become my lot.'

'Murder?' Martin almost jumped off the seat.

'Naturally.'

'It doesn't sound very natural.'

'As the King's Investigator, I have dealt with more than I care to think of. I am sure that I can help in your case.'

'My case? What case? Why do I have a case? And what does the king have to do with it?' Martin looked rather worried now.

Hermitage couldn't understand why the man was getting so excited about this. After all, he was the one who had come looking, it was no good getting all upset about it now.

'You have come to seek me out. Someone must have been murdered.'

'Why, for heaven's sake?'

'Why else would you want me?'

'Not a murder, that's for sure.'

Perhaps Martin was trying to block the idea from his mind.

'Come, Brother.' Hermitage tried to be soothing. 'You can tell me. I know it must be difficult.'

'No one has been murdered,' Martin insisted.

'Not that you know of,' Hermitage said.

'Not that anyone knows of. There is no murder.'

'Ah, Brother, there's no point keeping it from me, no matter the delicacy of the situation.'

'I promise you that no one is dead.'

'Are you sure?' Hermitage couldn't understand.

'I think it's the sort of thing I'd notice.'

'Maybe it's just a mysterious death, then?'

'Not even an un-mysterious death.'

'Not yet, perhaps?' Hermitage suggested. 'You have done well to come to me if there is a threat. Perhaps we can resolve it before any evil is done.'

'What threat, what evil?' Martin was becoming positively agitated now.

'The sort of thing I have to deal with, I'm afraid.'

'I don't understand,' Martin's voice broke a little. 'Why do

The Hermes Parchment

you keep going on about dead people?'

Hermitage could appreciate that ordinary folk might not be able to manage the reality of an unnatural death, but this Martin seemed to be confused by the whole business.

'As the King's Investigator, my encounters with murder have perhaps hardened me.' Even as he said this, he thought that he wasn't hardened at all.

'Ah,' Martin breathed deeply and seemed enormously relieved about something or other. 'There is no murder, Brother. That's not why I've come for you at all.'

'No murder?' Hermitage was now the one getting lost. What was the point of getting the King's Investigator involved if no one was dead? It would be a complete waste of time.

'No. No one is dead at all.'

Hermitage thought about this for a moment. 'You don't want me then.' He was actually quite relieved about this. Brother Martin had clearly come to the wrong place.

'Oh, I do. Most definitely, Brother Hermitage; there can't be another one.'

Hermitage had to admit that was unlikely, but if there was no murder then he should stay away. He shook his head slowly. 'I can assure you that you don't. Once the King's Investigator gets involved, death follows. It's become inevitable.'

'I am sure that in this case there will be no danger of that.'

'You don't know,' Hermitage warned. 'I have dealt with more murders than I care to think of. Everywhere I go, someone is either dead before I arrive or ends up dead soon afterwards. I wouldn't want that fate to befall you. Or anyone around you.'

'No one in this place is dead,' Martin pointed out, holding

his arms out to indicate Derby in general.

'They have been,' Hermitage said with grim seriousness. 'An investigation even fell upon this very town. A visitor wandered in, then there he was, dead.'[2]

'Good Lord.'

'Indeed. I have been all over this country and even to Normandy; and it's full of dead people. Just waiting for me. Or queuing up to die as soon as I get there.'

'I can see that would be a worry.'

'A worry?' Even Hermitage got agitated by this understatement. 'It's more than a worry, it's a danger. That's why I say you must not ask me to come to Lincoln. No one will be safe.'

Both monks were quietly thoughtful for a few moments.

'Surely, you don't really believe that people die because you are nearby?'

'Murdered,' Hermitage corrected.

'Quite. People can't really be murdered because you're in the neighbourhood. It must be because you are, what did you call it, investigating? Yes, investigating wrongdoing. You are going to it, not it to you.'

'Hm.' Hermitage had to admit that this was a very reasonable argument. Not that he was convinced.

'And there must be murders that happen, about which you know nothing?' Martin pressed the point. 'There could even be a murder happening somewhere right now. That one can't be your fault, surely?'

'I do tell myself that,' Hermitage said. 'Not that it's much comfort to think that people are still being killed.' He sighed heavily. 'I went to a weavers' moot once,' he said, the misery of his lot clear in his voice. 'A celebration of all things

---

[2] I'm not going to say, it might spoil the surprise.

weaving. And guess what happened?'

Martin chose not to answer.

Hermitage just sat and shook his head sadly. 'And I just happened to be passing through Shrewsbury once. A charming town, the very last place you would think needed a monk investigating murder. And it didn't until I walked through the gate.

'Would you believe I've even been to Wales?'

Martin did look impressed at that.

'Just in time for the murder,' Hermitage confirmed. 'And visitors from far-off lands?'

'What about them?'

'They travel halfway across the known world, get near me, and drop dead.'

Brother Martin looked thoughtful. 'Have you done anything apart from investigate murder?' he asked.

Hermitage sagged; it certainly didn't feel like it. 'In between murders, I come back here but no sooner have I sat down than another one arrives. Everyone brings them: Normans, other monks, merchants, you name it. Is Brother Hermitage in? Oh good, only we've got a murder here that he might like to have a look at.' He found himself feeling really miserable now, and he'd done that to himself.

Martin clapped his hands together and rubbed them vigorously. 'Then it is time you had some other function to carry out. I can see that doing nothing but deal with murder would drive anyone to distraction. I have come to you for another purpose altogether. One much more suited to your inclinations, I think, rather than your duty.'

That did raise Hermitage's interest, although he still wasn't convinced there wouldn't be a dead body in this somewhere; perhaps Martin was just trying to break the news gently.

'My inclinations?' He'd forgotten he even had any of those.

'Just so. I have come from the estate of Colesvain of Lincoln.'

Hermitage had heard the name. 'A supporter of William, is he not?'

'He is. And so he has kept his estates and his possessions. He is now making donations to the church. William expects it from his supporters, being a pious fellow himself.'

'Pious apart from all the murders,' Hermitage put in.

Martin ignored the comment. 'So, Colesvain is planning to give a great library into the care of the cathedral.'

'A great library?' Suddenly, Hermitage felt a lot better.

'Exactly. And I am making a catalogue of the contents so that we know what is where. Colesvain is no great scholar and so the place is a bit of a mess.'

Sorting out a library that was a bit of a mess? Hermitage felt as if he was being asked whether he was at all interested in popping into paradise for a while.

'And your reputation for the lexicography of the post-Exodus prophets is second to none. If we could persuade you to join our efforts, we would be profoundly grateful.'

Persuade? thought Hermitage. He'd been persuaded at the word "library".

Could he really afford to believe this though? 'And you're sure that no one is dead?'

'No one.'

'No shelves of books suspiciously fallen on anyone?'

'Certainly not.' Martin sounded quite offended at the accusation that the bookshelves were inadequate.

'Nobody quite old, about to die?'

'Not that I'm aware of.'

'Anyone with enemies who want them dead?'

'In a library?'

Hermitage forced himself to breathe very slowly as he let himself actually believe that this was happening. 'Brother Martin,' he said, as calmly as he could manage, even though he was jumping up and down inside. 'I would be glad to accompany you and do what I can.'

Martin beamed a smile. 'Excellent.'

'We'd better go to the workshop to let Wat and Cwen know about this.'

'Wat and Cwen?'

'Mistress Cwen is a fine weaver herself. They usually accompany me on my investigations, but this time they will not be needed. I can only imagine they will be delighted.'

Caput II The Big Book of Big Books

'You can't do it, Hermitage,' Cwen said. 'It's horrible.'

'What's horrible about it?' Hermitage was disappointed by her reaction.

'These perfectly innocent people in a library of all places. Do they know they're all going to get murdered soon after you arrive?' She then winked at Hermitage and gave him a broad smile.

'Oh, very funny, I'm sure.' He turned to Brother Martin. 'You see, even Cwen knows what happens.'

Brother Martin had been quite happy to go to the workshop of Wat the Weaver until he actually got there. As he stood on the threshold, it seemed that doubts troubled him. Doubts not helped by a grinning Wat, who greeted them with a rub of the hands and a disturbing, 'Oh good, brought us another monk then. This one will do nicely.'

Now though, they were settled in the upstairs chamber, taking wine and bread and discussing the plan. Hermitage had assured Martin that there were no tapestries about that would reveal anything he hadn't seen before.

Wat added glumly that every one of the characters in his new works had all their clothes on.

Martin had explained his mission to Wat and Cwen, who made it quite clear that organising a library must be lovely; for people who liked that sort of thing.

'How come this Colesvain has a great library at all if he's no scholar?' Wat asked.

'Built up by his family over the years, I believe.' Martin explained. 'His grandfather started it and his father continued. By the time Colesvain took possession, a librarian was installed who carried on with the acquisitions. I'm not sure Colesvain knows what he's got, and I am positive that he can't read anyway.'

'What a waste,' Hermitage sighed.

'Has the librarian not kept things in order then?' Cwen asked. 'From the way Hermitage goes on and on about librarians, you'd think they could organise the sea.'

'Unfortunately, the librarian, Elmund, was an enthusiast for acquisition, less so for the proper arrangement of what he acquired.'

'Was?' Wat asked with interest. 'You mean he's dead?' He gave Hermitage an encouraging look that there might be a death in this after all.

'Not at all,' Martin said, much to Hermitage's relief. 'He is now of great age though. Having built on an already fine collection, he spends his time perusing the volumes instead of cataloguing them.'

'Outrageous,' Cwen said, with a shake of the head. 'Who could imagine such a thing?'

'What manner of works have been secured for the library?' Hermitage asked barely able to contain himself.

'Oh, all sorts, really,' Martin said. 'From what we've seen so far there is everything from fully-bound volumes, to hundreds of individual sheets of parchment.'

'Hundreds,' Hermitage barely whispered.

'So, it's not just a case of making a note of the books; we also have to read the individual pages and record a title, if not a brief summary.'

'Read. Summary,' Hermitage sighed.

'And then there will be some searching to do as well,' Martin went on. 'Dear Elmund can't actually remember what he did with some of the volumes. He swears that he has a full set of the Decretus of Buchard, but we can only find the first fifteen titles.'

'Oh, my.' Hermitage was starting to feel a bit funny. And if he felt like this just talking about the books, what would he be like when he saw them?

'Are you sure you're up to this, Hermitage?' Wat asked. 'We know what you get like when you even see a book, never mind lots of them. It might be more than you can take.'

Hermitage thought that it might well be more than he could take, but he was going to give it a go. His courage was sound and his determination clear. He would tackle whatever great challenge the world put before him; even if it was a whole pile of books.

'How many pieces do you think there are in total?' he asked as calmly as he could manage.

'No idea, really.' Martin shrugged. 'Several hundred, I suppose.'

Several hundred? Hermitage was now overawed by the thought that the initial excitement he was feeling could last for many months.

'Do you want to go and have a lie-down?' Cwen asked. 'We don't want you getting over-excited.'

'How long is all this going to take?' Wat asked.

'Again, I have little idea. We have made a start, but have only really scratched the surface. Needless to say, the cathedral authorities have a completely unreasonable timetable.'

'And what is their timetable?'

'Six months, can you believe it?'

'No,' Cwen said blankly. 'Six months looking at books?' She just sat and shook her head.

'Six months.' Hermitage was almost standing up and sitting beside himself.

'I think we need at least a year,' Martin was serious.

'A year.' Hermitage was now in a complete daze.

'A year looking at some books eh?' Wat was clearly of a mind with Cwen that a few moments looking at a book from a distance would be quite sufficient. He turned to Hermitage. 'And what if the king wants you in the meantime?' he asked.

Hermitage looked at him and smiled, having heard some sounds but not discerned whether they were words or not.

'The King's Investigator business? Remember?'

'Oh, that.' Not only had the major dream of his life come true, but the weight of his duty had now been lifted. 'Well, I can't do it anymore, obviously.'

'Obviously?' Cwen did not sound so sure.

'Of course. I will be doing official work for the cathedral and for Colesvain.'

'Funnily enough, I suspect that King William will think he's a bit more important than them.'

'If William wants the work done, he will just have to find a new investigator.'

'I'm not sure it's going to work like that,' Wat said. 'I hate to drizzle on a lovely day, but if Le Pedvin turns up here asking for the King's Investigator, we're hardly going to say, "sorry he's busy reading some books", are we?'

Even the name of the dread Le Pedvin, William's right-hand man who killed with both hands, could not disturb Hermitage at the moment.

'You'll just have to tell him that I'm on official business.'

'He is official business. He's the definition of official business.'

'Well.' Hermitage waved the problem away. 'Just send him to Lincoln. I'm sure he knows the way.'

Wat looked over to Cwen, it being clear that there was no

way they were going to get through to Hermitage today.

'If he does come knocking,' Cwen said, 'you make sure you come and get us. We don't want you going off investigating on your own; goodness knows what would happen.'

Hermitage's mind wasn't anywhere near investigation at the moment, other than what went on inside the pages of a book, so he was ready to agree with anything. He just smiled happily at everyone.

'Lincoln then,' Cwen said. 'And for at least six months.'

Hermitage nodded from somewhere inside his stupor.

'What are we going to do without you?'

That did get Hermitage's attention. All his thoughts had thrown themselves headlong into books and libraries. He'd failed to work out that being in Lincoln meant that he wouldn't be in Derby anymore.

'I could go back to making profitable tapestries,' Wat said with a wry smile.

'Oh. Yes.' Hermitage was back with them.

'Thank you,' Wat said.

'No, no. I didn't mean that. I meant oh, yes, I won't be here.'

'Can't be here and there at the same time,' Cwen said.

'Well, quite. Oh.'

'You have to go, Hermitage,' Cwen encouraged him. 'Of course, you do. You know how much you like a book. And you see, six months will fly by and then what are you going to do?'

'I don't know.'

'Exactly. You can always come back here.'

Hermitage suddenly felt quite emotional. The excitement of being offered a library to play in had already put him off his balance. Now, the thought of leaving Wat and Cwen after all their time together was a bit more than he could cope with.

'I, er,' he said, suddenly unable to swallow anymore.

'Yes?' Cwen asked.

'I just, erm, need the, erm, privy.' With that, he stood and hopped down the stairs as quickly as he could, before he embarrassed himself in front of Brother Martin.

'Ah,' Cwen said as if seeing her baby take its first steps.

'Is he all right?' Martin asked.

'Do you mean now, or more generally?' Wat enquired.

'He'll be fine in a moment,' Cwen explained with a stare for Wat. 'We've been together for quite a while now, investigating this and that. Before he came here, Hermitage was at the monastery in De'Ath's Dingle.'

Martin crossed himself. 'I had heard that but wasn't sure if it was true or not.'

'Definitely true,' Wat said.

Martin was looking very puzzled, and not a little worried now. 'I have heard the most awful tales of that dread place.'

'Very dread indeed,' Wat confirmed. 'One of the dreadest I've ever been in. And smelly. That's where he and I met. I was on the way to Lincoln when I found him being attacked in some woods.'[3]

'Really?'

'And since then, that sort of thing's been happening all the time.'

'I see.' Martin's eyes were starting to wander around the room, perhaps confirming the way out.

'King Harold appointed him King's Investigator after he worked out who did what to some old monk called Ambrosius. And then, before we could get away, William turned up and did the same thing.'

---

[3] The Heretics of De'Ath; you must have read it by now…

'Did for an old monk?'

'No, no. Appointed Hermitage as his investigator.'

'I didn't know he needed one.'

'Us neither. But you wouldn't believe the sorts of things we've had to look into.'

'You, erm, all do this then?'

'Oh, yes,' Cwen smiled. 'Hermitage is very good at going "aha" at the very end and working out who actually did it. We're there to sort of line them all up properly in the first place.'

'A complicated business.'

'Frequently. And messy.'

'But don't worry,' Wat said quickly, spotting Martin's agitation. 'Hermitage never wanted to be an investigator.'

'Still doesn't,' Cwen added.

'He'd much rather be in a library dealing with books and stuff.'

'This Colesvain business will be a great relief. Investigating parchment instead of dead bodies.' The way Cwen said this made it clear that she'd rather do the dead bodies.

'But we've all been settled here for quite a while now,' Wat said. 'Anyone who's lived in De'Ath's Dingle is entitled to relax a bit. Moving out will be a shock, though.'

'I can see that,' Martin nodded. 'But it is as you said: once the work is done, he will be free to return.'

'Of course,' Wat agreed. 'But this has all come about pretty quickly, and Hermitage doesn't manage very well with surprises.'

'A bit of a drawback for an investigator of murder I'd have thought.'

'Absolutely. And that's just one of his drawbacks as an investigator of murder. He'll be much better off in a library.

The Hermes Parchment

Just promise no one is going to get killed.'

'I shall do my best.' Martin shook his head slightly.

'Actually,' Cwen said quite slowly, raising her finger. 'Haven't we got a bit of business to do in Lincoln?'

Wat frowned. 'Oh, that. Yes, I suppose so. No rush though.'

'But we could go now, as Hermitage will be heading that way.'

'I suppose we could.'

'Business in Lincoln?' Martin sounded a bit suspicious now.

'Oh, nothing like that,' Wat assured him. 'Although I have done quite a bit of business like that in Lincoln in my time. Very broad-minded folk in Lincoln.'

'I can imagine.' And from the look on his face, Martin could imagine but was trying not to.

'Some rich merchant wants a tapestry for his hall. I said I'd see him next time I was there. Not sure the hall's even been built yet.'

'A tapestry?' Martin inquired cautiously.

'Hunting and horses and that sort of thing, probably. Nothing out of the ordinary.'

Martin relaxed and turned as Hermitage came back up the stairs.

'Better now?' Cwen asked.

'I'm fine, thank you.' Hermitage sounded embarrassed at being asked how his trip to the privy had gone.

'Good news, Hermitage,' Wat said.

'Oh, yes? What's that?'

'We're coming with you.'

Hermitage just looked at them all. He was naturally delighted that he would not be saying goodbye to Wat and

Cwen as well as all the others in the workshop right now. The thought of long days in the library with Wat and Cwen there to share the excitement with him was wonderful. Then he recalled their general attitude towards literature and wondered why they would want to do such a thing.

'Will you find much to do in the library?' he asked. 'I suppose you could help as you do both read.'

'Good God, we're not going to the library,' Cwen said very quickly. 'We're going to Lincoln. There's some merchant there who wants a nice big tapestry.'

Hermitage frowned. It was one of his worries that if Wat and Cwen were left alone they might revert to old ways and old habits.

'A perfectly decent one,' Cwen insisted. 'But, as we've got to go there sometime, we thought we might as well come with you. Then we can say our goodbyes when we get there.'

Hermitage was delighted at that. It had been bad enough simply realising that he was about to leave. He didn't know what he'd do when the moment came to walk out of the door. Having all the time of a journey to Lincoln to get used to the idea would be a great help.

'And Lincoln's always been a good place for business, we'll probably be back again before long. We can pop in and see you.'

'And see the library,' Hermitage enthused. 'You could come and have a look at it now, and then look again in a few months to see the improvement.'

'Yes,' Cwen said very slowly, 'we could, couldn't we.' "But we don't want to", was silent.

'Oh, this is wonderful.' Hermitage beamed at them all. 'We could go now.'

'Need a bit of packing first,' Wat said. 'We can go in the

The Hermes Parchment

morning.'

'In the morning?' Martin sounded a bit worried about staying the night in the workshop of Wat the Weaver.

'It's all right,' Cwen said with the smile of a devil on her face. 'We can find room for you in the store. Just promise not to look at some of the older tapestries.'

'Or scream when you do look,' Wat added.

'Brother Martin will stay with me,' Hermitage said. Cautioning them both with a mild glare.

'Aha,' Martin's voice trembled.

'Come, Brother,' Hermitage said, standing to lead the way down the stairs. 'We shall find a spare cot, and then you can tell me all about the work you have done so far.'

'Er, right.' Martin followed Hermitage but kept looking cautiously back at Wat and Cwen. Wat didn't help by leering at him as he went.

'Ha, ha.' Wat rubbed his hands. 'We've got two monks to play with now.'

'You do realise what this means, don't you?' Cwen said when the monks had gone.

'That two Hermitages might be more than we can bear?'

'No.' Cwen held his gaze. 'Hermitage was going to this library on his own.'

'Yes, so?'

'And now all three of us are going.'

'Well done. You've kept up with the counting lessons, I see.'

'Brother Hermitage and Wat and Cwen the Weavers.'

'Is there a point?'

'The point is that we're all going to turn up.'

'So?'

Cwen simply shrugged insouciantly. 'It's now virtually

certain that someone is going to get murdered.'

Caput III Murder in the Air

This was one journey where Wat and Cwen were happy to tag along at the back and not get in the way. After only the first few steps, they concluded that they very much wanted to tag along at the back as they couldn't hear the conversation from there.

Hermitage and Martin were discussing the books and the parchments; continuously, neverendingly, and in the most appalling detail.

Surely, all there was to a parchment was what was written on it? Oh, no. Wat and Cwen only got a hint of the depths to which these two monks were prepared to dive before they hurriedly swam to shore.

Which animal it came from in the first place and what the preparation process had been? Could any properly be described as vellum, rather than parchment? When they got onto which stillborn animal had provided the finest quality material, the two weavers retreated at some speed.

'Good God,' Wat said. 'If I'd have known all this was going on just for a bit of parchment, I wouldn't have been so coy about my tapestry.'

'It's one thing getting the parchment from a pretty disgusting source,' Cwen replied. 'It's quite another to draw a rude picture on it.'

'At least we don't kill the sheep to get our wool. I think the weaving trade is positively wholesome now, compared to scribing. Who knew there was a trail of dead bodies leading to the scriptorium door? It's no wonder Hermitage became an investigator. He never told us any of this.'

'Weaving, in general, might be positively wholesome,' Cwen corrected. 'Your weaving isn't, or wasn't.'

'Yours neither.' Wat reminded Cwen that she'd produced her own range of tapestries that weren't discussed in polite company.

Cwen shrugged that there was no arguing with this.

'At least we didn't do a tapestry showing the production of vellum. That would have been quite revolting.'

From the drifting words coming back to them, the conversation ahead had moved on to a very excited exchange about the fact that some of the very old material in this library was actually written on something called papyrus.

As far as Wat could make out, this was some sort of reed. From his knowledge of reeds as long thin things that grew in rivers, he could only conclude that this would make the writing very difficult to read; and wouldn't the ink get wet?

He imagined that there was more to it than that. But he really didn't want to know.

'Newark for the night, then,' he said, as he and Cwen walked on. 'Be in Lincoln tomorrow.'

'Fine,' Cwen agreed. 'Where do you think the murder's going to happen then?'

'Oh, do stop going on about murder. You're worse than Hermitage. At least he lives in fear of one happening, you seem to be looking forward to it. This is nothing to do with his investigations. He's having a nice time thinking about books and he's going to a library. No one is going to get murdered.'

'Pah,' Cwen dismissed that nonsense. 'Could be Newark. We may not even get as far as this library before someone meets their end.'

Wat tried to ignore her. 'We'll just find some comfortable lodgings and enjoy a nice quiet evening.'

'With those two?'

The Hermes Parchment

'We don't have to sit with them.'

'We may not get a choice.'

'We'll start talking about the old tapestries; they'll soon move away.'

'So,' Cwen was not giving up. 'What do you reckon? The landlord of the lodgings?'

'What about him?' Wat looked a bit lost.

'Killed over some debt, perhaps? Or another guest? A mysterious fellow with a dark past he won't talk about, suddenly found dead in the morning with no explanation.'

'For heaven's sake.'

'Or a family is staying there. Son and father are arguing all night and then by sunrise the father is dead, and the son has a knife in his hand.'

'It sounds like it'll do you good to have Hermitage away in a library.'

'A Norman,' Cwen said with excitement.

'Where?' Wat quickly looked around, a worried expression on his face.

'Not here, in the lodgings. There'll be a big Norman, pushing everyone around. And then come morning he's dead. And it turns out he's a great friend of King William, so Hermitage has to investigate.'

Wat was looking askance at Cwen. 'I'm beginning to think there's something wrong with you. One too many investigations, perhaps.'

Cwen gave a careless shrug. 'You know that wherever he goes people die. I'm only thinking ahead.'

'Not everywhere. No one in the workshop has died, let alone been murdered in their bed.'

'But it all happens as soon as he goes out of the door.' Cwen nodded as if she had just expressed a universal truth that would only be revealed by time and events. 'And he's just gone out of the door. You'll see.'

'Maybe you could walk ahead ringing a bell. "Beware, King's Investigator approaching. Anyone who does not wish to be murdered, make way".'

'Couldn't do any harm.'

. . .

As they sat at their evening meal in the Newark lodgings, the four travellers responded to their surroundings in different ways.

Hermitage and Martin took no notice of them whatsoever. This was no surprise to Wat and Cwen, but they found it hard to believe that the pair of monks was still going on about parchment. In all the hours of their journey, they hadn't even moved on to the first book yet.

They had got on to the task of cataloguing, at least, but had got stuck on what should be recorded concerning the parchment itself, not even what was written on it.

They appeared to be in complete agreement that a copious record should be made of what material each document was written on, the problem appeared to be what order that record should go in.

From the short snatches of conversation that were unavoidable, it seemed that Hermitage favoured a chronological approach, while Martin was more supportive of an ontological structure.

There then followed a fascinating consideration of whether they might find some correlation between the two. The brothers were almost bouncing up and down in their habits as they reasoned that the nature of the material might relate

The Hermes Parchment

to the time of its production.

As a result of this utterly enthralling discussion, neither Martin nor Hermitage had the first clue who was in the lodgings with them.

Wat, on the other hand, was surveying the single downstairs room of the inn they had selected with barely disguised panic.

Cwen sat smugly on the other side of the table, her face was shouting out "I told you so" and it was clear that her voice would not be far behind.

There were Normans. How Hermitage had managed to ignore a group of six Norman soldiers was beyond belief. He normally collapsed into panic at the distant rumour of one.

These soldiers were making it perfectly clear that the country belonged to them now. That meant that everything in it was also theirs: including the inn, its ale, food and inhabitants. At least they appeared to be camped out near the Fosse Way somewhere and so wouldn't be staying the night; unless they felt like it.

The presence of these alarming figures had thrown a pall over the rest of the place, but it didn't stop the locals muttering in dark corners. Some of these mutterings, all in heavily accented Saxon, concerned doing things to Normans that would warrant investigation on the spot. Hence Cwen's smug look.

As if the Normans weren't enough, two locals were engaged in a very heated argument about something or other. They kept their voices low so that the soldiers wouldn't decide to get involved, but it was clear from the viciously pointed fingers that there was trouble afoot.

In another corner, a well-dressed young woman sat with her companion. This was a very large and very protective man, a long way her senior, who was doing his best to obscure her from the rest of the room with his bulk. He could be her father, wanting to avoid the attention of the Normans, or it could be something far more sinister. The woman did not look happy.

On top of this medley of muddle, the landlord of the place was having his own trouble. A drunk fellow, who looked like he had been in the tavern for at least a week, was taking the host to task over something or other. The landlord was urging quiet by holding his hands out and looking nervously at the Normans.

Fortunately, the drunk was slurring his Saxon words so much it was hard for a native to understand, let alone a Norman. There was something about "wife" and "recompense" but it wasn't clear whose wife, or whose recompense.

And then the door burst open.

The whole tavern turned to look at the priest who stood in the doorway. This man had a very angry look on his face, the sort of look that priests seem to be able to produce at will. It was also clear he had some very angry words to go with his face and was ready to shout them out for all to hear.

He then spotted that the majority of his audience was Norman and managed, with difficulty, to swallow his words. He now looked delighted to be here and held out his arms in happy welcome to one and all.

'I go for the large man in the corner first,' Cwen said, as she leaned over to Wat.

'Who?'

'The large man.' Cwen nodded her head in the right direction. 'And furthermore,' she looked very thoughtful. 'I'd say the small Norman soldier, by the tavern door, with a sword.'

'What?'

'The murder. That little Norman, who looks like a vicious so and so, will deliberately fall out with the large man and then draw his sword and kill him.'

'Oh really.' Wat said with some despair.

'Either that or the woman will kill him first. She looks like she wants to.'

Wat glanced over and had to admit that the look on the woman's face slipped between nervousness and hatred quite readily. It could well be that she was being taken somewhere she didn't want to go, by someone she didn't want to be with.

'Or the two locals,' Cwen offered. 'Take their argument outside and one of them doesn't come back.'

'No one is going to get killed,' Wat insisted. 'This is just a normal night in a tavern.'

'A normal night with the King's Investigator sitting here.'

Hermitage didn't even look up at the sound of his title.

'The landlord looks like he wants rid of the drunk,' Cwen went on. 'And the mutterings about the Normans are not very friendly at all. It could be that someone gets enough ale inside them that they think the country would be a lot better with one less Norman in it.'

Wat just shook his head.

'And if that priest isn't looking for someone to kill, then I'm a nun.' Cwen rounded off her summary of the room.

'You're forgetting one,' Wat said with a smile.

'Oh yes? Who's that?'

'The famous weaver who might kill if someone doesn't stop going on about murder.'

Cwen just gave this a little laugh. 'You couldn't do it,' she smiled sweetly at Wat.

'Because I like you too much?' Wat offered.

'No, because I'd pull your head off.'

Wat shrugged that she was probably right. 'Can we just get through the night without anyone being murdered?'

'You'll have to ask this lot.'

Wat spent the rest of the evening nervously looking around the room, fully expecting any one of these people to suddenly leap up and commit murder. Eventually, a realisation came to him and he relaxed a bit.

'You're forgetting one key feature of investigation,' he said to Cwen.

'Oh yes? And what's that?'

'No one gets murdered while we're watching.' He held his hands out as if this made everything all right. 'It always happens somewhere else and then we find out.'

'There's always a first time.'

'What would be the point of investigation if we're sitting here watching while someone sticks a sword in someone else? We could all say who did that. Be over in a moment. Even Hermitage could solve that straight away.'

'If you like,' Cwen accepted this. 'We'll wait till we go to bed then, shall we? Turn our backs for a few moments and the death can be delivered.'

Just as Wat thought he had no reason to worry, he now had a new one. He considered this problem. 'That's easy then,' he said. 'We don't go to bed. We keep an eye on everyone here until they're safely away.'

'Safely away to get murdered,' Cwen agreed.

'I begin to see how Hermitage feels,' Wat complained as he looked once more at those surrounding him and worried which one was going to do what to whom.

The Hermes Parchment

Eventually, the evening drew into night and the various individuals came to the ends of their days.

The Normans decided that they had had enough of stinking Saxons and staggered off into the darkness, singing a song in Norman French that sounded very rude, judging from all the grunting that had to accompany each chorus.

The large man and his young companion relaxed considerably at the departure of the soldiers. The woman even took the arm of the old fellow and kissed his cheek. He patted her arm in return and they left to find their sleeping quarters. As they passed, Wat could hear her mutter something about her father not needing to worry about her, she could take care of herself.

The two arguing locals had had enough ale to conclude that each was the other's very best friend in the whole world and that they'd actually forgotten what they'd been arguing about.

The landlord had resolved his issue with the drunk, who had decided that being married to the host's sister was the best thing that had ever happened to him.

Finally, the priest had passed out in the corner and was snoring loudly.

Hermitage and Martin seemed to suddenly realise that the inn had gone quiet around them and looked over.

'I must say, it's nice to have a peaceful evening out of the workshop without some murder popping up to bother us,' Hermitage said with a smile.

'You don't know what you've missed.' Wat sighed.

Hermitage looked around the room with a puzzled expression.

'It's all right,' Cwen said. 'Nobody dead at all.'

Hermitage nodded happily at this as he and Martin stood

and stretched, clearly looking forward to a night's rest.

'Yet,' Cwen added when she was sure they couldn't hear.

As they all left the room, Wat leaned over and whispered to Cwen. 'Not a single murder then. I should have put some money on it.'

'We've barely got out of the workshop,' Cwen replied. 'Plenty of time yet.

'Well, if you're so sure that we'll get one, I'll know what to tell Hermitage.'

'And what's that?'

'That you probably did it.'

Caput IV A Double Order of Colesvain

It was the end of the day by the time they took the last few steps into Lincoln. Unfortunately, the last few steps into Lincoln were all uphill.

The entrance into the town demanded the breath-taking climb up Steep Hill towards the old Roman gate. Hermitage had taken this route when he first arrived in Lincoln with Wat. And he still didn't have enough breath to do the job in one go.

Merchants, townsfolk, small children and the elderly strode past him as he panted on the side of the road.

'You need to get out more, Hermitage,' Cwen said. She was showing no ill effects from the climb.

Hermitage knew that the life of the monk should be one of toil and service. And in a monastery, the toil would be hard and relentless. Unfortunately, the amount of toil available in Wat's workshop was very low indeed. The weaver himself was not keen on toil and usually paid someone else to do it for him.

Hermitage had spent far too much time sitting and thinking about the post-Exodus prophets and considering his slim volume of prayers. His only real toil was to walk to the church so that he could refer to the priest's biblical texts and unpick any particularly knotty problems he had come across.

Other than that, he ate and drank well, slept soundly and had obviously lost most of his hill-climbing ability.

After a while, the huffing impatience of the others persuaded him to resume his efforts and they advanced up the hill towards the old gate. Close to the top, the last remains of old Roman steps peeped out from hundreds of years of neglect and these did help the final yards. Passing through what must have been a magnificent gateway, but was now a couple of tumbling columns, the four of them stood in the open area with the old Roman castle to their left and the building site of the cathedral to their right. The old Roman castle had been thoroughly trampled upon by a new Norman construction of wood and earth.

The standard approach of the invaders, or conquerors as they now insisted on being called, was to force all the locals to make a huge pile of soil, on top of which they would build their wooden forts. They would then peer down on all the locals and throw things if necessary.

Hermitage noted that the development of the cathedral was no further forward than the last time he had visited. There were piles of building material around, a few holes had been dug and some gatherings of idle craftsmen had been established. It was these last that looked as if they'd be around for centuries.

'Where do we find the Colesvain library?' Hermitage asked. His exertions on the hill were forgotten as the prospect of a big pile of books filled his mind.

'His house is just by the North Gate,' Martin said. 'It's only a short walk.'

Martin gestured that they should continue along the now reasonably level path of Bailgate.

'Cwen and I will come back and stay here,' Wat nodded his head over to the building that was now on their left.

Hermitage recognised this as the Hill Top lodging-house; a place of disgraceful luxury that Wat had used as their accommodation the last time they were here. Hermitage had been deeply ashamed to be in the place at all, but his shame was soon defeated by fine food, wine and a very comfortable bed.

The Hermes Parchment

After his struggle with the hill, he was starting to think that perhaps a spell of true monastic life would be good for him; body and soul. Perhaps the coming months in the library would give him that opportunity.

The walk up Bailgate was not long, and they passed a variety of traders' stalls and wandering townsfolk as they went. The remains of the old Roman market were quite clear here. Stubs of columns projected from the ground and large pieces of what must have been a roof, lay scattered like rubbish.

Re-use of this old and very solid material was quite common. One enterprising soul, having realised that the huge piece of Roman stonework that had fallen across the path would be impossible to move, had simply built his house on top of it, using it as the foundation. His subsequent home, as well as being a quite peculiar shape, was now so fundamentally in everyone's way that people had to walk around it.

Hermitage could see that it wouldn't be long before the route of the road changed to incorporate the new construction. He was sure that the Romans would have been horrified.

Moving beyond the traders, the town quietened as they approached the North Gate. The Roman arch here was still complete and in regular use. A rough wooden gate had been built within its walls, presumably to halt any aggressors. It looked like it barely had the strength to slightly delay a flock of marginally agitated sheep, let alone an invading force. Still, the Normans were here now, no one in their right mind would be invading anything.

To the left of the arch, some humble dwellings had been built; normal Saxon shelters sunk slightly into the ground with low roofs of grass to keep the weather at bay.

On the other side of the road, the Roman arch seemed to melt into a new construction; a quite magnificent house. It was two stories high and had shining glass in the windows. It was nothing like a Saxon longhouse, even one belonging to the most magnificent earl.

Hermitage gazed at it with some wonder. 'I don't remember this being here,' he said. He had walked this way back to his old monastery at De'Ath's Dingle; he was sure he'd have remembered something as substantial as this.

'Probably not,' Martin said. 'When the Normans confirmed Colesvain as their tenant-in-chief, he set about establishing himself properly.'

'By building the best house in town,' Wat commented.

'Quite.'

'Using most of the Roman stone that could be moved, by the look of it.'

'And most of the townspeople to build it for him,' Cwen snorted.

Martin shrugged and dropped his voice slightly. 'As you know, under Saxon rule, the king's appointed thegn would have to pay craftsmen for their efforts, and perhaps use his slaves for most of the work.'

Wat drew the conclusion. 'But if you're a Norman tenant of the new king, people do what they're told or face the consequences.'

Martin's face confirmed that this was the situation.

'So, Colesvain forced the people of Lincoln to build his nice new house for him in no time at all.'

'Probably asking if the Normans from the fort would come and offer some encouragement if the work slowed.' Cwen shook her head at the situation.

The Hermes Parchment

'Nice house for a not very popular man, I imagine,' Wat concluded. 'So, how did his library end up here?'

'It had been kept in various churches around the shire,' Martin said. 'But when Colesvain's new house was ready, it was all brought here.'

'Hence the librarian's enthusiasm for reading everything,' Hermitage said. Wat and Cwen looked at him, clearly not following. 'If the books had been scattered, he would not be able to review them all, the travel would be too much. Having them all gathered in one place would be marvellous.' At least, Hermitage thought it would be marvellous.

'Then Colesvain agreed to donate it to the church,' Martin said. 'Hence the task before us.'

Hermitage rubbed his hands in glee at what was behind those windows.

'Come then.' Martin held an arm out towards the magnificent front door of the house, a studded oak construction that looked like it would do a better job at keeping people out than the whole main gate of the town.

He stepped up and hammered on the door with his fist, actually making very little noise at all. He smiled at the others as he waited.

'Is it locked?' Hermitage asked, wondering why anyone would bother to lock the door of the king's tenant. Only a mad man would think of walking in and stealing anything.

'There are many treasures within,' Martin said.

'Books?' Cwen asked, clearly thinking that they didn't count as treasures.

'Among other things.'

'And there is a man inside who forced the local population to build his house for him,' Wat said. 'If I was him, I think I'd keep the door locked.'

After several moments of waiting, the sound of bolts being withdrawn could be heard before the door swung cautiously open. Through a crack only wide enough for it, a pale-looking face appeared and considered the arrivals. It nodded as it recognised Martin and drew the door back.

The figure of a thin, but well-dressed servant stood before them. He was a nervous-looking fellow who quickly beckoned them all to enter while he continuously glanced up and down the street.

'I'm not sure I want to be seen going in here,' Wat whispered to Hermitage and Cwen. 'Colesvain's clearly not a popular man with the locals and if we're seen associating with him...,'

'What?' Cwen asked bluntly. 'You'll be tainted? If I was Colesvain, I'd be worried about Wat the Weaver being seen going into my house.' She shoved him forward and they all entered.

The servant quickly shut the door behind him. 'I was only expecting one,' he complained, giving the small crowd a worried look.

'This is Brother Hermitage,' Martin said. 'He has come to work on the books. These are his, erm, companions, Wat and Cwen, who were travelling to Lincoln anyway, so we shared the road.'

The servant scowled but seemed to think this was an acceptable explanation. 'They'll not be staying,' he said, making it perfectly clear that they wouldn't be.

'No. It will be just Brother Hermitage, as agreed.'

'Hm.'

There was no movement to take them any further into the house or to show any hospitality at all, by way of food or drink. The servant just stood, looking at them, waiting for

The Hermes Parchment

Wat and Cwen to leave.

'Right then, Hermitage,' Cwen said.

Oh dear, thought Hermitage, was this going to be the goodbye?

'We'll go and settle ourselves in the lodgings and see if we can find our merchant in the morning.'

'Aha,' Hermitage said, very quietly.

'We'll come and see you before we go.'

The servant grunted that he hadn't been consulted about that.

'And perhaps you can show us a book.' Cwen offered, clearly hoping that it would only be the one.

'Of course, of course.' Hermitage smiled. That was something to look forward to.

The servant took a step towards the door, clearly very keen on seeing the back of Wat and Cwen.

'Who is it?' A voice boomed through the hall.

The servant released a great sigh. Whatever was coming, he had clearly hoped to avoid it.

They all waited to the sound of a heavy footfall before a large young man appeared from the back of the house. He was very well dressed, in what must be quite a large quantity of high-quality cloth. Fine boots, delicate decoration on jerkin and a very nice length of cloth tied neatly around his neck and shoulders, said that this was not another servant.

Hermitage assumed that this must be Lord Colesvain himself, although he seemed a bit young. He certainly played the part of a tenant-in-chief, looking as if he had taken most of the produce of his demesne, and eaten it.

'The monk for the library,' the servant explained with a bow.

'That thing,' the man almost spat, which seemed odd, if it

was his library.

He now positively stalked up to them and gave the sort of glare only a noble can drop on his inferiors; the first step being the automatic assumption that these people were his inferiors - probably by quite a long way.

'They aren't all monks,' the man astutely observed. 'In fact, one of them is a woman.'

The servant gave a rather impudent shrug that this really wasn't his problem; all he did was open the door.

'I am Brother Hermitage.' Hermitage bowed. 'Brother Martin has brought me to lend what assistance I can to the organisation of the library.'

'The library,' the young man sounded quite revolted. 'All I hear about is the wretched library. Father goes on about it all the time. We've got the useless Elmund who could be dead in there for all I know. People from the cathedral keep turning up asking where their books are, and now we've got yet another monk cluttering the place up.'

'I hope that I can assist getting it in order before your donation to the church.'

'My donation? It's not my donation, you wretched monk,'

Well, that was a bit rude.

'It's my father's donation. Why he wants to donate something of such value to the church, I cannot understand.'

Hermitage was very pleased to hear that despite his rudeness, this young man, who must be Colesvain's son, thought the books of the library important.

'It's ridiculous,' the objections went on. 'The church is awash with money, let them buy the stupid books if they want them. At least we'd get something out of it then.

'Simply giving them away is a very bad idea. One of my father's worst, and he has a lot of bad ideas.'

'His son being one of them,' Cwen whispered in Hermitage's ear.

'Ah,' Hermitage managed to ignore the comment. 'You are the son of Lord Colesvain then?'

'Of course, I am. Lord Picot, son of Colesvain.' Picot clearly thought that Hermitage really should have known this all along.

'I do beg your pardon.'

'Yes, well, you had better. And who are these?' Picot waved a rather disgusted hand towards Wat and Cwen.

'These are my companions, Wat and Cwen. They journeyed to Lincoln at the same time, but are now about their business.'

'Wat?' The young man peered hard at Wat. 'Not a weaver by any chance?' He did a very good impression of a snorting pig with its head buried in a trough.

'Weaver?' Wat asked. 'Certainly not.' He sounded as if he found the suggestion deeply offensive.

Hermitage was completely lost at this and didn't know what to say. He glanced at Cwen for an explanation but only got a wink, which didn't help at all.

'Well, it's been nice to travel with you, Brother Hermitage,' Wat said. 'But we'd best be about our business, as you say.'

'Ah, yes, just so.'

'We will see you before we depart again.'

'I look forward to it,' Hermitage said, and he really did. The joy of the library had just had some of its shine rubbed off by Picot. He hoped that the son of Colesvain would keep himself to himself as they worked through the books.

Ignoring them all completely, Picot turned on his heels and walked away muttering. 'For God's sake, the whole place will be full of library people before much longer.'

The servant sniffed at them all and turned to follow.

'Happy family, then?' Cwen noted.

'As you can see,' Martin explained. 'Young Lord Picot thinks that the library should be sold, not given away.'

'It doesn't look like he needs any more money for food,' Cwen said.

'Revolting,' Wat agreed. 'Don't you dare let on that I'm Wat the Weaver. I don't want that lump pestering me, particularly as he's the son of the king's tenant. He could make things very difficult.'

'I'll do my best,' Hermitage said. 'It doesn't sound as if he'll be engaging us in conversation anyway.'

'He loiters and complains quite a lot, but never invites a reply,' Martin said.

'Still,' Cwen said quite brightly. 'At least we're building a nice picture.'

'Nice picture of what?' Hermitage asked, not seeing much nice in this house so far.

'The murder.'

'What murder?' Hermitage almost hopped on the spot.

'The King's Investigator's murder. It could be Colesvain. The people of the town don't like him, and neither does his son. Then again, it could be the son, he's just plain revolting, anyone might want to kill him.'

In the face of Hermitage's open mouth, Wat took Cwen by the arm and bundled her back out of the front door.

'What?' she complained as they left. 'I'm only saying.'

Caput V Quiet in the Library

Hermitage felt some disappointment as Wat and Cwen left, but also a bit of relief. At least he couldn't hear Cwen suggesting there was going to be a murder anymore. And the next step was the library.

Picot and the servant had left them, and Hermitage looked expectantly at Martin.

'Very well, to the library.' Martin turned and led the way into the house, following the route that the surly servant had taken.

Across stone floors and past very oddly shaped walls they went, until they reached what must be the very back of the place. From here they turned left, Hermitage noting that one part of this wall contained the head of a statue of a man. Obviously taken from a Roman piece, this poor worthy, who probably held a position of honour in the marketplace, was now propping up a house.

The statue looked as if it wasn't really concerned about this ignominy, but Hermitage found the sight of the thing quite disturbing. He just hoped that he didn't have to pass this way at night. Heads in the walls was the sort of thing nightmares were made of, and he didn't need any more help making his nightmares.

Moving along the back wall of the house, they came to another great door, the equal of the one at the front. Brother Martin pushed this open and led Hermitage inside.

It is not true to say that breath is really taken away. If that was the case, Brother Hermitage would now be dead on the floor of Colesvain's library. It can, though, be postponed for a short period, while the breather concentrates on something far more interesting. Hermitage had unconsciously asked his breath to leave him in peace for a few moments.

His face had also ceased to concern itself with holding his chin up, and the function of blinking was considering taking the rest of the day off.

Books. And parchment. And more books. And books with parchment stuck in them. And parchment with books on top. And all of it scattered about as if a wind had passed through that only disturbed writing.

'It is a bit of a mess,' Martin observed with a shrug.

Hermitage had seen books before, of course, he had. And he had seen quite a lot of them in one place. The Archbishop of Canterbury's own chamber had contained more books than he had ever seen before.[4] But they were contained. It looked as if all the material in this room had made a break for freedom and had been caught in the act.

Books on shelves turned their backs on readers. They stiffened their spines and challenged anyone to rip them from their resting place. Their message was, "read me if you dare."

The books in this room were throwing themselves wide like the gates of some bawdy tavern, saying, "read me if you like."

Hermitage could just reach out and touch one. Which he did. A small pile of volumes lay on a desk just by his side and he ran his fingers over their covers.

'Ah, yes,' Martin said, glancing at the desk. 'A start, at least. The Liber Gomorriahanus and some minor volumes on the subject of clerical sin. Simony, clerical incontinence, that sort of thing.'

Hermitage quickly removed his fingers.

'Elmund insists we have a copy of the subsequent letter from Pope Leo somewhere, but we haven't found it yet.'

---

[4] But he wasn't allowed to touch them in The Bayeux Embroidery

The Hermes Parchment

Hermitage started to feel faint and told himself that now would be a good time to start breathing once more.

He also managed to close his mouth and blink several times, having realised that his eyes were becoming quite uncomfortable.

'I think part of the problem lies with the churches in which the material was stored,' Martin said. He spoke as if rooms full of loitering books was the most everyday occurrence. 'We know that many local priests don't read anyway, so a lot of them would have simply considered the volumes an inconvenience. No effort was made to catalogue them at all. Then, when they were summoned back here, they were simply piled into boxes and despatched.'

Hermitage nodded as he struggled to take in the full scale of the room.

It must be at least fifty feet square, taking up most of the space of the house. He imagined that the first floor contained the living quarters, although why anyone would ever want to leave this room, he could not imagine.

There were shelves around the walls, every one of them stacked with books in no obvious order at all. A great fireplace sat in the middle of the side wall, empty of fuel at the moment. Odd tables, desks and wooden boxes were scattered about, each of them piled to overflowing with written material of one sort or another.

A window at the far end looked out over the highway and the arch of the Roman gate, but it was mostly obscured by more piles of books that had simply been put on the floor when the rest of the space in the room ran out.

There wasn't even a way to walk from one end of the room to the other without winding your way through piles of books on the floor.

'And it would have been helpful if we had been here to supervise the unpacking,' Martin gave a little sigh.

Hermitage was still unable to speak but he did manage to raise his eyebrows, but only one after the other.

'Colesvain ordered his churches to send all their material here in one go. When it arrived, the boxes were opened and the books taken out. Until we ran out of room, then they were just left in the boxes.'

Hermitage swallowed at the inhuman treatment. 'They were unpacked like this?' he managed to croak out.

'Oh, no,' Martin gave a rather hopeless laugh. 'Colesvain had his servants put them in order.'

'Really?' Hermitage could see no sign of order.

'Yes,' Martin confirmed. 'If I recall correctly it was "big ones on the right and little ones on the left."'

Hermitage gasped.

'Quite. And the "odd bits and pieces in the middle."'

Hermitage had not moved since stepping into the room but now chanced a small pace forward. He didn't want to frighten the books away, but so dearly wanted to explore further.

'At this end of the room we have started to organise according to subject matter, but the far end is still a complete mess,' Martin explained. 'We thought that a rough categorisation, to begin with, might give us something to get our teeth into. No point cataloguing a volume on healing or physick, only to find the next is a commentary on the gospels.'

'Well, quite,' Hermitage agreed that such a situation sounded completely ludicrous.

'So, take your pick,' Martin held his hand out towards the rest of the room. 'Be careful though.'

The Hermes Parchment

Hermitage glanced down the room, thinking that perhaps some of the volumes were piled too precariously, and might fall if disturbed.

'It is too easy to be drawn into a volume and find that the day has gone by and all you've done is look at one book.'

That sounded like a pretty perfect day to Hermitage.

'Better to simply look at the first page or two to get an idea of the content. We can come back to the detail later.'

Hermitage knew that was sensible, he just didn't know if he'd be able to manage it.

There was one thing missing from the room though.

'The librarian, Elmund?' he asked.

'Of course,' Martin said. 'How remiss of me. Elmund!' he called out into the room. 'Where are you now?'

There was no sign of anyone else in the room, so Hermitage assumed the librarian must have stepped out, or be off somewhere else, lost in his volumes.

'Hm?' A voice drifted out from somewhere near the window.

Martin nodded and led the way across the room.

There, behind a huge pile of books that had created a little room of their own, they found Elmund.

He was as Martin had described, an old fellow, who looked like he would certainly not have the strength to be moving large quantities of books around. He sat in a low chair with a large book open on his lap, his attention still firmly fixed to the words before him.

A long grey beard just touched the edge of the page on his lap, and the unkempt theme continued over his head, where hair that had clearly not been cut for many years, was bound into a single cord that ran down the back of the chair.

His bare feet were stretched out in front of him and it

looked as if they had been washed sometime before his last haircut.

To Hermitage's surprise, he was dressed in a monk's habit; Martin had never referred to him as Brother Elmund.

'This is Brother Hermitage,' Martin announced loudly.

'Hm?' Elmund did not look up.

'Brother Hermitage, who has come to help with the library.'

'Excellent, excellent,' Elmund said, although it wasn't clear whether he meant Hermitage or the words on the page in front of him.

'As you can see,' Martin said gently. 'Elmund is little help when it comes to organisation.'

'Erm, Brother Elmund?' Hermitage asked, nodding towards the elderly man.

'I believe not,' Martin replied. 'I suspect Elmund's old clothes simply fell apart and this is what he found to replace them.'

Hermitage leaned forward, without disturbing Elmund from his studies, and glanced at the large work that was clearly so engaging. If there was one thing he found more uncomfortable than a closed book, it was an open one being read by someone else.

This volume had both writing and drawings, so was perhaps a work on medicine or architecture. Or anything else that required drawings, really.

It was difficult to read without facing the page directly, but at least the script was clear.

'Oh,' Hermitage said and stepped back smartly.

Martin raised a questioning expression.

'Simon Magus,' Hermitage hissed quietly.

'Quite possibly,' Martin didn't seem concerned.

The Hermes Parchment

'The book Elmund is reading appears to be a treatise on Simon the Sorcerer.'

Martin looked around the room. 'I don't think we've set aside a space yet for similar works.'

'Are there any?'

'Bound to be, I would say.' Martin gave Hermitage a frown. 'Does it disturb you?'

'Disturb me? No, I don't think so. It's just not what I expected, I suppose.'

'All sorts of things have been put to parchment over the years. If the library was garnered more as a result of random acquisition than any careful system, there are almost certainly going to be some very odd titles.'

'Elmund does seem to be engrossed in it.'

'He's usually engrossed in a book. He says so little that I have no idea where his real interest lies. He just seems to consume everything written down with equal fervour.'

Hermitage could sympathise with that. A new worry did nag at the back of his head though.

'If you'd rather not deal with the more, what shall we say, unorthodox material? I suppose that could be managed.' Martin did seem a bit disappointed at this.

'No, no,' Hermitage said brightly. 'I would be no sort of scholar if I decided not to read material I disagreed with.' He left a slight hesitation at the end of this.

'But?' Martin encouraged.

'If there is content here similar to that concerning Simon Magus, there may be other works that would not normally see the light.'

'I am sure that there are. But we will simply catalogue them, not act upon them. I imagine that they will descend into the cathedral library never to be seen again.'

Hermitage didn't quite know how to say this. 'I'm not necessarily thinking about mystical or even heretical texts.'

'Really. What then?'

'Well, it's just that my time with Wat the Weaver has opened my eyes to a whole area of human interest that I had never considered before.'

'Oho,' Martin smiled broadly. 'I can see that the old works of Wat the Weaver would be eye-opening in every way conceivable.'

'I'm sure. Not that I've actually seen any works of Wat himself, but I have seen those by others. Briston the Weaver, for example.'

'I have heard the name,' Martin confirmed. 'Another illustrator of those parts of the human anatomy that are best left unillustrated. Together with some exploration of what people do with those parts.'

'Quite.' Hermitage felt his face redden. 'And I can only imagine that if such subjects were made the topic of tapestry, they may also be in books.'

'I see, Brother Hermitage, I see.' Martin relaxed and patted Hermitage on the back.

'And they really may not be the sort of thing that the cathedral would want.'

'Should we even catalogue them?' Martin asked.

'Well, quite.'

'There's no need to worry, Brother.'

Hermitage sighed his relief at this.

'No indeed. Colesvain has made his instructions on that particular area very clear indeed.'

'Well, that's good.'

'Yes. He wants to keep them all himself. We've started a whole section by the door. You wouldn't believe how many of the things have been written. And most of them illustrated in a quite alarming manner.'

'Oh dear,' Hermitage sagged.

'There are some books from the east that you simply wouldn't believe.'

If there was a spare space to sit down, Hermitage would have done so.

'But you'll get used to it. As I say, no need to delve too deeply into the content of every book. With those particular volumes, a short peek inside the cover is enough to make their subject matter very clear indeed.'

'Aha.' Hermitage was pretty sure that he didn't even want to peek.

'You have to watch Picot though.'

'Really?'

'Yes. He keeps coming in and borrowing them.'

'There we have it!'

Hermitage jumped at the shout from Elmund. Even Martin looked surprised.

The old man slammed the book on his lap shut and stood from his chair.

'Something of interest, Elmund?' Martin asked.

'Interest? Interest? Oh, yes. Something of interest.' Elmund's voice matched the rest of him; rough with age but cut through with enthusiasm. 'Who's this?' he asked, staring at Hermitage.

'Brother Hermitage. I did tell you, but you were deep inside the volume on Simon Magus.'

'Who told you that?' Elmund demanded.

Martin frowned. 'No one told us. You were sitting there reading it.'

Elmund looked as if he was about to deny this but then

realised that there was no point. 'Brother Hermitage? Odd name for a monk.'

'He has come to help with the library.'

'Help with it? What's he going to do?' Elmund sounded very suspicious about this.

'He is a learned monk; his work on the post-Exodus prophets is renowned.'

'Oh, I wouldn't say that,' Hermitage was modest. All he'd really done was a very few scribbles following discussion with anyone who would sit still long enough to go over the topic.

'He's not taking the books,' Elmund insisted.

'No one is taking the books. At least, not until Lord Colesvain says so. He is here to help us catalogue. Well, he's here to help me catalogue, more precisely.' Martin made the comment on Elmund's level of helpfulness quite clear.

'Hm.' Elmund still wasn't happy about this and clutched his current volume close to his chest.

'What do you have, anyway?' Martin asked.

'Eh?'

'You said "there we have it", and jumped up.'

Elmund narrowed his eyes. 'Nothing.'

'Nothing? It didn't sound like nothing. It sounded like a discovery.'

'Not at all. Just a, erm, reference, that's all.'

Even Hermitage could see that Elmund was being rather evasive.

'Reference to what?'

'Saint Peter,' Elmund snapped at them.

'Well, there would be a reference to Saint Peter,' Martin said. 'It's known that Simon Magus argued with Peter.'

'Over the question of simony,' Hermitage put in.

'Exactly,' Martin nodded. 'So perhaps the volume should

The Hermes Parchment

go with the section on clerical sin?'

'Or at least some note made in its catalogue entry that it contains reference to the subject,' Hermitage suggested.

'A very good suggestion, Brother.'

'I'll catalogue this one,' Elmund said.

'You?' Martin now sounded even more surprised.

'Yes.' Elmund turned and took the book away with him to the far corner of the room.

Martin shrugged at Hermitage. 'I don't suppose we'll ever find out what he's so interested in. Still, at least it's got him cataloguing. Be the first book he's ever done; I'm surprised he knows how.'

Hermitage accepted this but did look over at Elmund, now hunched over his book on a corner table, a fresh piece of parchment close by and a quill in his hand.

He told himself that this was a library, this was not one of his murders. He was not here as the King's Investigator and so he should leave suspicion at the door.

But he couldn't help thinking that unwashed old men who wore monk's habits and sat in corners reading books about magic, warranted a modicum of suspicion.

Caput VI Beowulf Who?

Hermitage had to be forced to go to bed that night. Martin assured him that the books would not be going anywhere, and it would be better if he was alert for the work, rather than dozing off in the middle of some volume; literally.

He had seen the reason in this, and reluctantly left the task he was working on and began to tidy up.

'What are you doing?' Martin inquired.

'Oh, just clearing things away.'

'Why?'

'Why?'

'Yes, why?'

'Well, erm, you have to clear away your work at the end of the day.'

'Not if you're going to begin exactly the same work in the morning. Sounds like a bit of a waste of time.'

Hermitage could see the sense, but his old Scriptorium master would have taken his knuckles away for private punishment if he had left his station at the end of the day without everything cleaned and put away.

'Sound practice in a scriptorium, perhaps,' Martin said. 'When there are many brothers all working together and there's no telling which lectern you'll be on the next day. But here, there is only us. I should leave it where it is and then you can start again first thing. If I recall, it usually took half an hour to get everything ready in the morning, before you could do a stroke of work.'

Hermitage nodded that this was true. It still gave him the shivers to walk away from an open book with a quill just lying on the desk.

He had already got through several individual parchments,

The Hermes Parchment

which turned out to be simple letters of no real interest, and had embarked on his first real book. He was very excited by the age of this, as it appeared to be a much older manuscript bound into a new cover made of very fine skin. His hopes had risen as he found that the content was all in old English;

"Hwæt! Wé Gárdena in géardagum", he read.

"Listen! We of the spear-Danes in the days of old."

He had high hopes that this might be some great history of events back in the mysterious time after the Romans had left. In fact, it turned out to be a load of nonsense about monsters and dragons and someone called Beowulf - odd name for a hero. There was no point making much of a catalogue entry about this thing.

So, he was prepared to leave the volume for the morning; then he could start on a new one. Momentarily he wondered if he might take a book to bed. He almost giggled at such an outrageous idea.

Retiring for the night with more contentment and satisfaction than he had felt for longer than he could remember, Hermitage settled for an untroubled sleep. For once, he couldn't wait to wake up so he could pick up where he had left off.

...

The first light of dawn was a bit late for Hermitage, he was already awake and sitting on his cot. He thought that it might be a bit rude to go into the library before the others were up, but surely they wouldn't lie in bed after dawn.

He focussed his ears to pick up the slightest sound of anyone moving about. At the merest creak of a board, he was out of his simple room and heading for the library.

There wasn't actually anyone up and about at all, but now that he had started, he might as well carry on.

He pushed the door of the library open very cautiously, just in case the whole thing had been some marvellous dream; he didn't want to frighten it away.

But everything was still there. Just as he had left it. The books were still scattered, the various piles were still piled, and his volume of monsters still sat with his quill by its side.

He ran a hand across his head and down the side of his face, wondering why his cheeks felt slightly unusual. Perhaps he had slept in an awkward position. Then he realised what it was; he was smiling.

With a rub of the hands, he headed for his desk.

He stopped suddenly, as he heard a grunting noise from the back of the room. Had some animal found its way into this place when the door had been left open? That would be awful. Animals had no respect for the written word and could do untold damage.

His usual caution was cast aside as he strode towards the source of the disturbance. There were books to be protected here. If he had to face a wild beast, so be it.

Behind the stack of books by the window, he found Elmund sleeping soundly. Well, not quite soundly. The man was grunting and turning on a simple cot that had come from somewhere. He clearly occupied this space night and day. At least that gave Hermitage some comfort that the library would be protected at night. Protected from what, he wasn't quite sure, but the principle was sound.

Elmund's sleep was clearly disturbed by troublesome dreams. The grunting noises were obviously some sort of discussion that the librarian was having with his night visitors. And it was quite a lively discussion from all the

The Hermes Parchment

noises and the thrashing that now commenced as Elmund started waving his arms about.

Hermitage stepped quietly away, not wanting to wake the man. He glanced back as he walked off, having some sympathy for the poor fellow as he struggled with his nightmares. He also hadn't realised that sleeping in the library was an option.

Back at his desk, he took up his quill and simply gazed about in continued wonder. He didn't know which volume to tackle next. And part of the problem was that he had a choice. He wasn't used to being given choices about what he did next.

He opened his inkwell and dipped the quill a couple of times, examining the tip to make sure that the ink had taken. He then tested a line on the back of his hand, concluding that the instrument was fine, and wouldn't need sharpening for a while.

Next, he drew up the sheet of parchment that was to be a page in the final catalogue and considered what note he should make about this Beowulf rubbish.

With a slight sigh, he turned back to the text.

Well, that was odd. A frown rippled his forehead as he considered the words before him. This was a much later chapter of the book than he had been reading. Several pages had been turned by someone.

"Ðá se gæst ongan glédum spíwan," he now read.

"Then the Demon began to spew flames."

He could only think that Elmund had been wandering the library at night and had leafed through the book as it lay there. Doubtless, the old man was interested in knowing what the others were looking at. It was clear that Elmund was like Hermitage; he could resist an open book about as well as he could fly.

Still, it gave Hermitage momentary pause to note that Elmund had left the book on a page about demons spewing fire when he had been reading Simon Magus only the previous day.

He supposed it was quite legitimate that Elmund's interest could be in magic and sorcery and such, but purely from a literary point of view. Hermitage knew that there were many books on the subject going back hundreds of years. It was not a proper area of study, naturally, but books had to be catalogued, no matter what they contained.

If Elmund was compiling information on this topic, Hermitage would have to make sure that the catalogues were connected somehow. A reference in one place would have to refer to one somewhere else. What could he call it? A "cross-reference", perhaps? He felt a frisson of excitement at such an exhilarating concept. He would have to tell Martin about it. He felt an urge to rush upstairs and wake the man now, but maybe it should wait until he was up.

Back to this Beowulf character then. There was really very little to say about him, so Hermitage made a few notes, mainly about the size and shape of the book, as well as the language and a summary of the topic. "Child's story" seemed to fit the bill.

Now, what next?'

'Ah!' he cried out at the tap on his shoulder that was completely unexpected. He turned and saw Elmund leaning over him.

'Oh, good morning Elmund. You startled me.'

'Startled, eh?' Elmund said as if this was a confession of some sort.

'Yes, I thought you were asleep.'

The Hermes Parchment

'I was,' Elmund said, lending the words an unjustified aura of mystery. 'Dreaming, I was.' He looked at Hermitage with eyes wider than was really necessary.

'Oh, erm, good.'

'Reading the book then?' Elmund moved his eyes to the volume of Beowulf.

'Oh, no,' Hermitage shook his head. 'There's nothing of real interest here. Just some tale to amuse folk around the campfire.'

'Is that right?'

'Well, yes. Do you think there's more to it?'

'Oh, no,' Elmund said in a light and casual tone. 'Nothing at all.'

Hermitage considered the book again and wondered if something else might be hidden within its pages. It was not uncommon to find different books contained within the same binding. After all, binding a book was an expensive process; you might as well get as much between two covers as you could. He gave himself a note to check all the books in future.

'Thank you, Elmund.' he said. 'I shall make sure I quickly check that all the pages are consistent.'

Elmund scowled at him as if that wasn't what he'd meant at all.

As Hermitage had not the first clue what the librarian meant, he had nothing to say.

He couldn't take the discussion any further as the door opened and Martin arrived; not that he had any idea where the discussion could go, or even if it was a discussion at all.

'Ah, good morning, Brother,' Hermitage called. 'I have just had a marvellous idea for the connection of references across different catalogues.'

'That does sound intriguing.' Martin didn't sound

particularly intrigued. 'But I am afraid we have another issue to deal with just at the moment.'

Another issue? Hermitage thought. Had more books arrived? That would be wonderful.

'The representative of the cathedral is coming to see how we progress.'

'Bah!' Elmund almost spat on the floor. He waved his arms in the air and stomped back to his lair behind the books.

'Is this a problem?' Hermitage asked.

'It's always a problem,' Martin said with a heavy sigh. He came across the room and joined Hermitage at his desk. He could not help but cast an eye on the volume Hermitage was working on.

'Some nonsense tale called Beowulf,' Hermitage explained.

'Never heard of it.'

'I'm not surprised. And once we've catalogued it, I don't think anyone will hear of it again.'

'Ah, like that, then?'

'Complete waste of parchment. But it is quite old, so we'd better preserve it.' Hermitage knew perfectly well that you preserved all books, no matter what they had in them. 'But it was Beowulf that gave me the referencing idea I was talking about.'

'Ah, yes. But we must review that later.'

'This cathedral representative?'

'Just so. Obviously, our work here has only just started, and it will be many months before we are complete. That doesn't seem to stop the cathedral demanding that we work quicker and pass over material as soon as possible.'

Hermitage shook his head in sad sympathy. 'And he is coming today?'

'She is.'

The Hermes Parchment

'She?' Hermitage had naturally assumed that this cathedral representative would be a cleric of some sort. He supposed that it could be a nun.

Hermitage knew that he was as mild-mannered a fellow as he had ever come across. No one else he ever met seemed as mild-mannered as he found himself to be. He thought the best of everyone and gave them the benefit of any doubt available; a major failing for an investigator of murder, as Wat kept telling him.

Despite all that, he did not care for nuns. He had several bad experiences to call upon, and never held out any hope that the next encounter would be a good one.

'By the name of Ardith.'

'Ardith,' Hermitage considered the meaning of the name. 'The one fighting a good war?'

'She does that well.'

'Sister Ardith?'

'No, she's no nun.'

Well, that was a relief.

'She's an organiser, apparently.'

That didn't sound much better. 'Organiser?' Hermitage puzzled over the word. 'From the Latin organizatus or perhaps organum, an instrument of implementation?'

'She's certainly that.'

'What does she organise, then?'

'Everything. Everything and everyone. And Lord Colesvain's no help in stopping her organising us. Stand still too long and you'll be organised before you know what's happened.'

A grumbling noise emerged from Elmund's direction.

'I think our librarian is the only time she met her match. And then it only really ended in stalemate. They've taken to just avoiding one another.'

'Why is she coming now?'

'She's probably heard of your arrival and expects things to speed up. She's already convinced that she could have had the job done by now if she was doing it.'

'But she's not a librarian?'

'Lord, no. Some reading, but not much. Probably thinks books are a distraction from organising things.'

'Oh dear,' Hermitage sighed. His idyll of choosing what to do and when to do it was coming to an end far too quickly.

'We'll just have to listen to what she wants and deal with her accordingly.'

'Do you know when she's coming?'

'It was the first news the servant gave me on waking. She tends to turn up with first light. Even her days are organised.'

As if someone had been outside the door listening, there was now a hammering on the front door, followed by the sound of the servant scurrying to answer.

'Let's get it over with,' Martin sighed as he stood and turned to face the door.

This opened to reveal the servant, who was quickly bundled out of the way by a woman who was all purpose. Her walk, her expression, her dress, her face. They all said that she had things to do and that if they knew what was good for them, they would get done as quickly as possible. Even her long hair was tied back in an organised manner.

She must be at least thirty years of age or so, but the restless energy within gave her the presence of someone much younger.

'Mistress Ardith,' Martin bowed. Hermitage followed suit. 'May I introduce Brother Hermitage.'

Hermitage gave another bow, thinking that two might

make a better impression than one.

'Yes, yes,' Ardith said as if introductions were a waste of productive time. 'So, where are we?'

'We continue,' Martin said, with a very slight edge to his voice. 'Much as the last time you visited. Was it only last week? My, my.'

'And what do you have ready for me?'

'Ready for you?'

'Books, man, books. That is what you're doing here.'

'Of course, we are.' Martin's voice was hardening. 'But as I have told you before, the material must be reviewed and catalogued. Once it has been done, the books will be ready for the donation.'

Ardith gave a great condescending sigh. 'I know that you need to review and catalogue. I am aware of that. And presumably, you can only do one book at a time?'

'Well, yes,' Martin seemed a bit confused by this statement of the obvious.

'So, once one book has been done, you can hand it over.'

'One book?'

'One less than two,' Ardith explained.

'You want us to pass the library over one book at a time?'

'Ah, you have it. Well done.'

Martin just gaped.

Hermitage could see that the working relationship between Martin and Ardith was not a good one. He could also see that transporting one book at a time would be a complete waste of effort and would destroy their ability to make a sensible catalogue. Ah, he had it.

'Cross-referencing,' he said.

'I beg your pardon?' Ardith looked at him as if he had just made the most disgusting suggestion.

'Cross-referencing.' Hermitage smiled and nodded.

'Is he all right?' Ardith asked Martin.

'It's quite simple,' Hermitage said, thinking for a moment that Ardith might think he was criticising her lack of knowledge. He carried on regardless.

'We need to cross-reference the books. A topic in one book may be covered in another. If we've passed that book over to you, we wouldn't be able to complete the reference properly.'

'What?' Ardith sounded quite annoyed now.

'Take this volume, for instance.' Hermitage said. 'It's something called Beowulf. An old nonsense tale of dragons and monsters and heroes and the like.'

'Fascinating.' Ardith did not sound fascinated.

'But we have found reference to demons in it.'

'Demons?' Now Ardith seemed to be much more engaged, even worried, perhaps.

'All very silly of course, but then we have several books of the bible where demons are mentioned and so we will need to make note that there is connection between the different works.'

'Your point being?'

'That there will be another book in the library with a reference to something from Beowulf.' He glanced down at the text. 'The people of the Geats, for example. There could be a volume in here that has the full history of those folk. If we let you take Beowulf away, we would never be able to add to its catalogue properly. You see?'

Ardith clearly didn't.

'Cross-reference,' Hermitage explained again.

The woman from the cathedral looked as if she was trying to come up with a counterargument to this, or even to understand it at all. Instead, she just pointed a finger. 'Just get on with it,' she ordered as she turned and stomped from the room.

'Brother Hermitage,' Martin said in admiring tones. 'Well done, indeed. Who'd have thought, what did you call it, cross-referencing, would deal with a troublesome soul so effectively?'

Hermitage shrugged that he was glad to help.

'Mind you, she'll probably spend the rest of her day working out how to get around it, so we'll have to come up with something else for next time.'

'She did seem alarmed by the thought of demons,' Hermitage said.

'She did, didn't she?' Martin nodded slowly. 'We might be able to use that; get some demons together for her next visit. They'll be better at dealing with her than I am.'

Caput VII You Just Can't Get the Staff

Their next disturbance was Colesvain himself.

The morning had been long and productive, and thoroughly enjoyable as far as Hermitage was concerned. He had put down the ridiculous Beowulf thing with some relief and moved on to a single sheet from a commentary on the Gospel of Paul, by someone called Arethius. He was sure that the name of this Arethius would be lost to history before long. Not only was the commentary incomplete, but it was also wildly inaccurate and just plain wrong in most respects.

Still, a catalogue was a catalogue and it had to go in. Hermitage briefly considered whether a catalogue of the catalogue might be in order; one step at a time, he told himself, don't get too excited too early on.

Picot sidled in at one point and took a title from the pile by the door, mumbling about wanting to just check on something.

It was after the noon meal that there was a great commotion in the house.

The servant ran into the library, gave it a quick look and then ran out again. Shouts could be heard around the place; instructions were issued and responded to and complaints were made and ignored.

'Sounds like the master's home,' Brother Martin observed without looking up from the text he was considering.

'Really?'

'Whole place gets into a complete panic whenever he shows his face.'

Hermitage was a little worried by this information. 'Is Colesvain a hard master then?' The only nobles he had ever had to deal with were difficult people; if being difficult involved death threats whenever they didn't get their way.

'Not at all,' Martin replied. He put down his quill and leaned back in his chair. 'He's absolutely fine. The problem is that his household takes advantage of his absence to pursue their own interests, instead of doing what they're told.'

'Really?'

'Oh, yes. Repairs come to a halt. The stable block he wanted built hasn't even got its timbers ready. No one bothers organising his personal papers or dealing with his business. And Picot spends all his time in his room considering exotic texts.'

'Oh, dear.'

'Quite. Personally, I find Colesvain to be one of the better nobles, but then I'm getting on with my job. Like any man in his position he can get a bit cross when things aren't done.'

'So why don't his staff simply do the things? If they know he's going to come back and berate them, why don't they get on with it?'

Martin shrugged. 'Lazy?'

Hermitage shook his head slowly. He was sure that he'd glanced at a parchment somewhere that appeared to be a treatise on apathy. Perhaps the staff might like it read to them.

The noise outside reached a whole new pitch, which Hermitage assumed was the actual arrival of Colesvain, followed by his discovery of the progress made since he was last here; namely none.

There was an awful lot of shouting after that, some threats got through the library door and made Hermitage squirm, even though they weren't directed at him. Eventually, there were some loud bangs of something heavy and metal being struck vigorously on the fabric of the building. This was followed by many scurrying feet and then the peace after the storm.

The door to the library opened and what could only be the figure of Colesvain entered. The king's tenant-in-chief shut the door behind him, leaned on it and closed his eyes. 'Good God almighty above and all his little cherubim,' he said angrily. Fortunately to himself.

Hermitage had a moment to consider the new arrival and "noble" screamed out at him. And "important noble" at that. Colesvain was wearing far too many clothes of far too great a quality to be anything but noble. If he had just got off a horse, Hermitage could only imagine that the horse was very grateful.

Gold dripped from the stitching of his cloak, the completely unnecessary tassels that hung from its hem, and in the form of a chain worn around the neck.

Gloves and boots were of the very highest quality, and there was even a cloth hat of the deepest blue with more gold stitching around the edge.

Colesvain himself must be about fifty but appeared to be in rude good health. His face was round, but not fat, and it looked accustomed to anger.

The eyes opened now and considered the room before him.

'What am I going to do with them, Martin?' he asked, as he walked over and took a seat by the empty fireplace.

Brother Martin had no reply to offer.

'And where's dear Elmund?' Colesvain called. 'Another of my staff doing nothing useful?' He shouted these last words as if he knew perfectly well that Elmund would be behind his wall of books, reading something. 'If my father hadn't appointed you, I'd have you out on the street with the rest of them,' he added. This still got no response from Elmund.

The Hermes Parchment

'You're almost as useless as that son of mine. I haven't even seen him. Probably for the best.' He took breath. 'And who's this then?' Colesvain looked at Hermitage.

'This is Brother Hermitage, the monk I told you about. He is very learned, and we have already made good progress in the one day he has been here.'

'Someone's doing something, then.' Colesvain said, with no other acknowledgement of Hermitage's presence. 'Found anything of interest?' His gaze wandered around the room as if expecting to see something other than a book.

'Brother Hermitage discovered a volume entitled Beowulf.'

'Beowulf? What's a Beowulf?'

'It is a tale of a hero who slew monsters and dragons,' Hermitage said. 'All nonsense, really.'

'Slew monsters and dragons, eh?' Colesvain looked thoughtful. 'Doesn't live around here, does he? I could do with someone to deal with my staff.'

'Er, Denmark, I think.'

'I suppose I could send them to Denmark, and he could slaughter them there.'

'From what I could discern, the tale was already old some hundred years ago.'

'Probably dead by now then,' Colesvain observed. 'Anything else?'

'Ardith has been round again,' Martin said.

'Good, good. And were you able to give her anything?'

'Well, no. The cataloguing of the library is going to take quite some time, even with Brother Hermitage here to help.'

Colesvain released a great sigh as if he was profoundly disappointed that the people inside the library were proving to be as useless as those outside. 'It's no good me telling King William that he can't have his books because you're still looking at them, is it?'

Hermitage knew from personal experience that it was no good telling King William anything at all.

'I suppose not.'

'So, get on with it.'

Martin considered the floor at his feet. 'We need to cross-reference the books.'

'You need to do what to them?' Colesvain sounded quite disgusted.

'As we look at each one, we make a note of its contents. Then, when we discover a later book with the same subject, we can make a note on the first one's catalogue. And vice versa.'

Hermitage nodded that this was a very good explanation.

Lord Colesvain was looking at them both as if his horse had started talking.

'So, if we've given the first book away, we wouldn't be able to do that.' Martin's explanation trailed off as he realised that Lord Colesvain didn't understand it and wasn't interested anyway.

'Give her the books,' Lord Colesvain instructed very slowly. 'As quick as you can.'

Martin nodded acceptance of the instruction. Even Hermitage could see that "as quick as you can" could still be quite slow.

'God above,' Colesvain swore. 'We could do with that Beowulf. Or any sort of wolf, come to that.'

'My Lord,' Martin bowed agreement. 'And how fares the estate?' he asked, clearly anxious to move the conversation on from the slow progress of the library.

'Out there, you mean.' Colesvain waved towards the window. 'Fine. It all goes well. A few of the old landowners still don't seem to understand that they don't own anything at all anymore, but they'll come round. I ask you. Huge tracts of land out there managing perfectly well, and my wretched hall servant can't even clean the windows.' Colesvain now scowled at the window he'd been looking out of.

'You,' he said, nodding to Hermitage. 'What did you say your name was?'

'Brother Hermitage, my Lord.'

'Hermitage?'

'An odd name for a monk,' Hermitage said.

'If you say so. Well, Brother Hermitage, make yourself useful and tell one of my wretched servants to bring some wine, would you?'

Hermitage glanced over at Martin, who nodded.

'Of course, my Lord.' Hermitage stood from his desk, making sure not to disturb anything, and made for the door.

'And if any of them say they can't manage it at the moment, you have my permission to throw them out.'

'Aha, thank you, my Lord,' Hermitage said, knowing perfectly well that he would be able to do no such thing.

Once out of the library, Hermitage looked left and right but saw no one. The only places he'd been were his room, the hall and the library, so he had no idea where to look for any servants.

They obviously vanished somewhere when they weren't wanted. There must be a room.

He wandered back into the hall and around the area of the main staircase. Behind this, he discovered a door he had not seen before. Pushing this open, he found a long corridor leading away from the back of the house. Presumably the servants' quarters.

It only occurred to him now that this house must have a

kitchen of some sort, for the preparation of the food he'd been eating. It would also need stores for food and fuel, as well as somewhere for the servants themselves to live.

All these practical details were not the sort of thing that impinged on Hermitage very often, and they certainly weren't going to be able to penetrate a room full of books.

He trod cautiously down the corridor, thinking that one of the servants would burst out of a door at any moment. Another fresh revelation was that there was probably more than one servant.

Once more, he told himself that he really must pay attention to the practical elements of life. And once more, he knew that he wasn't listening.

Carefully pushing one door to the side of the corridor open, he found the wine store. It was a small room with barrels against the wall and skins, jugs and goblets ready and waiting. He wondered if it would be easier for him to simply bring Colesvain's wine himself.

His natural inclination not to upset anyone told him that he had better do as he had been told. The master of the house would probably be cross that his servants were again not doing their jobs, and the servants would be angry that Hermitage was doing their work for them. There was no pleasing some people.

Leaving the wine store, Hermitage moved on down the corridor. Now, he could hear voices drifting to him from further on.

He ignored the next two doors, which were closed and quiet, and then came to a very well used entrance. The wood of this door was scuffed and damaged as if it was barged aside on a daily basis. This could be the kitchen.

If it was the kitchen, it currently had too many cooks. The

noise was coming from here and many voices were raised in argument, all at the same time. He couldn't pick out what was being said, but no one inside was very happy.

Doubtless, it was unpleasant being berated by your master for not doing your job; and even more unpleasant being found out. The natural response of any God-fearing Englishman was to respond to this sort of thing with profound contempt and hatred for the one telling you what to do. It was clear that the staff here were concentrating on their contempt, and not getting on with all the things they'd been criticised for not doing.

He knew how these things went. It wouldn't be long before the tumult died down and people would wander off, complaining how unfair it was that they were now being forced to do the things they should have done in the first place.

Monks were no different. Attending daily orders was both a duty and a pleasure. Being told to attend by a prior or abbot made the whole thing much more irritating, somehow.

Such was the level of dispute behind the door that he was very reluctant to enter and ask for Colesvain's wine. If the master himself did it there would be no argument; Hermitage might get things thrown at him.

And it was most likely that all the noise was not even a dispute. The servants would be loudly agreeing with one another that their lot was awful, their master was worse and that it simply wasn't fair. Each would be vying with the other to make their agreement louder than anyone else's. Or one would have some particular point on the whole unfairness question that the others hadn't grasped properly.

The best thing to do was to wait. Let the tide of annoyance go out, and then he could make a cautious entry. Of course, he couldn't tarry too long. Colesvain was expecting wine, and he wouldn't wait all day for it.

He started hopping up and down on the spot as the time dragged on. There was no let-up in the volume of complaint from beyond the door and he really didn't want to step into the middle of it.

An instruction from a person of authority versus a rabble of difficult common folk? This really wasn't the sort of dilemma Hermitage was built to resolve.

He was just about to turn and go back to fetch the wine himself when there seemed to be a lull in the arguments going on. He decided that he would chance opening the door very slightly to see if he could tell what was happening. If it was bad, he would fetch the wine himself. If it was good, he could relay Colesvain's order.

Pushing slowly on the door so that there was a small enough gap to see through, Hermitage pressed his face to the space. Fortunately, no one inside had noticed the slight movement.

It was the kitchen. Pots and pans were hung around and the large fireplace with its glowing logs stood ready for the spit or the pot.

There were about six men and women inside that he could see, and probably more out of sight. They seemed to have made all their arguments and were now just standing about muttering, largely to themselves. Any moment now, normality would resume and the wine could be safely ordered.

One voice did speak up, but Hermitage could not see who it was. It sounded as if it might be a ringleader or one of the more senior servants, as the others all lent their ears. Perhaps he was going to sum up the situation and draw the only reasonable conclusion; that they all needed to get back to work.

Hermitage listened to the message and froze. He even stopped breathing. There was no question of him being able to move, and so when the servants came out of this room, they would find him standing there; and that would not go well.

Fortunately, there was another outburst of noise at the words of the leader, and Hermitage managed to use that moment to take two quick steps back from the door.

He still held his breath but was soon satisfied that he had not been spotted and that no one was going to burst from the kitchen to deal with him.

Not willing to turn away, he stepped backwards up the corridor until he reached the wine store. He considered this and what his next step should be. He could certainly not tell Colesvain what he had just heard, he would need to consult Brother Martin first.

Slipping into the wine store, he bent and filled a jug from the tap on one of the barrels, fortunately discovering that it was wine and not beer. He grabbed a goblet from a shelf and made to leave. He peered very carefully around the edge of the door and breathed out when he saw that the corridor was still empty.

Skipping as quickly and as quietly as he could, he went back up to the door into the main hall and slipped through this with an enormous sense of relief.

He could now breathe normally and he panted with the exertion of the last few moments. He even found that he was shaking slightly.

Giving himself a moment to calm down, he held jug and goblet firmly and returned to the library.

'Good God, I thought you'd gone back to your monastery,' Colesvain said. 'Where's the servant?' he asked, clearly annoyed that Hermitage was bringing the wine instead of the person who was supposed to do it.

'Oh, erm, they're all busy doing, erm, things.'

'Busy, eh? About bloody time somebody was.' Colesvain took the goblet and the jug and stood from his seat. 'Well, I'll leave you to get on with it. Quickly.'

'We will,' Martin confirmed as he stood and bowed.

Hermitage managed to give a sort of nod as he passed by.

Hermitage waited until Colesvain had gone and shut the door. He then went over to it and put his ear against the wood.

'What are you doing?' Martin asked.

Satisfied that all was quiet, Hermitage moved away from the door and sat opposite Martin. He even brushed some parchment out of his way, without even looking at what it said.

'I was just down by the kitchen,' Hermitage hissed in a quiet and urgent whisper.

'That's all right. You're allowed.'

'And I heard them.'

'Heard who?'

'The servants.'

'Complaining about the master coming back to his own house, I imagine. Disturbing their peace and quiet.'

'Yes,' Hermitage said, trying to look and sound as serious as he could. 'But then I heard one of them talking about what they were going to do about it.'

'Do about it?' Martin looked puzzled now. 'What can they do about it?'

Hermitage took a breath and held Martin's eyes with his

own, just to make sure that the message would get through.
  'They're going to kill him.'

Caput VIII Open the Box

'Kill him?' Martin asked, in a voice that said he clearly didn't believe this.

'I told you,' Hermitage wailed now. 'I told you that everywhere I go there is death and murder and killing. It's happening again. I've only been in the library a day and already the master of the house is about to be murdered.' He was still feeling very odd. 'At least I'll know who did it. The investigation won't take long. Perhaps I'll follow Colesvain around until it's done, then I can be a witness!'

'Calm yourself, brother,' Martin urged. 'What do you mean, they're going to kill him?'

Hermitage pulled up a chair and sat close by Martin. 'I heard them talking in the kitchen. They were complaining about their lot, as everyone does, and then it went quiet. I peeped around the corner of the door and could see them. One who was hidden spoke up. He said that there was only one thing to do; kill Colesvain.'

'Servants talking of killing their master, eh?'

'Exactly.' Hermitage was glad that Martin had got it. He was surprised when Martin laughed.

'Well, of course, they were. All servants want to kill their masters. It's perfectly normal. I should think it's a common topic of conversation in servants' halls up and down the country. Wouldn't it be better if the master or mistress was dead? Oh, yes, that would be lovely. No one ever does anything about it.'

'No one has the King's Investigator in their house at the time.'

'Brother, Brother. Surely you have been privy to the dormitory speculations about what would happen if the abbot died?'

'Well, yes, I suppose so.' It was common in monasteries for monks to engage in speculation. After all, once darkness had come and the orders were complete, there was very little else to do. Obviously, the truly pious and devoted would not reduce themselves to such tittle-tattle; but then in most monasteries, the truly pious and devoted were a tiny minority.

Guessing which monk would die next was a common theme, along with planning for what they would do in the morning when they all woke up; but discovered that the abbot hadn't. And the worse the abbot, the livelier and more detailed the planning.

'But this fellow sounded terribly serious.'

'There's usually one,' Martin got back to his work. 'The more serious they sound, the less likely they are to do anything themselves. They're the sort of people who want to encourage others to do evil, then stand by and watch. Or better still, be miles away so they can claim it was nothing to do with them.'

Hermitage started to relax a little in the face of Martin's lack of concern.

'And can you imagine what would happen to them if they did kill Colesvain?' Martin said, without looking up. 'King William's nominated tenant-in-chief? I truly dread to think.' Martin gestured around the library with one arm. 'And I've read some pretty horrible things.'

Despite the assurances, Hermitage knew that this would continue to bother him. Martin didn't seem at all concerned, which gave him some confidence that the servants weren't about to slaughter their master, and probably everyone else in the house.

He would do his best to just add it to the stock of general worries that he always kept about him. He would keep an ear on the servants though. Perhaps he might warn them that their discussion had been overheard, by giving them a pointed raise of the eyebrows at the right moment.

Instead, he tried to take his mind back to where he had left off before Lord Colesvain had interrupted. He did wonder if it was now getting too late to start something afresh. Perhaps it would be better to get another night's sleep and then begin again. He gave a short laugh at such a ridiculous idea and stood to decide which part of the room to approach for his next task.

There really was no sense to the order of material at all. Fantastic tales, religious texts, simple records of trade, family notes: all of them jumbled as if they had been tipped out of a giant sack. There was no telling what he would pick up next. How absolutely wonderful.

He momentarily thought of Wat and Cwen, and whether they were settled in their lodgings. They hadn't come back to say they were leaving, so they must still be working in the town. Whatever they were doing, he was sure they weren't having as much fun as he was.

His mind soon returned to the library. A book or a parchment then? Which should he choose? He'd done a book with that Beowulf thing, then he'd done a few parchments. Perhaps another book then. Maybe, and he chided himself for such selfish indulgence, a great big one. The bigger the better. He rubbed his hands with glee and looked around the room for the very biggest book that ever there was.

Aha, there. By the door, there was a large wooden case that had clearly been dispatched from one of the churches. It was quite possible that the church had never opened it in all the years of its possession. Such was the size, at least four feet square, it must have taken at least four men to lift it. Hermitage almost giggled with excitement at what might lie within.

Someone had taken the lid off, just to check that it was books perhaps, and not dirty vestments, but then it had been left. Hermitage would explore.

He had been horrified to discover that some of the books in the place had been attacked by mice. Doubtless shredded to make their nests, the horror of such desecration was unbearable. At least this box was good, solid wood, and would be proof against the wretched creatures. Creatures of God, he reminded himself, but still wretched.

As he drew up to the box and peered over its lid, he noted that it was of very solid construction indeed. This had not been banged together from some left-over bits of firewood. This had been made by a carpenter. The corners were properly jointed, and wooden pegs had been driven through to hold the whole thing together. It was a lot of trouble to go to for some books.

Hermitage approved, of course, but he knew what the ordinary man was like. A fine box like this would be good for a collection of precious artefacts; but then to Hermitage, that's what books were.

It was probably the only thing they had available when word came to despatch their books to Lord Colesvain. In itself, the box was quite a valuable thing to have given away.

The lid had been put loosely back in place and Hermitage moved this to one side. It was quite a large and heavy piece of wood in its own right and he wondered about calling to Martin for help. He saw that his Brother was engrossed in his own work and so didn't want to disturb him.

He moved the lid over as far as he dared so that it would not tip off and crash to the floor. Then it tipped off and crashed to the floor.

'Sorry,' he called as Martin looked over.

Even Elmund stuck his head over his pile of books, before dropping down again when he saw there was nothing of interest.

'From a long-dead monastery named Rooksby, I believe,' Martin said. 'We've had a quick look through as far as we could get. Just to check it's not full of rats.'

Hermitage hadn't thought about rats; he did now and shuffled backwards slightly.

'Rooksby?' he asked. 'I've not heard of a monastery of Rooksby.' He was aware that being in De'Ath's Dingle was a solid shelter from civilised life, but he knew most of the houses in this area. Rooksby was not a name he had ever heard.

'Gone for many years, I think. There is very occasional reference to it in some of the records I have come across, but no detail at all. It must have been somewhere near or the box would not have come here.'

'Who sent it then?'

'Not sure,' Martin said, which seemed odd for a great big box. 'Whatever happened to Rooksby, its contents would have been dispersed. Some other house got the box and simply passed it on when they were told.'

'We don't even know where that other house is?'

Martin shook his head. 'Shocking I know.' He laid down the parchment he was working on. He also dropped his voice and gave a cautious glance towards Elmund's end of the room. 'Before I got here, can you believe that no one was making any note of where material came from?'

'No!' Hermitage was horrified at this; genuinely horrified. A killer in the kitchen was one thing, but not making proper records? Unthinkable.

'Obviously, we're doing a bit better than that now, but the box was here when I arrived. Who knows where it came from? Elmund certainly can't remember.'

'How do we know it came from Rooksby, then?'

'Some hot tool has been used to burn the name into the side of the box. Just on the inside.'

Hermitage chanced a peer over the edge of the box; carefully, in case one of the rats was still in there, hot tool at the ready.

Just below the edge, he could see the word "Rooskby" branded into the timber. 'An expensive box,' Martin explained. 'They'd want everyone to know who it belonged to.'

Hermitage could see that this was reasonable.

'Fascinating,' he said. 'I shall have a look and see what there might be of interest.'

'Please do,' Martin replied. 'We've got to start on it sometime. Try not to add to the mess on the floor, if you can avoid it.'

Hermitage felt guilty that he was indulging in this box of treasure when he could be clearing up the material that was still just lying about. 'I shall catalogue it assiduously,' he assured Martin.

He did momentarily wonder if it might not be a whole crate full of copies of Beowulf; that would be a huge disappointment.

Martin returned to his work and Hermitage went and found a candle that he could place nearby. It was getting darker now and he wouldn't be able to see the inside of the box.

Just below the burned-in name "Rooksby", the books began; tempting him by just lying there like that. And there did appear to be a lot of them. They were all sizes, small, large and everything in between. They looked very comfortable as if they had been living contentedly in their box for many a year.

Despite Martin's warning, Hermitage thought that he'd better take them out of the box before he did anything. It really was too murky in the room to consider them without the full light of the candle. He got quill and parchment to hand so that he could at least make a note of any titles as he pulled them out. He could always put them back again afterwards. No, come to think of it, he couldn't; he wasn't capable of putting a book back in its box.

As he found that taking the first book from the top of the box only revealed another one underneath, he had to look at that one as well, didn't he?

Rather than remove a slice from the top, he thought he would burrow downwards. Despite the fascinating nature of the first volumes, something told him that the deeper he went, the more interesting things would get. After all, the lower books would be older, wouldn't they? And how else could anyone define "interesting".

The first two or three he took out were gospel commentaries. In Wat's workshop, he would happily have gone to his grave for a couple of pages from one rather poor commentary on a gospel. Now he had a whole room full, discovering another one was a bit of a let-down.

Four layers down, he came to something that looked very interesting. It had a well-tooled cover, with gold edging and

The Hermes Parchment

was obviously a highly valued piece. He lifted it out and propped it on the side of the box. Bringing the candle close he opened the cover and turned the first page of what was a very thick piece of parchment.

He closed the cover again, very quickly, and wondered whether to put the book straight back in the box, or whether he should do the proper thing and add it to the pile that took so much of Picot's interest.

He had no idea what language the book was written in. The words, if they were words at all, seemed to be random collections of lines gathered together in little squares.

The pictures were another question altogether. They were very plain in their language and the very best place for them was at the bottom of a much, much deeper box.

Still, he could not let the fact that the content of this book was just plain disgusting detract from the fact that it was a book. If he gave it a suitably vague title in the catalogue, there was a good chance no one would ever look at it again; or even find it.

Wherever this monastery of Rooksby had been, it had very questionable taste in books.

Putting this volume down on the floor with some relief, Hermitage bent back into the box. He felt down and discovered that he had come to the bottom. Only a smooth face of wood presented itself to his fingers, which was a shame.

He stepped back and moved to start on the next pile. Then he looked at the box and frowned.

He was no great expert in, what was it called? Geometry? Something like that; from the Greek anyway. But he thought that the inside of a box could not be less deep than the outside. There was certainly more room for the books to go further down than he had reached.

Perhaps he had touched a book with a wooden cover? He had heard of such things but had never seen one. Well, now he would.

He dived back into the box, his enthusiasm in danger of burning his name in the wood all on its own.

Moving the candle to the very edge of the box, telling himself to make sure he didn't let any wax drop in, he leaned over and found the wood at the bottom once more.

He had to move the layers of books at the side so that he could get clear access but was disappointed to discover that it really did seem to be the bottom of the box.

But that couldn't be. He looked at the outside of the box again. Then once more at the inside. Then he had an idea of which he was quite proud.

He removed the rope cincture from around his waist and dangled one end into the box, marking the depth with his thumb. He then removed the belt, keeping his thumb on the right spot, and held it against the outside of the box.

Then he did it a couple more times before he realised what the conclusion was. There was something inside the bottom of the box. Another box, perhaps?

At the sight of one box full of books, Hermitage's curiosity had been running around like a puppy chasing a kitten's tail. A box inside a box full of books was almost more than he could bear.

He bent in again and cleared more space inside the box. Volumes of potentially great interest were scattered around him. He'd promised Martin that he would put them back, but he had to solve this mystery. With a beaming smile, he realised that this was the sort of investigation he liked. Why couldn't King William ask him to look into boxes of books

The Hermes Parchment

more often?

With most of the inside of the box cleared, Hermitage saw that there was a handle buried in the box in what was obviously a false base.

A rat with a tool fresh from the fire could have come and branded the names of all its children on the back of Hermitage's hand and he wouldn't have flinched.

He took the handle and pulled. Nothing happened. Then he pushed. The same result. Then he pulled again. Then he let go and looked at the handle. It was made of a bright metal and was sunk into its own recess from which it could be easily prised.

Instead of pulling this time, he twisted it one way, then the other. Something gave. He twisted harder and the thing seemed to release against some internal catch.

Now he pulled, and the whole bottom of the box rose up. He was right, it had been a false bottom and was a simple sheet of wood, although made by a craftsman to fit exactly.

He wrestled the wood, which was the same size as the box, after all, until he could get it up and out of the box completely.

'Good heavens,' Martin said from his desk. 'What have you got there? We don't need to dismantle the boxes.'

Hermitage was too excited to reply. He looked back into the true bottom of the box now and saw a single book nestled in protective wood shavings. And it was huge.

His knees gave way and he had to hang on to the side of the box to avoid collapsing on the floor.

He had no idea what the book was, but it was enormous and of an incredible quality. Even in the dim light of the candle, gold shone from the cover. There even seemed to be some sort of great jewel buried in the leather, if it was leather and not something far more costly.

At Hermitage's estimate, the book must be two feet high and at least a foot and a half across. He couldn't tell how thick it was, but the space in the bottom of the box could house a very long work.

Judging from the size of the thing, he wouldn't even be able to get it out on his own.

He turned to call for Brother Martin but found that he was already at the box.

'Great heavens,' Martin breathed.

Hermitage nodded.

'What is it?'

Hermitage managed to shake his head. There was no way he could talk at the moment.

'If you climb in, Brother, we can lever it out,' Martin said.

Hermitage didn't really understand what that meant just at the moment, but he soon realised. He hitched his habit up and lifted a leg over into the box, being very careful not to come anywhere near the magnificent find.

Standing in the wood shavings, he very gently slid his fingers under the top edge of the book, feeling a huge pride that he was the first one to touch it in untold years. As he did so, he saw that the book was as thick as its promise. Pages and pages of parchment must be contained between its covers. It was so thick that large yellow metal clasps were fitted across it, to stop it from falling open and to protect the contents.

Following gestured directions, he tipped it over until Martin could take hold of the edge and hold it steady. Hermitage then bent to the other end and lifted the bottom until they had the weight of it between them. And it was heavy.

The Hermes Parchment

They manoeuvred the book until it was resting on the edge of the box. Hermitage then climbed out and they moved it onto a strong desk, hastily brushed clear of loose pages of parchment.

As Hermitage looked at it in the dim light of the room, he thought that he had never seen anything so wonderful in his entire life. Even whole bibles in the possession of Archbishops were not as magnificent as this. He wondered what it might contain for a moment, before concluding that it would naturally be some great compilation of books of the bible.

From the size of it, he dared speculate that it might even be the whole book in one volume. He felt faint and had to sit down.

Martin examined the cover, which they could now see was extravagantly decorated. Jewels, large and small, were laid out within a pattern of embossed leather that must have taken the finest craftsman months to produce. There was no sign on the outside of what the contents would be.

Martin took a deep breath. 'You open it, Brother,' he said.

Hermitage looked at him from within his stupor. 'Me?' he managed to croak.

'Of course. You made the discovery. The monastery of Rooksby is long gone, and it could be very many years since this book was last opened. Someone went to a lot of trouble to hide it away, so it is only fair that its finder opens it first.'

Hermitage stood now and gave Martin a very sincere bow. He wasn't sure if he wanted this moment to actually arrive or always to be just there, waiting for him.

He stepped forward and laid his hands on the cover of the book. He held his breath as he slipped his right hand around the edge and unclipped the mighty clasps that held it shut.

Clasps that felt suspiciously heavy. Could they be gold?

In silence, he lifted the cover and folded it back. The leather creaked and complained at this unfamiliar treatment, while the parchment inside crackled in excitement at its release.

He looked at the first page, wondering how long ago the last eyes had seen this.

Great, flamboyant letters presented themselves, even these edged in gold and red. 'Greek,' he said.

'Just so,' Martin agreed.

Hermitage was so confused by this whole experience that it took a moment for him to get the Greek language back in his head.

'Erm,' he said as he read the words. 'Oh, my,' he added.

Martin spoke the name emblazoned there slowly as he read the letters; Hermitage seemed to have ground to a halt.

'Hermes Trismegistos.'

'Where?' They were both startled by the bark that came from Elmund.

Caput IX Tapestry for the Pious at Heart

Wat and Cwen had gone about their business with vigour, once they had the day free of Hermitage's library - as they now thought of it. They'd had a very pleasant evening at the Hill Top lodging house, but then that was the general idea. Each of them ate and drank more than Hermitage and Martin had managed between them. They retired to comfortable beds where the food and drink inside them carried on carousing, while they tried to sleep.

Leaving their packs in the morning, they set off to find their merchant. Directions were given by the very quiet man who ran the lodging, and who seemed to know everyone in Lincoln personally; who they were, where they were, and what they got up to when they thought no one was looking.

'How long do you think we're going to need here?' Cwen asked as they walked around the building site of the cathedral and off towards the eastern wall of the old town.

'No telling, really. In the old days, Godrinius was a pretty sharp merchant; knew what he liked and when he liked it.'

'Godrinius?' Cwen gave a little snort at the name.

'Yes,' Wat agreed. 'He always did have a lot of ideas about himself; mainly good ones. Insisted he was descended from the Romans and was probably the rightful emperor.'

'I imagine a lot of us are descended from the Romans.'

'Probably. But Godrinius even had a list.'

'A list of Romans?'

'That's it. His father and his father's father and so on.'

'All the way back to an emperor?'

'At least one. Still, if a man with lots of money wants to call himself an emperor, who are we to disagree?'

'Particularly if we want some of that money.'

'Exactly. If Godrinius wanted a tapestry showing him as a Roman emperor in the middle of a what-do-you-call-it, then so be it.'

'What-do-you-call-it?'

Wat was clicking his fingers as he thought. 'The Romans had a word for it.'

'Hermitage would know.'

'Well, whatever it is, Godrinius was in the middle of it, if you know what I mean.'

'I can imagine, this being in the "old days" of Wat the Weaver.'

'Quite.'

They walked on without having to be explicit about the subject matter of Wat's old tapestries - and Cwen's come to that. Both of them were quite capable of being more explicit than decent people wanted to hear about, let alone see come to life in wool.

'I do love rich people,' Wat mused.

'All of them?'

'Every one. All you have to do is tell them that they're getting something no one else has got and they pay stupid amounts of money.'

'The more they pay, the better they enjoy it,' Cwen agreed.

'I had the idea of inviting one to the workshop once, you know, for a very personal discussion about a particular work I knew that only they would be interested in.'

'Did he come? They usually make you go to them.'

'Ah, yes, but this was so exclusive I couldn't possibly trust it to the open road.'

'Clever.'

'I showed him the work, he was overawed and snapped it up at four times the price I had in mind.'

'And now you're one of the rich people.'

'Oh, no. I've got a lot of money, but I'm not one of them. How can anyone be so clever and stupid at the same time? They haggle their ways to every deal imaginable, taking crumbs from the mouths of babies if there's a penny to be made, yet hand over vast sums for next to nothing.'

'Still, at least your man went away satisfied.'

'He did. And so did the one who came the next day and bought the same tapestry,' Wat grinned. 'And the one the day after that.'

Cwen shook her head, part in disappointment and part in admiration. 'Aren't you worried they're going to meet?'

'And talk about their Wat the Weaver tapestries? I don't think so.'

They'd arrived at the Roman east wall of the town now and turned left to head towards the old gate. This was where they'd been told they'd find Godrinius. Apparently, he made himself available for business by the east gate most days.

Roman wall was a bit of a misnomer; it was more like a builder's yard of Roman rubble, just waiting for someone with the right equipment to come and take it away.

The east gate itself hadn't actually been a gate for as long as anyone could remember. Two haphazard piles of cream-coloured stone sat on either side of a gap, so they called it a gate.

'Godrinius isn't likely to want a repetition of your old stuff,' Cwen said. 'Not with William-the-Godly on the throne.'

'Lord, I should think not. I hope not, anyway. What would Hermitage say?'

'He'd be appalled, I think that's the word.'

'That's the one. And think how bad we'd feel, having to

keep it a secret from him.'

'You wouldn't.'

Wat shrugged. 'Godrinius really does have an awful lot of money.'

'He did have an awful lot of money.'

'That's true. His fortunes may well have fallen. Mind you, with Colesvain the Saxon running Lincoln, instead of some Norman madman, things might have continued as normal round here.'

Cwen's eye developed a mischievous shine. 'Perhaps, you know, what with the Normans being in charge and Godrinius needing to show what a fine citizen he is..?'

'What?'

'He wants his money back?'

Wat almost fell to the ground on the spot.

'That's a horrible thing to say. I give you shelter, I take you into my workshop and let you weave, against the very specific rules of the guild, and this is how you repay me?'

Cwen had a good chortle as they walked on.

At the remains of the eastern gate, there was quite a gaggle of people. This was obviously a popular meeting spot and it was clear that quite a bit of trade was being done.

It was not a full market; there was no exchange of goods or provisions, but some intense discussions were going on, regularly punctuated by sombre shakes of hands.

Wat could tell that this was the sort of spot where business was done that Lord Colesvain really didn't need to know about. After all, if he knew about it, he'd tax it, and how would that help anyone? Particularly the merchants.

There was no missing Godrinius in the middle of things. A very well dressed and very large fellow, his display of wealth was blatant. People of obviously lesser status swarmed around him like bees around a particularly stinking flower.

He shook hands, passed smiles around and patted people on the back; the way pickpockets do.

Despite the fact that he was talking to others, he had an eye on his surroundings at all times. Probably so that he could spot a tax man coming. This time he saw Wat, who gave him a broad smile.

Finishing off a conversation, Godrinius quickly moved away from the crowd, indicating that Wat should not come any closer.

'Well, well,' the rich merchant said as he came over to Wat and Cwen.

'And I hope you are,' Wat replied, his eyes dragging themselves to Godrinius's magnificent purse before he could stop them.

Godrinius looked at Cwen and raised an eyebrow.

'This is Cwen,' Wat said.

'The weaver,' Cwen added.

'My, my. Not the same Cwen who was rumoured to work with Briston the Weaver?'

'That's me,' Cwen said with some pride, stepping slightly in front of Wat as she did so.

Godrinius gave her a bow. 'I bought a work from Briston once.'

'Did you?' Wat didn't sound happy about that.

'And I could not believe that he had done it himself, his previous work being of a lower standard.'

'Generally pretty poor, I think,' Wat said helpfully.

'So I prised it out of him. He had another working for him.'

'With him,' Cwen corrected.

'Quite. He didn't want to tell me of course, but I said I

wouldn't buy another thing from him unless he told me honestly.'

'Briston honest, eh? That'd be a first,' Wat said.

'It is a pleasure to meet you, Mistress Cwen.' Godrinius bowed again. 'Who'd have thought, eh? From such delicate fingers and from so gentle a visage, images of such entertainment could have come.'

'Yes, well.' Cwen was now a bit more reluctant to be acknowledged as a weaver of that sort of thing.

'I particularly enjoyed the series, Fifty Days in the Hay, but I only got up to number four.'

'All that sort of thing has come to a halt now,' Cwen said, making it clear that Godrinius wouldn't be getting day number five from her.

'Oh, quite, quite. That's why I put word out that I would meet with Wat again when he was passing.'

Wat acknowledged this with a small bow, during which his eyes managed to snatch another quick look at Godrinius's purse.

'Lord Colesvain tells us all that we need to make a good impression on the Normans.'

'Not an easy task,' Wat said. 'We've met a few of them and they don't impress easily.'

'Of course, the instruction is entirely for Lord Colesvain's benefit.' Godrinius didn't seem to think this was unreasonable. 'If Colesvain is to keep his title and his lands, he needs a good loyal county at his feet.'

'Not just Colesvain,' Wat cautioned. 'If the Normans take a dislike to the man in the street, they bury him at the side of it.'

'Really?' Godrinius was definitely more engaged now.

'Oh, yes. It doesn't do to upset a Norman. Any Norman.

The Hermes Parchment

The king and his man Le Pedvin are the worst, but the rest of them are trying to catch up.'

'I see.' Godrinius looked as if his mind was made up about something. 'A God-fearing man, our King William, I hear?'

'I imagine it's mutual,' Wat said. 'I've not met God yet, but William scares my leggings off.'

'You've met him?'

'Several times.'

'Good Lord.'

'He doesn't seem to know anything about Wat's old trade,' Cwen explained.

'And it's best that he doesn't,' Godrinius said. 'Nor any information about your old customers.'

'Rest assured, he's not going to hear anything about anything from me.'

'Excellent.' Godrinius was actually looking a bit worried now; probably the way very rich people did when they met someone even richer. 'Pious,' he said.

'Beg pardon?' Wat was confused.

'Pious. That's the order of the day. Our noble monarch supports the church and so must we.'

'Sounds quite wise.'

'Can you do pious?'

'Can I what? Do pious?'

'Yes, you know. Your old works were most certainly not pious, eh? Eh? Har har.' Godrinius reached out and punched Wat lightly on the shoulder. 'But those days are gone. I need to be seen as a man of William's own heart. Defending the church, standing firm against the encroachment of evil; that sort of thing.' Godrinius waved his hand to indicate there was probably a lot more of "that sort of thing", but he couldn't be bothered to think about it now.

'I see.'

'So, can you do pious? Can you make a nice pious tapestry? One that I can have on the wall for when the Normans come round.'

'Oh, right, I'm with you. Yes, yes, I can do pious.'

'We,' Cwen said.

'Yes, we. We can do pious, no problem at all.'

There was a bit of mutual nodding.

'I've got a monk now,' Wat said as if this were proof he could do pious.

'Oh, yes?' Godrinius laughed in a horrible way and winked at Wat.

'Not like that. A real monk. He, erm..,' Wat was about to say that Hermitage lived with him, but that didn't sound right. 'He stays at the workshop and makes sure we're all on the straight and narrow path.'

'What does that mean?'

'It's from the bible, apparently.'

'Saint Matthew,' Cwen said.

'Good Lord.'

'Exactly.' Wat shrugged

'You really have got a monk, haven't you?'

'Certainly have.' Wat was back to business. 'So, pious is not a problem for us at all. Cwen's made a marvellous saint. The Archbishop of Canterbury even wants to see it.'[5]

'Really?' Godrinius was hooked now.

'That's right. King William's own Archbishop of Canterbury. How much more pious can you get? You'd be using the Archbishop's own tapestry workshop.'

'That's pushing it a bit,' Cwen commented under her breath.

---

[5] In the middle of The Bayeux Embroidery, somewhere.

The Hermes Parchment

'Which saint is it?' Godrinius asked.

'Patrick,' Cwen said.

'Ooh,' Godrinius didn't sound so keen. 'Snakes, eh?'

'One or two,' Cwen agreed. 'But they're very pious snakes.'

'I can't do with snakes.'

'No problem,' Wat said. If the very rich man who wanted to buy a pious tapestry couldn't do snakes, then snakes were out. 'Got anything in particular in mind, or should we consult our monk?'

Godrinius didn't sound that interested in the content, as long as it was pious. 'Don't mind really. As long as it's got the main character.'

'The Son of God?' Cwen checked.

'No, me.' Godrinius looked a bit puzzled about why he'd want a pious tapestry with someone else in it.

'Of course,' Wat said quickly, while Cwen was busy looking stunned.

'How about me supporting the Normans and some saints?'

'Piously,' Cwen confirmed.

'I'm sure we can do that,' Wat said. 'Big I assume. Pious is coming out big these days.'

'Of course,' Godrinius agreed. 'The bigger it is, the more pious I'll look.'

'Well, exactly.'

'And I imagine you will need something for supplies,' Godrinius chuckled as he reached for his purse.

Wat's hand reached up to wipe the dribble from the corner of his mouth. 'You'll be able to impress the Normans by telling them you've already paid towards the work.'

'How long then?' Godrinius asked.

'As long as you like,' Wat said, gazing with rapture at the gold coins in his hand. 'Four feet, five?'

'Time, you greedy weaver. How long until I get my tapestry?'

'Oh, right. Two months?'

'Two months it is.'

Wat knew that with Godrinius, this actually meant two months and not the three or four he could sometimes get away with.

'Although,' Wat said slowly.

'A problem?' Godrinius sounded as if he didn't like problems.

'No, no. I'm just thinking that there may be more people here who want a nice pious tapestry. Now that the Normans are in town.'

'Could be,' Godrinius accepted cautiously. 'Although mine will be the first and the best. And biggest.'

'Of course, of course, no question.'

'The piousest,' Cwen confirmed.

Wat suddenly stiffened, smiled broadly and raised a finger.

'You have clearly just had a marvellous idea,' Cwen observed.

'I certainly have. Why have we come here in the first place?'

'To talk to Godrinius.' She gave the merchant a sympathetic look that they were going to have to put up with Wat.

'Before that.'

'Erm, Hermitage?'

'What Hermitage?' Godrinius asked.

'It's the name of our monk; odd, we know.' Cwen shrugged.

'Hermitage came here to work on Lord Colesvain's library. The library being donated to the cathedral.'

'Piously, I expect,' Cwen noted.

The Hermes Parchment

'And what sort of place is going to want a huge number of pious tapestries to hang around the place? A cathedral.' Wat held his arms out to show that the entire output of his workshop was as good as sold.

'That place?' Godrinius was very dismissive of the idea.

'You think they won't?'

'I'm sure that they will, but you and I and our children and our children's children will be long dead before that place opens its doors.'

'Really?'

Godrinius gave a little laugh. 'They've been building that cathedral for as long as anyone can remember; or rather not building it. We suspect it's some church scheme to keep their money out of the king's coffers. Oh, we can't pay taxes Majesty, we're building a magnificent cathedral in Lincoln. Perhaps, now that the Normans are here, they'll get on with it.'

'But,' Cwen frowned. 'Hermitage has come to catalogue the books so they can be given to the cathedral library.'

'What library?' Godrinius snorted at the very idea. 'If your monk can catalogue bricks, he might be some use. Library, ha!'

'There is no library?'

'There's no two walls standing up next to one another, never mind an actual room.'

'Then why is Colesvain having his books catalogued?' Cwen asked.

'To look pious?' Wat suggested. 'Tell William he's giving all his books to the cathedral. Sounds pretty pious to me.'

'Didn't Picot say that people from the cathedral library kept turning up asking for the books?' Cwen recalled.

'He did,' Wat's frown was now disturbing what had been a

very good day, so far.

'What people from the cathedral?' Godrinius scoffed. 'There is no library so there are no people from it. The entire working population of the cathedral consists of a few masons and carpenters; most of whom don't do anything all day. I don't know who Picot's been talking to, but then he is an idiot child.'

'Well,' Cwen said brightly. 'We must have got the wrong end of things completely. No library, no cathedral, no tapestries.'

Wat looked at her as if she'd got the wrong end of something.

'We'll go and check on our monk and then get back to work.'

'Good plan.' Godrinius bade them both goodbye and headed back to the east gate to make some more money. He called, 'See you in two months,' over his shoulder.

'What's going on, then?' Wat asked as they turned away.

'It's obvious, isn't it,' Cwen said.

'Is it?'

'Of course, it is. It's all part of the murder.'

Caput X It's All Greek to Everyone

Hermitage and Martin were brushed aside as an energetic Elmund emerged from his den and made straight for the book. He ran his hands over the open page and had a look of rather wild excitement in his eye.

'Now then, Elmund,' Martin complained.

'Hermes,' Elmund seemed to be partly dazed and partly triumphant. 'The source of all wisdom,' he mumbled. He now looked back over his shoulder at Martin and Hermitage, before he slammed the book shut. 'I'll take this,' he said.

'Oh, really?' Martin folded his arms.

'Yes, yes,' Elmund almost dribbled. He leaned across the table and put his arms around the book. His attempt to take it failed as he discovered the thing was simply too heavy for him.

'I think not,' Martin said.

'Bring it, bring it.' Elmund stepped back and gestured the other two to pick it up for him.

'Certainly not,' Martin replied. 'This book belongs to Lord Colesvain and must be catalogued.'

Elmund gave Martin a very nasty look. 'You,' he turned to Hermitage. 'Help me.'

Hermitage was seldom roused to ire of any sort, but someone trying to take a book away from him was making a big mistake.

'I work with Brother Martin,' he said, quite firmly, he thought.

Elmund began hopping on the spot in frustration that he wasn't getting his way. He even looked around the room quickly, as if there were someone else who could help.

With a glare at them both, Elmund skipped over to the

door and went out.

'Quickly, Brother,' Martin said. 'Let us move the book to a safe spot.'

'A safe spot?'

'I suspect Elmund has gone to fetch some of the house staff to help him take it away.'

Hermitage had too many questions about this to get any of them out.

'He will use his influence as Lord Colesvain's librarian to instruct the servants,' Martin explained. 'They tend to do what he tells them, mainly because he is so difficult I think.'

'What will he do with the book though?'

'Spirit it away somewhere.'

'It's a bit big for that.' Hermitage considered the huge volume sitting on the table. 'Where would he put it so that we couldn't find it again?'

'I don't know, but I worry. He seems more excited about this than I have ever seen him. And we know that there are volumes in the library that we can't find. Elmund could have a secret store somewhere.'

'We probably can't find the books because they're already here.' Hermitage glanced around the room, which still looked most like a library after a longship full of Vikings came to take a book out.

Martin lowered his voice a bit. 'And, to be honest, I begin to share some of your concerns.'

'My concerns?' Hermitage felt that he hadn't had a concern for weeks.

'About Elmund's favoured topic.'

Hermitage thought for a moment. 'Oh, Simon Magus.'

'Exactly. If Elmund's interest is in the area of sorcery and magic, who knows what else he has. And who knows what his plans would be for the work of Hermes Trismegistus?'

'Ancient knowledge,' Hermitage nodded that he understood.

'Exactly. This is a book of legend.' Martin was serious and took a deep breath. 'This volume could be the single greatest find in the country, let alone this library.' He laid a hand on the cover. 'I have never heard of a single book containing his works, have you?'

'Well, no. We've all heard that Hermes was a source of learning for the early Christian fathers, but that was only in short passages.'

'Quite. And the rumours of what else he taught continue to circle. Magical powers, the ability to summon and banish demons, spells for good and ill. Hermes Trismegistus is the source of it all.'

They both considered the book, as if cautious about ever opening it again.

Hermitage felt that he had something else to add. 'I did find that Elmund had turned the page on that Beowulf book to a passage about demons.'

'Oh, dear,' Martin was clearly worried.

'But surely his interest will be in the books themselves, nothing else?'

'Who knows? If his interest is only in the books, he could still secrete them away from the library. And if his interest is their contents?'

Hermitage couldn't immediately follow that line of thought. 'He can't actually believe any of that nonsense, can he?'

'Who knows what a man believes.'

'But there's nothing in it,' Hermitage insisted. 'The church has made it quite clear that there's no such thing as magic.

Anyone who believes it is in error.'

'Just so.'

'And Hermes Trismegistus,' Hermitage warmed to the subject. 'From my own recollection, even the martyr, Clement of Alexandria, acknowledged that there was a number of specific writings by Hermes in ancient Egypt, a very particular number that I can't quite recall at the moment. Anyway, he saw no trouble in them. Very appropriate works referring to the power of God, as I recall.

'And Saint Augustine himself refers to Hermes. He says that he's wrong, obviously, but there's no suggestion of magical powers. It's just ridiculous.'

Martin held his arms out to indicate complete agreement. 'What we know and understand may be of no interest to Elmund. If he is convinced there's something in it, who knows what he will do with the book?'

'I still don't really see what he can do with it. It's simply huge. It must be the largest book in the entire library.'

Martin nodded that this was probably right.

'If Elmund wants to study it, he can do so here. Not that it will do him any good.'

Hermitage carefully opened the cover of the book once more and read the name. 'It's simply a remarkable artefact. Goodness knows where it came from, but it has been well kept in all the intervening years.' He turned the first page over and considered the finely written Greek text. 'My, this will take a great deal of scholarship to untangle. I fear my Greek is not up to the task.'

'Mine neither,' Martin looked as well. 'There seems to be a name there.' He pointed to one word. 'Poimandres?'

'Very peculiar,' Hermitage shrugged. 'Do we know if Elmund has much Greek?'

The Hermes Parchment

'No idea. He could be fluent, for all I know.'

The door opened again and Elmund returned, with two servants in tow.

'Aha,' he said. 'Now we see you.'

'We've not gone anywhere,' Martin said.

'Reading the book, eh?' Elmund made it sound like an accusation.'

'We were just saying that we can't. Our Greek is not up to it.'

'Greek?' Elmund sounded surprised.

'Of course,' Hermitage said. 'The work is in Greek. A very fine hand, by the look of it, but it would take me years.'

'All of it?' Elmund was sounding quite angry now; angry with the book. 'Greek?'

'I believe that was Hermes Trismegistus's origin,' Martin explained. 'If not Egyptian, and goodness knows what language they wrote.'

'Egyptian, presumably,' Hermitage offered helpfully.

'Blast,' Elmund muttered under his breath.

'So,' Martin whispered to Hermitage. 'He doesn't have Greek, then.'

'You.' Elmund gestured to the servants. 'You're witnesses.'

The servants didn't look very happy at being witnesses, whatever it was they were witnessing.

'Come, come.' Elmund scurried over to the table, beckoning the servants to follow. They did so reluctantly, looking around the room at the books as if they were about to be jumped on by a particularly vicious volume.

'There we are, you've seen it now.'

The servants nodded that they had indeed seen a book in a library. They did seem a bit more interested in this one though, or rather, more interested in the jewels that sparkled on the cover.

'If it goes missing, you'll swear that you saw it here.'

The servants gave the sort of nods that indicated that they sort of might, if it ever came to it, which they hoped it wouldn't.

'How can it go missing?' Hermitage asked. 'It's too heavy for one person to move.'

'Yes, but there's two of you.'

'We don't want it. It belongs to Lord Colesvain. We can't read it anyway, it's just a fascinating object. It'll be in the cathedral soon enough.'

'The cathedral?' Elmund seemed horrified at this suggestion.

'That is where all the books are going,' Martin reminded him.

'No, no, no. They can't have it.'

'Can't have it?' Martin was surprised by this suggestion. 'I think you'd better take that up with Lord Colesvain.'

Elmund was so flustered that he didn't seem to know what to do.

Martin gently gestured that the servants could leave now. They did so with shrugs of acknowledgement that everyone in this house was mad, apart from them.

Elmund was now walking back and forth between his resting place behind the books and the table with the book on it. He seemed to be wrestling with a problem of what to do.

Hermitage and Martin just stood and watched him come and go. Eventually, with more glares at them both, he came up to the book and reached for the cover.

'If I may?' he asked, rather sarcastically.

'Of course,' Martin said. 'Help yourself. It's not going

anywhere.'

Elmund huffed at that and opened the cover. Turning past the title he moved on to the first page of text.

There was no denying that this was a beautiful book. Whatever the words were, whatever tale this thing had to tell, it was a wonder to look at.

And Hermitage stood looking at it. The parchment was of the most wonderful quality. If he had his dates right, the original work would have been written on papyrus. That would have been the version considered by Clement and by Augustine. This must be a later copy; but what a copy.

Months, if not years, must have been spent in a scriptorium producing this work. The cover could have been created while the writing was going on, the two being brought together at some later date.

The quality of the writing was superb. It was clear and neat and was obviously the work of a master scribe; more likely several. The book was so thick, no one man could have produced it in a single lifetime.

Each page was ornamented with fine coloured scrollwork and decoration. There were no figures in the decoration, as there might be in more local pieces; no fantastic animals paraded, no faces stared out.

The fact that the language was too difficult to decipher with ease, did not detract from the beauty of each page; at least it didn't for Hermitage.

Elmund was grumbling and muttering to himself as he considered the words before him.

'What's that?' he pointed at one letter on the page. Hermitage leaned over.

'Well, it's Pi, isn't it,' Hermitage said, thinking that was one of the easier letters. If Elmund didn't know that one, he had no chance translating any of this at all. He also wondered how a librarian had managed to cope without being able to read the basic Greek alphabet.

'Pah,' Elmund growled at the book. He looked at Martin and Hermitage with quite an aggressive expression. Hermitage felt that this was most unjustified. After all, it wasn't his fault the man hadn't learned his Greek.

'I'm going out,' Elmund said.

'Going out?' Martin sounded as if he didn't know what the words meant. 'What do you mean, going out?'

'Into the town.'

'Into the town?'

'God above. Into the town. And don't you two touch that book while I'm gone. I'll be back soon enough.'

With another nasty look at them both, Elmund stomped to the door and walked out, slamming it shut behind him.

'We might need to move it,' Hermitage called after him. 'It is a bit in the way here,' he trailed off as it was clear Elmund could no longer hear him. Instead, he just reached forward and gently closed the book, as if shielding its sensitive pages from such rough goings-on.

'Well, I never,' Martin said when the silence of the library returned. 'In all my time here, I have never even seen Elmund leave the room, let alone go out of the house.'

'Really?' Hermitage asked, with a little worry about the domestic arrangements.

Martin coughed. 'I believe he does his business in the fireplace.'

Hermitage looked at the fireplace and decided that he would not be warming himself by that hearth.

'I wonder where he's gone?'

'Wherever it is, it will be something to do with this book.'

The Hermes Parchment

Martin laid a hand on the huge volume.

Hermitage nodded that it was the book that seemed to have prompted Elmund into action. 'Perhaps he's gone to find someone who can read Greek?' he suggested.

'In Lincoln?'

'You think not?'

Martin gave it some thought. 'I suppose that there are merchants from around the world who have settled here. It's possible someone might have some Greek. We've got a Welshman.'

'Does he read Greek?'

'I doubt it.'

They both looked at the book now, but it offered no revelation.

'What does he think is in here that is so important?' Hermitage pondered.

'I have no idea, and I don't think he's going to tell us.' Martin folded his arms and looked thoughtful. 'We might get Lord Colesvain to persuade him.'

'Would he?'

'You've seen that he is very anxious that we complete our work promptly, doubtless encouraged by the king. And he has very little time for Elmund. It's probably our duty to report a find of this importance straight away. After all, the book looks very valuable, if nothing else. I imagine those are real jewels in the cover.'

'They certainly look like it,' Hermitage said, never having seen any real jewels close up.

'And we wouldn't be moving the book.' Martin's mind seemed to be made up. 'I will go and get Lord Colesvain now. Then, when Elmund returns, he can explain himself to his master.'

Hermitage thought this sounded a bit provocative, but as someone else was doing it, it was probably all right.

He waited by the book while Martin went off. He opened the cover once again and looked at the marvel of the work. It was wonderful to have these few moments alone, just him and the book. He stroked the front page and could feel the gold sitting proud of the parchment itself.

He'd already looked at the first page, so he took a great leap of courage and put his fingers into the side of a page about halfway through. He pulled this open and saw that the quality of the work continued. Here though, was a diagram of some sort.

In the middle of the page, a five-pointed star was drawn in thick, dark ink. Outside of this was a circle, and on the outer edges of the circle, words were written. He bent to look at these and saw that they weren't even Greek. He had no idea what this language was, which surprised him. He knew what most languages looked like, even if he couldn't read them.

There had been that very rude book with its square lines that might have been words or not, but this was very strange. It looked very similar to eastern or Greek writing but was just different enough to put his eye off completely.

Above the circle, some very fine lines led upwards towards the drawing of a pyramid, and inside that was a rather alarming image of an eye.

Hermitage started to worry about this drawing, it was making him feel quite uncomfortable, for some reason.

He took half a step away from the book as if to get the whole thing in proportion. As he did so, the page came into focus and he saw what it was. The star, the circle, the pyramid, the eye and the writing all formed parts of a giant face. The face of what he could only describe as a demon.

The Hermes Parchment

He gave a small gasp and stepped up to hurriedly close the book again. He would have to tell Brother Martin about this. Perhaps this was the sort of thing Elmund was looking for.

He calmed his breathing and told himself not to be foolish. It was only a drawing, after all.

His breathing stopped as the room suddenly darkened.

It was as if night had been crouching behind the windows and had just this moment leapt up to obscure the daylight. He turned towards the dusty and mostly obscure windows of thick and distorting glass, and he saw a huge ghostly shape bobbing up and down outside. Or was it outside? It was hard to tell if the figure was in the room, outside, or somewhere inside the glass itself.

'Ooh,' Hermitage whimpered quietly to himself.

Before he could get any more worried, the figure spoke. A deep, booming voice imposed itself on the quiet of the room.

'Brother Hermitage,' it said. 'I want you.'

Caput XI One Book Short of a Library

'What is the matter with you?'

Hermitage could hear Wat's voice but wasn't sure if he could trust himself to open his eyes. He was clearly lying on the floor; he could feel the hard surface beneath him. How he had got here, and what Wat was doing with him, were questions he didn't have answers to. That was why he thought that keeping his eyes closed was probably for the best.

'Are you all right, Hermitage?' Well, that was Cwen. Things must be reasonably safe if Cwen was here as well; wherever here was. He opened one eye as a first step.

Wat was looking down on him, as was Cwen. To their sides stood Brother Martin and Lord Colesvain.

'What happened?' Martin asked him.

Hermitage risked propping himself up on his elbows. Nothing untoward happened, so he sat up.

He knew what had happened, but as he thought about it he concluded that it all sounded rather silly.

'Oh, nothing really.' He tried to sound as if he'd just tripped and hadn't been lying unconscious on the floor at all. 'I was looking at the Hermes book when there was, erm, someone at the window who called my name. It was a bit of a shock, that's all.'

'It was me, you idiot,' Wat said.

'I see,' Hermitage said. He didn't really see at all. Why would Wat do that instead of coming in through the front door?

'I wanted to get your attention.'

'Well, you did.'

'You weren't supposed to faint. Must have been a very

The Hermes Parchment

scary book.'

'Not at all. It was just that my mind was fully engrossed; you know how it is.'

It seemed pretty clear that the others didn't know how this was at all.

'I didn't expect people to come creeping up at the window.'

'I wasn't creeping.'

'You did creep,' Cwen accused him. 'You said it would be funny if you gave Hermitage a bit of a shock.'

'Yes, well. I didn't expect him to fall down.'

Brother Martin was looking on at this conversation and started shaking his head slowly, in bewilderment. 'Why didn't you just knock on the door?'

'Ah,' Wat said, with some excitement. 'I had good reason for that. We had good reason for that, didn't we?'

'I suppose so,' Cwen admitted.

'Who the devil are you people anyway? And what are you doing in my house?' Lord Colesvain asked now. He had his arms folded and was clearly not too happy with strangers turning up frightening people in his library.

'Oh, we're, erm, friends of Brother Hermitage. Travelled with him.'

'Fascinating. And your reason for creeping up at the window?'

'The cathedral,' Wat announced.

'The cathedral? Your good reason for not using the front door is the cathedral.' Lord Colesvain took a seat. 'I look forward to hearing this one.'

They got Hermitage back to his feet and made sure he was able to stand without falling down again. They then all gathered stools to join Lord Colesvain by the fireplace. As Hermitage did so, he noticed for the first time that it did smell a bit.

'Where's Elmund?' Colesvain called out.

'He's not here,' Martin said.

'Not here? What do you mean, not here? He's always here.'

'He said he had to go out.'

'Go out? He's never been out in his life as far as I know. What made him want to go out now? Is he dying and wants to see the sun one last time before he goes?'

'Not that we're aware of. We discovered a very particular book, or rather, Brother Hermitage did.' Martin nodded an acknowledgement to Hermitage. 'And Elmund seemed to get terribly excited about it.'

'That great big thing on the table?' Colesvain asked with some interest.

It was hard to miss the massive bejewelled volume in the room, but the unconscious monk on the floor had taken priority.

'That's the one.'

'What is it?'

Hermitage saw Martin's unspoken invitation that he could explain, but he really didn't feel up to it at the moment. He gestured that Martin should carry on.

With the briefest of pauses, Martin announced the title with great significance. 'It is the work of Hermes Trismegistus,' he intoned.

No one else in the room got the significance, although they did register the intoning.

'Hermes, you say?' Colesvain said. He sounded as if was trying to show that he knew the name when he didn't. 'Remind me?' he instructed.

'Hermes Trismegistus.' Martin repeated this as if he hadn't said it properly the first time, and that his audience would understand now.

They didn't, but Lord Colesvain nodded as if this was exactly what he'd been expecting and wasn't particularly impressed.

'It's very, erm, big,' Cwen offered.

'And expensive-looking,' Wat added. 'Are those real jewels on the front?'

'God,' Colesvain sighed. 'Don't let Picot see it. He'll be prising them out of the leather so he can sell them.'

Hermitage noticed that Colesvain was now looking at the book with some interest. He imagined that offering to donate books for King William was all well and good, discovering that some of them were jewel-encrusted might be a bit of a disappointment.

Martin seemed anxious to get them back to the most important aspect of the book. 'It is the work of Hermes Trismegistus.'

'Yes, just so.' Colesvain acknowledged.

'It is in the original Greek.'

'Fascinating.'

'It is, without doubt, the single most significant volume in the entire library.'

'I imagine it would be.'

Hermitage recognised the signs of someone trying to sound knowledgeable about something of which they had no knowledge. It was all a bit awkward when the person in question was the local lord.

'Go on then,' Wat said, relieving the tension. 'I'll bite. Who is Hermes Trismagismus?'

'Trismegistus. No one knows, really.'

'Well, that's helpful. Not likely to come asking for his book back, then.'

'He lived and died thousands of years ago,' Martin said, clearly hoping that someone in the room would take this seriously.

'Thousands?' Cwen scoffed a bit.

'Thousands. It's not known exactly, but his works have been considered since before the birth of our Lord.'

Hermitage was pleased to note that they did all look at the book with a bit more interest now.

'That thing?' Cwen asked.

'That thing,' Martin confirmed. 'Obviously, we don't know when this volume was created, but it has been protected and cared for over many years. It came in the collection of the monastery of Rooksby, a place that has itself vanished in the mists of time.'

'Mists of time?' Cwen frowned a bit and looked out of the window as if expecting to see this mist.

'I mean it's very old.'

'Ah. Hermitage says that very old books are the best,' Cwen nodded profoundly.

'This book, this very volume in the room with us, may be older than the Bible,' Martin said.

Now they were taking it seriously.

Colesvain stood and walked over to the table to look at the book. He admired the cover, running his hands over the jewels and nodding with admiration. He then opened the cover and considered the first page.

'And this is Greek, is it?'

'It is.' Martin joined Colesvain at the table and the others crowded round to look.

'Why are all the letters wrong?' Cwen asked.

'Wrong?' Hermitage had to speak up. 'What do you mean, wrong?'

'Well, they aren't proper letters at all, are they. They're just funny shapes. I can see an O and an M and a Y, but what's that one?' She pointed at one odd shape.

'That's Sigma, it's the S sound.'

'S? It looks more like a three.'

'A three if it was the wrong way round,' Hermitage pointed out. 'The Greeks had a different alphabet.'

'How did they read it then?'

'What?'

'How did they read it if the letters are all different?'

'They weren't different to the Greeks, you lump,' Wat laughed. 'This is the way they wrote and read everything.'

Cwen frowned at the words, and then kicked Wat to make herself feel better.

'And their reading and writing probably came before ours,' Hermitage added.

'Very old, eh,' Colesvain commented thoughtfully.

'Absolutely,' Hermitage assured him. 'Some of the early Fathers of the Church referred to Trismegistus. In many ways, he could be seen as a prophet of sorts. Not guided by the Holy Spirit, of course, so still wrong, but I gather a lot of his work is about God's creation.'

'You've not read it, then?'

'Never. I have only heard reports and seen the odd commentary. And the Greek in this book is a little too much for either of us. We can get through one letter at a time, but it would take forever to read the whole thing.'

Colesvain lifted another page of the book but saw that it was more of the same and put it down again. 'So, why did Elmund get so excited about it?'

Hermitage and Martin exchanged glances. They had their own suspicions about Elmund's interests, but how much should they reveal to Lord Colesvain? Particularly as they had no real proof of Elmund's motives.

'We don't know,' Martin said. 'Although, I would have to say that Hermitage and I are pretty excited about it ourselves.'

'But you haven't run out of a library you've spent at least the last thirty years living in.'

Hermitage couldn't stop a wishful thought crossing his mind about living in a library for thirty years.

Colesvain looked thoughtfully at the book, before closing it again. 'You don't think he's trying to sell it?'

'Sell it?' Hermitage didn't understand.

'For money,' Colesvain explained. 'If this thing is as rare and important as you say, people would pay good money for it. Well, I assume someone would.'

'If Elmund were after money, he could have been selling the books of the library for years,' Hermitage said.

'Do we know that he hasn't?' Colesvain asked.

Well, that was an awkward question.

'Martin, you told me that part of this job was finding the books that are supposed to be here. Somewhere.' Colesvain held his arms out to draw their attention to the shambles that was the library.

'Well, yes,' Martin said slowly.

'So, how do we know Elmund hasn't been quietly taking books and selling them?'

'I suppose we don't,' Martin admitted. 'But if he has, what's he been doing with the money? He's certainly not spending it on clothes.'

'Hm.' Colesvain appeared to reluctantly accept that Elmund did not look like a man who had any money at all. 'Perhaps he's just keeping it to look at and count. Some people do.'

Cwen coughed loudly in Wat's direction.

Wat held his hands out to display the fine clothes he was wearing, and presumably the money they must have cost.

Martin shook his head. 'I don't think so. I've not been here long, but I've seen no evidence that Elmund is interested in material wealth.'

'Well,' Colesvain said brightly, appearing ready to change the subject. 'We might find out when he comes back. If he comes back. Perhaps the thing scared him and he ran away.'

'Scared him?' Cwen asked carefully.

'Elmund always has been a superstitious old fool.'

'Really?' Martin asked. Hermitage could tell he was trying to sound nonchalant; the others might spot that he wasn't.

'Oh yes. Going on about secret knowledge and mysteries and the like. I sometimes think he's safest in a library. If he started talking about that sort of thing outside, someone from the church would be having a serious talk with him.' Colesvain returned to his seat by the fireplace.

'Has that thing got anything mysterious in it?' he asked, nodding back towards the book.

'Not that we've seen,' Martin said. 'And of course, the Greek language makes it difficult.'

Hermitage didn't like to mention the fact that he'd found a demon in the pages. He thought it would drive the discussion in a very difficult direction, and someone might ask why he hadn't said something earlier. He'd discuss it with Martin and the others once Colesvain had gone.

Lord Colesvain was looking thoughtful. Eventually, he took a breath and said what was on his mind. 'We can give it to Ardith, then.'

'Give it to Ardith?' Martin sounded as shocked as

Hermitage felt at the prospect.

'Of course. If you can't read it, it's no good here, is it? And she keeps going on about wanting books, so she can have this one. Keep her quiet for a bit. Be a good one to tell the king we've handed over as well.'

Hermitage was wishing he'd kept quiet about not being able to read it. That would have been completely dishonest, of course, but at least he could have kept the book.

'I think we'd better keep an eye on it for now though,' Colesvain said. 'If Elmund does have designs on it, we may need to keep him away until Ardith comes back. Can one of you stay in the room at all times?'

'Oh, yes,' Hermitage blurted out. He was very willing to stay in the library at all times. He might even bring himself to use the fireplace for its alternative purpose. The thought of losing the Hermes book was too much.

'Sooner we get the thing into the cathedral, the better,' Colesvain said.

'Ah,' Wat said. 'The cathedral.'

'Your reason for frightening monks through the window.' Lord Colesvain turned to Wat.

'That's it. We were talking to Godrinius today, about a tapestry.'

'Godrinius?' Colesvain asked with real interest. 'You didn't manage to get any taxes out of him, did you?'

'I didn't know we were supposed to.'

'Everyone in my household is supposed to. If anyone sees the man, they are to take whatever money he has on him at the time. He never pays his taxes anyway, and this seems to be the only way of getting anything out of him.'

'We'll remember for next time,' Wat said. It being fairly clear that there wouldn't be a next time.

'The point is, he told us that there is no cathedral.'

'Well, of course, there isn't,' Colesvain said. 'It's not built yet, is it?'

'No, it isn't. And that means the only people working on the cathedral are builders; carpenters and masons and so forth.'

Colesvain didn't seem concerned about this.

'So, there's no library. No librarian, no people working in the library.'

Colesvain did scowl now. 'I'm sure Ardith is preparing the library. There's probably a lot going on that isn't actual building.'

'But where are the books going to go, if she hasn't got a room to put them in?'

'Are we sure she's from the cathedral?' Martin asked.

'Where else would she come from?' Colesvain sounded angry now. Probably angry that he might have been tricked.

'How did you come to meet her?' Cwen asked.

Colesvain growled a bit. 'I am not accustomed to explaining myself to strangers who wander into my house uninvited.'

Cwen tried to look apologetic, but she could never do it very well. 'Just worried about Elmund.' She smiled sweetly, which she could do very well indeed.

Colesvain's softening was almost visible. 'There was a meeting with King William,' he muttered. 'He summoned all his tenants, and there was no question of not going. When he asked what support and gifts we were going to offer to our local churches, we had to come up with something. I said I had a great library that I would donate to the new cathedral. He seemed pretty happy with that.'

'Considering he can't read,' Cwen complained.

'And was Ardith there?' Martin asked.

'No. She arrived here a week or two later to get the donation for the cathedral.'

'And she's been back regularly asking for the books,' Martin said.

'When, as far as we know, she has nowhere to put them,' Cwen said.

'They'd be better off staying here,' Hermitage said. 'After all, we're cataloguing them anyway. If we get that done, the cathedral can take them when the work's finished. I've told her all about the cross-referencing problems it would raise if she took books too soon.'

'Have you,' Wat said. 'That's good then.' He gave Cwen the look that said he had not the first clue what Hermitage was talking about.

'Does anyone know where she lives?' Cwen asked. 'Obviously not in the cathedral.'

'There are several houses in that area. The church officials, you know,' Martin said.

Hermitage certainly did know. His whole life as an investigator had started off in the bishop's house by the cathedral, under the wretched instruction of the even more wretched church official, Nicodemus. At least he wasn't still about, having been exiled after he was eventually found out for the dishonest schemer he was.[6]

'Let's go and find her, then,' Cwen said, sounding very anxious for some action that wasn't library-based.

'She'll turn up soon enough,' Colesvain said. 'When she does, just give her the book and have done with it.'

'She might be connected to Elmund. Maybe he's run off to see her?' Cwen suggested.

---

[6] In the beginning, was The Heretics of De'Ath

The Hermes Parchment

'He's never given her the time of day before,' Martin said.

'But they both seem to be overly interested in the books,' Hermitage said. 'She's very keen to get hold of them, and after seeing one book, the man who never leaves the library has left.'

'Do as you please,' Colesvain said as he stood once more. 'But get that book to Ardith. Quite frankly, this library has been nothing but a nuisance all my life. I'll be glad to see the back of it. I've got more important things to do anyway. I'll tell you what.' He rubbed his chin in thought. 'If Elmund does come back, don't let him in. It's one very good way of getting rid of the wretch.' With that, he strode from the room.

After a few moments, in which no one had anything useful to say, the door opened again, very slowly.

Picot appeared, obviously having made sure his father had gone.

'So,' he said, striding into the room as if he owned it now. 'What's this about a book with great big jewels in the cover?'

Caput XII Suspicious? Who Cares?

𝔓icot was eventually persuaded that he didn't need to take the jewels from the cover of the book, "just so that he could get them checked by a trader he knew". The persuasion centred on what his father would do to him if he interfered with this volume; and what King William might do when he found out that the cathedral donation had been robbed before it even got there.

Much against his better judgement, Hermitage used the very dubious volume he had found in the Rooksby box, to tempt Picot away from Hermes Trismegistus. He felt very bad about it, but Picot was very easily tempted and happily went off to his room, the volume clutched under his arm.

'What are we doing?' Wat asked once he had gone.

'What are we doing?' Hermitage didn't understand the question at all.

'Well, not us, specifically. I'll re-phrase the question. Cwen, what are you doing?'

'Me?' Cwen sounded as surprised as Hermitage to hear that they were doing anything at all.

'Yes, you. What's all this about going to find this cathedral woman and seeing where Elmund has gone?'

'Well, it is a bit odd, isn't it?' Cwen said.

Wat looked at her blankly. 'And perhaps you can tell me who cares?'

'Pardon?'

'Who cares? Who cares where a librarian has gone? Hermitage might, but then he likes that sort of thing. We've got tapestry to make for Godrinius, so what we need to do is go back to Derby and set the apprentices to work.'

'A tapestry?' Hermitage asked, feeling a touch of worry

about what sort of work this might be.

'Don't worry, it's very pious,' Wat said.

'In fact, pious was the very word Godrinius used,' Cwen added.

'Well, that's good.' Hermitage was pleased to hear it but was still prepared to get a nasty surprise when he saw what Wat's idea of pious looked like.

'So, I don't know why we're asking questions about the library that are nothing to do with us.'

'It's all very suspicious,' Cwen said. 'Godrinius told us that there isn't a cathedral library, so what's going on?'

'I'll say it again, who cares?'

'It could be part of something bigger.'

'Something bigger?'

'A bigger scheme or plan, involving goodness knows what.'

'Murder?' Wat suggested.

'Murder?' Hermitage squeaked.

'Who knows.' Cwen sounded sombre and serious.

'I do,' Wat said. 'This is a library and they've misplaced a librarian, that's it. You've been going on about murder since Hermitage was asked to come here. I think you'd rather like there to be one.'

'Not at all,' Cwen protested.

Wat folded his arms and looked very superior. 'Oh, yes you would. I think you like it when there's some murder to investigate. People to question, killers to chase. In fact, I think you'd rather like to be King's Investigator yourself.'

Hermitage would be quite happy about that.

'That's ridiculous.' Cwen dismissed the idea.

'Think of all that power,' Wat said temptingly. 'You could barge into places, threaten people with the king's authority and bring murderers to justice.'

'You're getting completely the wrong end of things.'

'Good. Let's go back to Derby and get on with the tapestry then.'

'Doesn't it bother you at all that Hermitage is here sorting out a library that is being donated to the cathedral at the king's behest, and then we find out there is no cathedral?'

'Erm, let me think. No.'

'You're not in the least curious about who this Ardith is or where Elmund has gone?'

'No.'

'Or what happens to these books once they're handed over?'

'Ah, now on that topic I am absolutely clear.'

'Good.'

'Absolutely clear that I absolutely do not care.'

Cwen sidled a little closer to Wat and almost hissed the next words into his ear; rather like a snake in a tree with something special to offer in the way of apples. 'Not even books with great big jewels in them.'

Wat could not stop his eye wandering over to the very valuable-looking cover of the Hermes book. 'Great big jewels that belong to the king's tenant-in-chief, and will soon be donated to the cathedral, as King William expects.'

'But what if someone is stealing jewels from under the king's nose?'

'The king needs a bigger nose. Which most definitely is not our problem.'

'You tell him, Hermitage.'

'Tell him what?'

'That this is all very suspicious.'

'Is it?'

'There you are.' Wat was happy. 'Even the duly appointed

The Hermes Parchment

King's Investigator can't see that this is suspicious.'

'Yes, but he misses suspicious things most of the time.'

Hermitage had to accept that this was true.

'I expect Elmund will turn up,' he said. 'It's true, he did get terribly excited about this book and ran out, but there could be good reason.'

'Such as?' Cwen asked.

'I don't know.' Hermitage glanced at Martin, who had been watching this exchange with complete bemusement.

'Well,' he added. 'Perhaps that's not strictly true.'

'Oh, yes. Go on.' Cwen sounded intrigued, which drew a huge sigh from Wat.

Hermitage took a moment before he explained. 'I didn't want to say anything in front of Lord Colesvain, but Elmund did seem to have a particular interest in writings with a, what can we say, magical aspect to them.'

'Magical?'

'Yes. You know, Simon Magus for example. All nonsense of course. There's no such thing as magic, the church has confirmed it. But he also looked through Beowulf for the passage on demons. And now he's got terribly excited about Hermes Trismegistus.'

'He looked through what?'

'Beowulf. It's a book I found with a lot of nonsense about monsters and heroes and the like.'

'And demons.'

'One or two, yes.'

'And people like that sort of thing, do they?'

'Someone went to the trouble of writing it down, so I'd say yes.'

'Hm.' Cwen sounded as if Beowulf would be the last thing she'd read.

'I thought you said this Hermes fellow was a prophet and inspired church people?' Wat asked.

'Well, yes, that's true. But there are other passages that are a bit less orthodox. And in the middle of the book, I found this.'

Hermitage went over to the book and opened it to the middle once more. He didn't find the right page immediately, so turned a few backwards and forwards until he found what he was looking for. 'There,' he held his hands out.

The others all gathered around to consider the page.

'What is it?' Cwen asked.

'I have no idea, really. The writing is in some arcane language that I've never seen before, and what the diagram means is a mystery. But, try standing back and looking at the whole thing.'

They stood back.

'What?' Wat said, not seeing anything.

'Ooh,' Cwen said. 'It's a demon.'

'Where?' Wat squinted.

'Oh, yes,' Martin agreed. 'How ingenious.'

'Where's a demon?' Wat pressed.

'Here,' Cwen demonstrated by pointing at various points of the picture. 'That's his eye, there's his ear, these lines are the hair, and the pointy star thing is his mouth.'

Wat turned his head this way and that. 'I don't see it. You're just making things up.'

'We can all see it, can't we.' Cwen looked to the monks who nodded.

'Seeing demons in books, eh?' Wat scoffed. 'Right.'

'Did Elmund see this?' Cwen asked.

'No,' Hermitage shook his head. 'He jumped up when we mentioned the name of the book. He wanted to take it away for himself.'

'A bit big for that,' Wat noted.

'Exactly. He couldn't move it. He got some servants to come and look so that they could say they'd seen it. Then he discovered it was all in Greek and rushed out.'

Wat clapped his hands together. 'Well, I'm glad that's all sorted out then.'

'Sorted out? Cwen asked. 'Nothing's sorted out.'

'Everything's sorted out that is of any interest to us, I mean. Elmund's got excited by a naughty book about demons and has run out. Hermitage says he'll come back soon enough. End of problem. End of our problem, anyway.'

'Something is going on,' Cwen enunciated very clearly.

'Lucky old something. While it's going on, we can go on back to Derby.'

'Pah,' Cwen snorted. 'We can't go back until tomorrow anyway.'

'And why's that?'

'Because, if we set off now, we won't even get to Newark before dark. Then we'll have to stop again before Derby. Two nights' expensive lodgings instead of one. Leave at first light and we'll do it in two days.'

'Hm.' Wat didn't sound happy but couldn't deny the sense in that. Then he snapped his fingers. 'But that'll be cheaper than staying at the Hill Top another night.'

'We won't be staying there though, will we? We'll be staying here.'

'Here?'

'Of course. This is where all the suspicious book stuff is happening. I'm sure Lord Colesvain won't mind. He's got so many rooms he probably won't even notice.'

Wat just shook his head, clearly having given up all

resistance. 'I think you need to concentrate on weaving a bit more. Hermitage is a bad influence.'

Hermitage had never been a bad influence on anything before. It sounded quite exciting.

'And who knows,' Cwen said. 'Elmund might come back and we can sort everything out before we go.'

'Or he won't, we won't, and we still go anyway.' Wat made the position clear.

Cwen shrugged that she was willing to accept this. 'What do we do with the rest of the day then?' she asked.

'Well,' Hermitage said. 'Martin and I have more than enough work to be getting on with. Elmund's absence won't be a hindrance because he didn't actually do much anyway.'

'And we could start sketching out the tapestry for Godrinius the pious,' Wat said. 'Make some use of this enforced idleness.'

'Aha,' Hermitage said. 'I might have something of interest.'

Wat looked as if he thought that was very unlikely.

Hermitage went off to one corner of the library where he had already started a small pile of books. 'Where is it?' he mumbled to himself. 'Ah, yes, here we are.'

He returned to Wat and Cwen, struggling to hold a big thick volume in his hands.

'Oh,' Wat said as if receiving a gift. 'It's a book, you shouldn't have.'

'Not just any book. Look inside.'

Hermitage put the book on a table near them. Like the Hermes volume, this too had a magnificent cover, inset with jewels, although it was much smaller. Cwen opened it. Inside, each page was a blaze of glorious colour. Magnificent illustrations took up whole sides of the open book, while pages of Latin text appeared throughout.

The Hermes Parchment

Gold and red patterns interwove on some pages, while clearly religious illustrations of the Virgin Mary and various saints dominated others.

'You'll probably find something quite pious in there.'

'Wonderful,' Cwen breathed as she looked through it, each page stiff with age as she turned it. 'What is it?'

'It's the gospels,' Hermitage said quite casually. 'It's a very nice one, but we've got quite a few here.'

'Who made it?'

'No idea. Quite a lot of people, I expect, it is quite a big work. As far as I can tell from some other notes, it came from a place called Lindisfarne.'

'Lindisfarne Gospels, eh?' Wat gave it a cursory look. Despite himself, he seemed quite impressed. 'There might well be some ideas here.' He gave a little laugh. 'Who'd have thought a book would come in useful.'

...

They all worked quietly on their own for the rest of the day, and there was no sign of Elmund or of Ardith. Picot didn't bother them, and they all got on with their tasks.

Hermitage found some more gospels to add to his growing pile, his smile broadening with each addition. Martin was engrossed in a box full of parchment, while Wat and Cwen had started sketching out some ideas for the Godrinius tapestry.

They'd asked if they could tear some pages out of the Lindisfarne Gospels to take away with them, but Hermitage had nearly fainted again at the suggestion and had to be revived with some wine. They satisfied themselves with some rough copies they made.

As the evening drew in, Martin suggested that they should retire for the night as it had been a trying day.

Hermitage was very happy to volunteer to be the one staying in the library all hours, as Lord Colesvain had suggested. He could keep himself occupied for quite some time yet, and when he did need to sleep, he thought that any disturbance would wake him.

He did take advantage of the offer to slip out and use the privy before he settled in. Following Elmund's habit of the fireplace didn't appeal at all.

When he returned, Martin had produced a bed sack full of straw from somewhere and had laid it out in one corner along with a small jug of wine.

'We'll go and get our things from the Hill Top,' Wat said. 'Don't wait up.'

Hermitage imagined that getting their things from the Hill Top would involve some wine in comfort before they returned to whatever space could be found in Colesvain's house.

Martin bid him goodnight and said that he would tell the servants what was happening. If Elmund did return, they would all want to be present, to find out just what the librarian was up to.

With the library to himself, it was several hours later that Hermitage finally had to admit that he needed to sleep. And those hours had been most uncomfortable. He wanted to settle down and delve deep into one volume or another, but then all the others kept calling to him and he had to get up and browse them. That would reveal some new fascination, which was itself broken by the sight of another work, sneaking into the corner of his eye.

Eventually, he went over to his makeshift bed and settled

down for the night; with only three or four books at his side, "just in case."

He didn't recall the moment of going to sleep, but then who did? As far as he could recall, his sleep had been undisturbed and peaceful, although he did not feel terribly refreshed as he started to wake. In fact, he felt quite peculiar. Maybe this was because Cwen appeared to be shaking him vigorously and calling his name with some anxiety.

He tried to speak but found that he couldn't get any words out. He told himself to wake up, but sleep kept dragging him backwards. All he needed was another hour or two, then he'd be fine.

There was some shouting going on now, but he mixed it in with his dreams and let the real world slip away once more.

When the bucket of water was thrown over his face, he found that he could wake up, after all.

'What?' he spluttered and coughed as he sat up. 'What was that for?'

'To wake you up,' Cwen said urgently. 'It didn't look like you were going to. Ever.'

'Ever?' Hermitage did not know what was going on. He could see that Martin and Wat were in the room and that Cwen was holding a now-empty bucket. He might have thought it was some sort of joke if they weren't all looking so serious.

'What is it?' he asked. 'What's going on?'

'I was wrong,' Cwen said.

'Wrong?'

'I'm prepared to admit when I'm wrong.'

'No, you aren't,' Hermitage heard Wat mutter.

'And this time I was wrong.'

'Wrong about what?'

Cwen squatted down at his side and laid a hand on his shoulder. Now he knew something was amiss.

'Colesvain was not going to be murdered.'

'Oh, well, that's good,' Hermitage said. He'd never really thought he was.

'It was Elmund.' Cwen nodded over her shoulder.

Hermitage glanced in that direction and saw the body that was lying on the floor. 'Oh, no,' he groaned. 'Not another one.'

Caput XIII Normal Service is Resumed

His feelings at the sight of dead Elmund were very mixed. On the one hand, he was appalled that the poor old fellow was dead. On the other, he had an overwhelming urge to say "I told you so".

Then he was horrified that this body was in the room with him and might have been for some time. How could he have slept while someone arrived in his makeshift bedroom and then died on the floor?

Finally, he felt shame that the very reason he had been sleeping in the library in the first place, to watch out for Elmund, had come to pass, and he'd slept through it.

He put his hands behind him and turned to hoist himself onto his feet; a bit too quickly, it seemed, as his head spun. Once he'd got his balance back, he looked at Elmund.

Cwen had said that he was murdered, and he had thought that this was a bit of a bold assumption to make on the basis of someone lying on the floor. Could it be that Elmund wasn't dead at all? Or if he was, it could be entirely natural.

He considered the deceased librarian and thought that it probably was murder.

The man was laid out on the floor, face down, with his arms stretched out on either side. His legs were apart, and he looked just like a penitent who has thrown himself before the altar.

Although most penitents tended not to bleed quite so copiously.

'It is Elmund?' he checked. With the face down and the cowl drawn up it was quite possible that this was someone else; someone else who had been murdered in the library.

'Definitely Elmund,' Martin said, Hermitage only now

noticing that he was in the room.

'And, erm, how was he..? That is to say, how did he..? I mean, all his blood? It seems to have, sort of, come out?'

'It certainly has,' Wat said. He was standing closest to the body, but still some distance away so that he didn't get any of Elmund's vital fluid on his shoes.

'A knife?'

'Pretty much essential, I'd have thought,' Cwen said. She then took a deep breath. 'But I am afraid there is worse, Hermitage.'

'Worse?' He looked quickly around the room, wondering what could be worse than a dead librarian in a pool of blood.

'I think you better sit down.'

Hermitage frowned at her but complied. He was still feeling peculiar from his deep sleep and a sit down would be nice.

As he did so, Cwen squatted at his side and put a consoling hand on his knee.

'What is it?' he asked in all seriousness. He really could not imagine what could be worse than this.

'I'm afraid,' Cwen said in a sombre tone, 'that your book has been murdered as well.'

That was ridiculous. You couldn't murder a book. And anyway, what did she mean, his book? 'My book has been murdered?' He gave half a smile at the very silly statement.

Cwen nodded her head over to the table in front of which Elmund lay. Hermitage followed her prompting.

There was the Hermes Trismegistus volume, its huge and bright cover dominating the space as it had when he went to sleep. He had thought about taking it to bed to study but reasoned that the thing was so heavy it might crush him if he fell asleep with it on top of him.

The Hermes Parchment

There didn't appear to be anything wrong with it, so he still couldn't see what Cwen was going on about. Then he noticed that the cover was sitting at a rather peculiar angle. It wasn't lying flat as it had been. The spine of the book was still solid, but the outer edge of the book had sunk, somehow.

He stood now and went over to it. He had a horrible sinking feeling about this. Cwen would not have warned him in so serious a manner if there wasn't something to worry about.

As he drew near to the book, he saw that there was something very wrong with it indeed. The cover was still there, but it wasn't covering anything anymore. The entire contents of the book had gone.

He pulled the front cover open with surprising strength and gazed at the ruin before his eyes. Stubs and fragments of charred and burned pages lay against the back cover like the remains of last night's fire.

A corner of the title page remained in place, and he could just make out EPMOY TPI, Hermes Tri, as he would say it. He gazed at what remained of the book for several long moments. The others maintained a respectful silence.

That such disaster should befall this great volume, only the day after he recovered it from its hiding place, was beyond bearing. It was the most magnificent volume he had ever seen; or rather, it had been. Of inestimable value, both for the knowledge it contained and its more worldly price, it was now gone. It was simply unbelievable, and he really couldn't take it in.

'How is this possible?' Hermitage breathed.

'We know,' Cwen said, with genuine sympathy.

Hermitage put a hand to his mouth and shook his head very slowly from side to side as he looked at the book and what remained of its contents.

Then he looked at the inside of the cover. Then he closed it and looked at the front again. Next, he turned the whole thing over and repeated the process with the back cover.

'It's gone, Hermitage,' Cwen said. She was clearly thinking that Hermitage was hoping his eyes deceived him and the contents of the book were still in there somewhere.

'I mean,' Hermitage said, his puzzlement hopping around inside his head. 'How is this possible?'

'Books have to go sometime,' Wat said with a shrug.

'I know that.' Hermitage was feeling quite lively. 'What I mean is how is this possible.' He even pointed at the book, to bring their attention to the contradiction it presented.

'It burned,' Cwen said.

'No, it didn't.'

'Erm.' Cwen looked at the others as if expressing her concern that Hermitage was not taking this at all well and that she might need some help dealing with him in a moment or two. 'All the pages. They've gone. They burned away.'

'How?'

'Fire?'

'A fire that burns the contents of a book to a charred mess, but doesn't touch the cover?'

It was Cwen's opportunity to frown. 'Oh.'

'Oh, exactly. And this was a big book. If the pages in this had caught fire, they would likely have taken the whole library with them.'

'Then, how?' Cwen asked.

'That's what I said,' Hermitage confirmed. 'How does the entire inside of a very large book burn away, while the cover remains untouched?' He flipped the cover back and forth. 'There isn't so much as a stain on it.'

The Hermes Parchment

'That's very odd,' Martin said, as he came over.

'It certainly is. More than odd, I would say. Here,' he held the remaining front page between his fingers. 'You can just make out the first Greek letters. From the colouring that remains, it's clear that this really was the front page. But, like the others, it has obviously been burned.' He crumbled a bit of the ash between his fingers now. 'Yet the front cover, that was sitting right on top of this page, is completely free of any mark.'

Martin now moved the book around, opening and closing the cover and considering what remained of the interior in close detail. He even got his face down and sniffed at the interior.

'The smell of burnt parchment is clear.'

'There is no doubt that the pages have been burned away.'

Martin shook his head. 'I really don't understand how this is possible.'

Hermitage just held his hand out to remind them all that that was just what he'd said.

Martin looked at the table the book was sitting on, the floor by its side and even up at the ceiling. 'There's not even any sign of the fire spreading beyond the contents of the book.'

Hermitage nodded agreement.

'Not even a trace of ash anywhere else at all,' Martin went on. 'I did have to burn some old ragged ends of parchment a while ago,' he said.

Hermitage was positively alarmed at that statement and obviously looked it.

Martin waved the problem away. 'There was nothing written, they had clearly been off-cuts of the main sheet.'

'I see.'

'And, erm, Elmund had used them in the fireplace.'

Hermitage really was revolted by that. There were some things that one simply did not do with parchment, and that was the very first of them.

'Your point?' Wat asked.

'The point is that when I burned them, they spread ash all over the place. They caught in the draft from the chimney and left a residue everywhere. With this burned book, there isn't so much as a speck of ash anywhere. Apart from in the book.'

Hermitage had managed to move on from his horror at the sight of the destroyed masterpiece and was now thoroughly intrigued about how it might have happened.

He said the problem out loud, hoping that hearing the words might help find a solution. 'We have a book on a table, the inside of which has been completely burned away. The cover of the book is not scorched, touched or marked in any way. There is no sign of ash or the remains of the pages anywhere in the room.' He looked to the others to see if this had helped. It certainly hadn't helped him.

The only possible answer that kept pushing on the inside of his head was magic. He certainly wasn't going to even consider that nonsense.

'There is one other thing we're not talking about,' Cwen said.

'Hm?' Hermitage was staring hard at the book as if his gaze would force it to give up its secrets. 'What's that?'

'The dead librarian in the room?'

'The one with all the blood,' Wat added.

'Oh, yes.' Hermitage was ashamed that he'd completely forgotten about the remains of Elmund.

'At least he's not been burned,' Cwen said.

The Hermes Parchment

'Bit of a coincidence though, isn't it?' Wat said. 'Dead librarian and burned out book. I bet you don't get that very often in a library.'

Hermitage scowled at his levity. 'I suppose we had better see if we can find out what happened to Elmund.'

'I think we can see what happened,' Wat said, clearly not wanting to get any closer. 'He had a lie-down and all his blood came out.'

'Or vice versa,' Cwen suggested.

Wat nodded that this was a reasonable alternative.

'But how?' Hermitage asked. 'People's blood doesn't just come out of them. As Cwen said, it needs a knife or something similar.'

'Even librarians?' Wat asked.

'They are normal human beings,' Hermitage said.

'Really?' Wat sounded quite surprised by this.

'We need to turn him over.' Hermitage nodded towards Elmund, hoping that someone else would do it.

'Off you go, then.' Wat nodded towards the large pool of blood.

'Here, move the table.' Martin stepped forward. Wat joined him, and they took the table with the Hermes volume on it and moved it away from Elmund's body. Around the head, there was less blood on the floor, and so it was possible to reach the librarian without stepping in some of his mortal remains.

'There's no sign of anything on his back,' Martin reported. 'The habit looks clean and untouched. Well, not clean obviously, but no sign of attack.'

He got down on his hands and knees and moved the cowl back from the head. 'Oh, dear, poor fellow.' He crossed himself, and the others joined in. 'He was a most difficult man, but no one deserves this fate.'

Martin nodded at Wat and made it clear that he wanted some more assistance.

With a reluctant sigh, Wat joined Martin and they both grasped Elmund's shoulder, heaving him over onto his back.

'That'll be where the blood came from then,' Cwen observed.

Hermitage turned away and dashed for the fireplace, in case he needed to leave his stomach there.

'It's well known that all the blood of the body is kept in the throat,' Martin said. 'That's why it comes out when you get cut there.'

Wat and Cwen squinted at one another that they weren't quite sure about that. Still, it wasn't worth arguing about right now.

'And Elmund has definitely been cut there,' Cwen confirmed.

'And all his blood came out the hole,' Wat said.

Hermitage swallowed hard and concentrated on the mess that was in the fireplace.

'No sign of a weapon, though,' Cwen said. 'Whoever did this didn't leave their knife behind.'

'And he didn't do it himself,' Wat added. 'Not unless he went and put the knife away before coming back.'

'I hardly think tidying up would be his main concern.' Cwen tutted.

'And there's no sign of blood anywhere else,' Martin pointed out.

'But why laid out like that?' Wat asked, being a bit more serious now. 'If you want to cut someone's throat you just do it and let them drop.' The others looked at him. 'I imagine,' he added. 'He must have been attacked and then put here.'

The Hermes Parchment

'The alternative being that he lay down and then he was murdered,' Cwen said. 'Which would be an odd thing to do.'

'Odd,' Wat repeated. 'Yes, it would definitely be odd.'

'And then there's the book,' Cwen said. 'Not only was Elmund laid out here on the floor with his arms out, but he was also facing the book. The one that was burned to death without damaging it.'

Hermitage managed to emerge from the fireplace now. He had got his stomach under control and was sure that as long as he didn't look at Elmund too closely, he would be all right.

With his senses getting themselves back in some sort of order, he was reaching his old conclusion once more.

'This time, I was even in the room,' he said quietly.

'Pardon?' Cwen said.

'The King's Investigator and all the murders. This time I was actually asleep in the room when it was done.'

'Yes,' Wat said. 'How did you manage to sleep through all this? Burning books, dying librarians, you'd think there would have been a bit of noise.'

'I have no idea.' Hermitage shook his head.

'It was hard enough to wake you when we tried,' Cwen said. 'It took a bucket of water to get you in the end. Setting light to books and murdering librarians might well have not been enough.'

'You don't usually sleep that heavily.' Wat noted. 'Slightest noise and you're up worrying what it is.'

'An unnatural sleep,' Martin said, with a horrible seriousness in his voice.

'Unnatural?' Hermitage didn't like the sound of that.

'Of course. Sleeping through the murder of Elmund. Then you can't be woken'

'And I still feel a bit peculiar.'

'Unnatural.' Martin looked around the room as if taking the whole ghastly place in. 'We must tell Lord Colesvain about all of this, of course. But before we do, I think there is one thing we must consider. And I would rather Colesvain was not privy to it.'

'Really?' Hermitage asked, a bit intrigued, despite himself.

'Putting this whole situation together, along with what we know about Elmund.'

'Go on,' Cwen instructed.

Martin still seemed a bit reluctant but took a breath and went on. 'The book of Hermes Trismegistus is burned from the inside out without any trace of the fire damaging anything else at all. Elmund is found dead and prostrate at the table where the book is resting. Finally, Brother Hermitage has an unnatural sleep, just as all this is happening.'

Hermitage nodded that this was a reasonable summary.

'And we know which books were of particular interest to Elmund.'

'We do,' Hermitage confirmed. 'Magic.'

'Magic.' Cwen huffed as if she couldn't see any connection.

'Of course,' Martin went on. 'And the picture of the demon is now gone. That was in the middle of the book, wasn't it?'

'Erm, yes, roughly,' Hermitage said.

'So that's where the fire could have begun.'

'With the demon?'

'Precisely. Elmund could have come back intending to take the book, or at least do something with it. He casts a spell on Brother Hermitage to make him sleep, and then begins his work.'

Hermitage, Wat and Cwen were looking askance at this suggestion, but Martin seemed to be taking it very seriously.

'But it all goes wrong. Elmund tries something, I don't know what, but it causes the demon in the book to come alight.'

'And then jump out of the book and cut his throat?' Cwen suggested with a snort.

'Who knows?' Martin said. 'These are demons we're dealing with.'

Cwen now gave a short laugh. 'Hermitage, you tell him.'

'Tell him what?'

'That there are no demons. You said yourself there's no such thing as magic.'

'That's true,' Hermitage agreed. 'Definitely no such thing as magic.'

'There you are then.'

'But demons? Well, that's another question altogether.'

Caput XIV Colesvain All Round

'What the devil?'

Hermitage thought this a most inappropriate expression in the circumstances, but Lord Colesvain was entitled to use it, what with finding his librarian dead on the floor.

'What in God's name happened?' Colesvain squatted at Elmund's side and considered the very plain fact of the death, and the method of its delivery. 'What has this idiot done to himself?'

Hermitage was a bit surprised by that remark.

'His throat's been cut,' Wat pointed out.

'You don't say?' Colesvain spared Wat a glare.

'Bit tricky to do it to himself?' Wat suggested. 'In which case, someone did it to him? And if that is so, we could ask who did it, and why?'

'Much better questions,' Cwen observed rather smugly. 'Who committed the murder and why, eh?'

Colesvain frowned deeply now and stood to consider the room. 'What are you two doing here again? You can't just walk into my house off the street, you know.'

'Of course,' Cwen bowed her apology. 'It's just that we usually help Hermitage investigate his murders.'

Colesvain didn't have anything to say to that. It looked very much as if he hadn't actually understood the words at all.

Hermitage dropped his head. He knew that Elmund was dead. He knew that it was murder. He knew he was King's Investigator and this sort of thing was bound to happen. He just wished no one had mentioned it.

Lord Colesvain found his voice. 'His murders?' You mean he did this?' He considered Hermitage quite closely. 'He doesn't look the type.'

'No, no. He doesn't do them. He investigates them.'

Colesvain looked at Cwen, silently demanding an explanation.

'It means he tracks who did it.'

'He tracks who does murders?'

'That's it.'

'And that's a job, is it, tracking murderers?'

'Oh, yes. He's an investigator.'

'That's ridiculous. Whoever heard of such nonsense? I tell you what, though. Elmund was perfectly all right until you three turned up.'

'That's what I said,' Hermitage felt as if he was in a world of his own. A world where inevitability followed him around like a dog. If he didn't keep feeding it, it would bite his leg off.

'You what?'

'I said there would be murder if I came here. I warned Martin, didn't I?'

Colesvain now passed his glare to Brother Martin.

'It's not like that at all,' Martin pleaded. 'Brother Hermitage has had to investigate murders so often that he believes they happen when he's near, which is nonsense, obviously.'

Colesvain nodded towards Elmund's body. 'I think I'm with Brother Hermitage, so far. And you brought him here despite the warning?'

'The murder has happened, and we are fortunate to have Brother Hermitage with us.'

'I'm not sure Elmund sees it that way. And I think we need to know a lot more about this monk and his friends. Before they were here, we had a lot fewer dead librarians.'

Despite his horror at the murder, Hermitage felt the

suggestion that he had something to do with it was unfair. Yes, it had happened when he was near, but he hadn't done anything. In fact, he'd slept through the whole thing. He did feel that the murder of a librarian was a more unspeakable act than most; even if the librarian concerned wasn't actually very nice.

Of all the dead people he'd had to deal with, he had found that quite a lot of them actually deserved it. It was only the instructions of the king or the fact that he found himself there at the time, that made him investigate anything at all.

He tried to maintain the conviction that there must be murders going on all over the country, that he knew nothing about, and so he couldn't be the cause. The more they happened close by, the more doubts he had.

But librarians? If people were going to go around murdering librarians, they needed to be stopped.

Colesvain was frowning at Hermitage now. 'How does a monk get a job investigating murder anyway? I've never heard of it before. I've got a Shire Reeve to track killers. Not that I like people being murdered in my library.'

Hermitage found that, despite himself, he really did want to look into this murder. The books, the librarian…, the books. Could he really walk away? He knew that there was one thing he could say to make sure he was not dismissed.

'The king.'

'The king?' Colesvain looked thoroughly confused, and a bit worried.

Hermitage tried to look modest and unassuming and as if he was only being forced to reveal this information. 'King William made me his investigator.' He shrugged that this really couldn't be his fault.

'King William?' Colesvain responded in just the way

The Hermes Parchment

Hermitage expected; suspicious, but very cautious.

'And before that, King Harold.' Hermitage completed the picture.

'I didn't know King William had an investigator.' Colesvain sounded very suspicious.

Hermitage could only look apologetic. 'I've had to look into various matters for him and Le Pedvin.'

'Le Pedvin?' Colesvain swallowed now.

'Dead nuns in Kent, dead nobles in the garderobe, dead Saracens, Normans and Druids.'[7] Hermitage sagged as he realised how long the list was.

'Druids?' Colesvain spluttered.

'Never done a librarian before,' Cwen put in.

Lord Colesvain was now looking very confused. 'And you brought him here?' he turned on Martin.

'Not for that,' Martin explained. 'Brother Hermitage is a learned monk. He is an expert on the post-Exodus prophets. It is for his learning that I fetched him.'

'But he warned you there would be a murder?'

'Well, yes, but that was ridiculous.'

'So ridiculous it has left a huge bloodstain on my library floor.' Lord Colesvain now paced up and down the room a bit, clearly trying to reach a decision about what he had to do.

'And you two follow him everywhere, do you?'

'Oh, yes,' Cwen nodded.

'So, how do we know it's not you causing the murders?'

'I only met Hermitage after he'd already done two.'

'Very comforting, I'm sure. And you?' he asked Wat.

'I've been in since the start.' Wat smiled that he should be recognised as the more senior of the investigator's assistants.

'It could be you, then.'

---

[7] And every one has their own book!

Wat showed not the least sign of concern at this potential curse. Briefly, it occurred to Hermitage that they might be able to share it; he soon concluded that it was for him alone.

Colesvain shook his head. 'I suppose you want to investigate Elmund?'

'I'm not sure, "want to" is the right expression,' Hermitage said. 'But I am here and Elmund is here.'

'Yes, he is, isn't he.'

'And there's the book to consider.' Cwen reminded them.

'What book?' Colesvain asked, which seemed an odd question in a library.

'The great big one. Hermes, what's-his-name.'

'What?' Colesvain seemed to ignite at this news. 'What about it?'

'It's burnt.'

'Burnt?' Colesvain shouted out.

'I'm afraid so,' Hermitage confirmed, nodding towards the remains of the book.

Colesvain quickly stepped over to the table and considered the book.

'At least the jewels are still there,' Wat observed.

Colesvain opened the front cover of the book and simply stared at the contents. 'How is this possible?'

'That's what I wondered.' Hermitage stepped over to join the owner at his book, well, at its cover anyway.

'As you see, the contents have been completely burned away, yet the cover remains untouched. Brother Martin has pointed out that there is not even any sign of ash in the room.'

Colesvain quickly looked around, as if confirming this was the case.

'And there's a dead librarian stretched out in front of it,'

The Hermes Parchment

Cwen pointed out for all their benefit; in case they'd forgotten.

'And you can investigate all this, can you?' Colesvain asked.

'I can try,' Hermitage shrugged. 'All I ever do is try.'

'And you succeed?'

'Well, he's still alive,' Wat said. 'None of the killers has got him and William hasn't done the deed.'

Colesvain nodded as if this was the best mark of success there was. 'And they're connected? The death of Elmund and the book?'

'Who can say?' Hermitage considered telling Lord Colesvain their concerns about Elmund. After all, if he had been in the household for years, Colesvain might have information about the old librarian that would be of use. Suggesting the involvement of devils and demons seemed to be going a bit far. 'It is a bit of a coincidence,' was the best he could come up with. 'Man and book, both dead in the same room.'

'And where had he been?' Colesvain asked. 'The man who never left the room went out. Where did he go? Who did he see? Could they have anything to do with this?'

Hermitage thought that they sounded like very good questions indeed. He must remember to try and find out the answers.

'We shall have to go out into the town and see if anyone saw him,' he said.

'Yes.' Lord Colesvain looked very thoughtful. 'You do that.' He patted the cover of the Hermes volume. 'And you report to the king, you say?'

'Oh, er, well.' Hermitage didn't really know how to answer this. There was something in the manner of the question that gave him pause; he didn't usually get pause and act upon it.

'Not necessarily,' Wat said.

Hermitage was a bit surprised by that answer. It wasn't one he'd have come up with.

'We're obviously not here on the king's business,' Wat went on. 'William has not instructed Hermitage to come and investigate, so why would he report back? This is a purely local matter.'

'Hm,' Colesvain's thoughtfulness was not going away. 'But one of the volumes that was going to the cathedral has now gone. A very valuable volume.'

'But not one that was in the catalogue,' Martin spoke up.

Hermitage didn't understand what was going on here, but he could tell that it was something.

Martin shrugged the problem away. 'It can't go in the catalogue now we don't have it anymore. All we could put would be, "cover of a burned book". I'm sure the king wouldn't be at all interested in that.'

'And I'm absolutely positive that he's not in the least bothered about dead librarians,' Wat added.

Colesvain seemed satisfied with this. 'Or Le Pedvin,' he said.

'We never tell Le Pedvin anything,' Wat said in all seriousness. 'Unless it's completely unavoidable.'

'Right. So, we forget the book, but we find out who did for Elmund. Never mind the king, I'm the tenant-in-chief and I can't have people murdered in my own house.'

'Quite right too.' Cwen nodded as if it was an outrageously rude thing to do.

'What would William think?' Colesvain shook his head.

Hermitage looked at the body of Elmund and chastised himself once more for being asleep while the deed was done. How was that possible? He had a thought; one he was quite proud of. 'Perhaps someone in the house heard or saw something?' he said.

'Hm,' Lord Colesvain was thoughtful. 'Flog a few servants, you mean?'

'Pardon?' Hermitage was taken aback by this suggestion. It sounded as if it was the way Colesvain started each morning. He had heard of such things, and he had seen the way the master dealt with his staff but was it really routine to flog them?

'See if one of them has something to say.'

Hermitage thought that "stop flogging me" might spring to mind.

'The door should have been locked, and the useless staff are supposed to deal with this sort of thing.'

Hermitage didn't imagine that "this sort of thing" was a regular occurrence, but he took the point. It would be bad enough if someone had broken in and taken the book; leaving a dead librarian on the floor was going a bit far.

He considered the floor of the room and couldn't see blood anywhere else. All of Elmund's must have come out where he lay. It was thus reasonable to conclude that he had been murdered in the library, and not killed outside and then brought in. Quite what help this conclusion was, he was not at all sure.

Lord Colesvain strode across to the library door, threw it open and bellowed that everyone was to "get in here this minute". He then returned and took one of the seats by the fireplace.

It seemed that the staff were used to instructions like this, as it wasn't very long at all before the first face appeared around the door. The face then disappeared again, the look clearly saying that there was no way it was going to be first. It reappeared quite quickly as someone from behind had obviously given it a push.

The first fellow on the scene was a young boy, small and meek and pale. He obviously had some function in the depths of the house, as the way he blinked at the windows made it quite clear that he hadn't seen daylight for quite some time.

His gasp at the sight of Elmund on the floor was loud and alarming.

'Ignore the dead librarian,' Lord Colesvain ordered. 'It's him I want to talk to you all about.'

The young lad was followed by a more robust looking older man, who pushed and shoved the boy to make sure that he was closest to Lord Colesvain in case there was any physical discussion to be had. He seemed less concerned about a body in the room but did his best to keep away from it.

Hermitage watched with growing astonishment as people continued to file into the room, each of them considering the corpse with a variety of reactions. Some almost tutted as if they saw things like this most days of the week. Others turned away and clamped hands over mouths and looked like they wanted to leave the room quite quickly.

There were more boys, men, women and girls. He recognised several from his wine-seeking expedition, but most of these people were complete strangers. How many people did Colesvain need to run his house?

As the arrivals petered out, one final old man came into the room, a floppy cap clutched to his chest as he looked around the room in astonishment. From the grime on his hands, Hermitage assumed that this was an outside worker. It also seemed reasonable to assume that he'd never actually been in the house at all before.

The ones at the back couldn't see the body, so had to take reports from those in the front row.

Lord Colesvain stood to see all the faces arrayed before him. There must be twenty people in the room now. He peered over heads as if making sure that everyone was here.

'Where's that useless son of mine?' he called out. 'Picot? Where are you hiding?'

There was no reply to this.

'Shall I go and fetch him, my Lord?' the servant who had opened the front door to them spoke up. This was obviously one of the more senior members of the household. He was one who had cast a glance at Elmund and then sniffed as if to say he might have known.

Hermitage tried hard to think whether the voice was the one from the kitchen that had talked of killing Colesvain. From the few short words, it was too hard to tell.

Colesvain simply waved the man away, and he scurried from the room.

'And if he's in the middle of doing something revolting,' Lord Colesvain called after him, 'bring him anyway.'

The master of the house seemed quite content to simply stand in front of his staff in complete silence, appraising them all with a cold eye.

Even though Hermitage didn't live here, he found the examination uncomfortable. Most of the staff seemed to share this as they all chose a part of the floor for their most earnest attention.

After several moments, the door opened again, and the servant returned.

'Where have you been?' Colesvain demanded, clearly thinking that this shouldn't have taken so long.

'I can't find him, my Lord.'
'Can't find him?'
'No, my Lord. He is not in his chamber, or anywhere else in the house.'
'Where's he gone?'
'I don't know, my Lord.'
'Well, that's no good, is it? Who here last saw Lord Picot?' he asked the crowd.

There was no answer.

'Come on, come on. Someone must have seen him today, or last night?'

When there was still no answer, one very nervous looking woman put her hand up.

'Who are you?' Colesvain asked.

'Edyth, my Lord. I'm a kitchen drudge.' She sounded as if she were horrified that she was having to speak not only in front of the master of the house but actually to him.

'And what do you know about my son?' Colesvain sounded quite appalled that such a lowly creature would even have laid eyes on Picot.

'Nothing, my Lord, Nothing. It's just that I saw him leave last night when I was putting the slops out.'

'Leave? What time was this?'

'Dark,' Edyth replied. 'Middle of the dark, it was.'

Hermitage could see that "light" and "dark" were probably the only differentiators of time this Edyth would need.

'And he just left.'

'That's right, my Lord.'

Colesvain frowned that this was not much help.

'It was about the time of the gurgling,' Edyth added.

'The gurgling?' Colesvain clearly thought she was mad.

'That's right, my Lord.'

'What gurgling?'

'The gurgling that was coming from in here.' She pointed at Elmund. 'I expect it was him doing the gurgling. Master Lordship Picot come out of this room, shut the door and run out the front. I Iad a terrible look on his face he did. And blood all over his hands.'

Caput XV Devil of a Job

Lord Colesvain leapt into action as only a tenant-in-chief of the king could leap. He barked out orders to various servants and snapped at them when they didn't leap as quickly as he did. He ordered one man to summon the Shire Reeve; he instructed others to get out into the town and start looking for his son and had yet more scouring the house and every corner of it to see if Picot was hiding somewhere.

He completely ignored the people in his library, including Elmund, and strode from the room cuffing the nearest servant round the back of the head, probably to make himself feel better.

'Oh, my,' Hermitage said, when they had the room to themselves once more.

'Well, well,' Cwen added.

Wat and Martin just exchanged looks.

'That's a bit suspicious, isn't it,' Hermitage offered when no one spoke.

'Really?' Wat asked, sounding surprised. 'Son of the house goes running from the room where a man has been murdered and he has blood all over his hands? Of course, I'm not the King's Investigator, so don't have your expertise, but I suppose it could be suspicious now you come to mention it, yes.'

'All right,' Hermitage could now recognise when Wat was being critical. 'It's very suspicious.'

'Why would Picot kill Elmund?' Martin asked, gazing at the body that still lay on the floor. 'I never had him as the type.'

'The type to cut peoples' throats?' Cwen asked.

'The type to actually do anything. He talks a lot, and

complains a lot, and moans a lot and tells people to do what he wants because he's the son of Colesvain, but that's about it. If he could, he wouldn't even pick up his own knife to eat his meal, let alone put one in someone's throat.'

'All talk and no action,' Wat summarised.

'Exactly. If he didn't have his father's name to bandy about, someone would have done something crude and unnecessary to him in an alley somewhere by now. He's very annoying.'

'Well, it's still suspicious,' Hermitage concluded, considering the body of Elmund, which was unavoidable. 'Do you, erm, think we should do something about him?' He nodded towards the corpse.

'It's a bit late to try reviving him,' Cwen said.

'Obviously. I mean should we move him, put him somewhere more dignified? I know he was a difficult soul, but he's just lying there on the floor in his own blood.'

'We are sure it is his own blood?' Cwen asked. 'Picot was covered in blood as well, we're told.'

'Edyth didn't mention Picot having a big hole in his throat,' Wat said. 'And he was still moving, of course. I reckon this is Elmund's.'

Cwen folded her arms. 'Hermitage is a monk,' she said.

'Erm, yes?'

'So he's Christian and forgiving and tolerant.'

'With you so far.'

'I'm not. One more clever remark from you, master weaver, and there'll be one more damaged body in the library.'

Wat held his hands out in mock horror.

'Brother Hermitage is right,' Martin said. 'We can't leave him here, and all the servants are off doing their master's bidding.'

'Is there somewhere suitable we might lay him?' Hermitage

asked quietly.

Martin looked around and gave it careful thought. 'The fireplace?' he suggested.

'The fireplace?' That didn't fit Hermitage's idea of dignified or suitable.

'He did spend quite a bit of time in there,' Martin pointed out.

'I'm not sure he'd want it as his last resting place.'

'It won't be the last. Just somewhere out of the way until he can be properly buried.'

'We can hardly put him outside,' Cwen said. 'The animals would have him.'

'And the Shire Reeve will probably want to have a look,' Wat added, a serious and sober expression on his face, clearly for Cwen's benefit.

'I'll do the feet,' Cwen said quickly.

Despite Hermitage's reservations, it seemed to be agreed that they would move Elmund into the fireplace.

Wat and Martin moved to the shoulders while Cwen and Hermitage took a leg each.

'I hope nothing falls off,' Wat said, to a very hard glare from Cwen. 'What? His throat's been cut, we don't know what's going to happen.'

Hermitage closed his eyes so he wouldn't have to see what happened.

On the count of three, they all lifted and shuffled sideways towards the fireplace. Hermitage was surprised at how heavy Elmund was. He was a fairly thin old man, and a lot of what had been inside him was now on the floor. It still took the four of them to manoeuvre him into the fireplace, with staggering steps and a lot of strength.

Fortunately, the fireplace was a large structure and there

was plenty of room for them all to walk in at the side of the fire basket. Wat and Martin went first and propped their end against the back wall. Once they had stopped moving, Hermitage put his leg down and opened his eyes.

He was grateful to see that all of Elmund had come with them, there was no need to go back for the leftovers.

They all stepped away and looked at the old librarian as if paying their respects. This was a touch difficult as the sight of a corpse propped in the corner of the fireplace was quite bizarre. It looked as if the old man had drunk too much the night before and was now having a bit of a rest in the only spot he could find.

That it was the spot he found for most of his other bodily functions, was an added insult in Hermitage's mind. 'Should we cover him with something?'

Cwen immediately pointed an accusing finger at Wat. 'Whatever you're going to suggest, don't.'

'I wasn't going to say anything,' Wat protested; although it looked like he was.

'Just ignore him,' Cwen told the others.

'Wat or Elmund?'

'Both, Hermitage.'

They turned back to the room now.

'Oh,' Hermitage said. 'Look at that.'

They all considered the spot where Elmund had lay.

'As soon as the servants come back, I'll get someone to bring a mop and bucket,' Martin offered as he turned up his nose at the pool of blood. It somehow looked even more unpleasant, now that it didn't have a body in the middle as some sort of explanation.

'No, I mean the marks. I don't think they were there before.'

They stepped up close, as close as possible without getting blood on their feet and peered at the floor.

Emerging from the edges of the blood, where Elmund's head, hands and feet had been, clear lines could be seen drawn on the floor. Drawn in chalk by the look of it, as if someone had gone to the trouble of drawing around the body as it lay there. But the lines were straight, rather than following the contours of arms and legs.

'They certainly weren't there before,' Martin confirmed.

The lines were invisible under the blood itself, but now that the body was out of the way they could see that the lines formed a very specific pattern.

'It's that shape,' Cwen said.

'What shape?'

'The shape that was in the book.'

'The shape that was in the book?'

'The burned book, for goodness sake, Hermitage. It's the same shape that made the demon's mouth. The five-pointed star.'

'Oh, yes,' Hermitage was quite intrigued now. 'I wonder why Elmund would have done that?'

'I don't think Elmund would have done it,' Wat said with a bit of a sigh. 'Why draw a nice star on the floor and then lie down in it while someone cuts your throat?'

'Someone else did it?'

'The lines go under the blood, so they were drawn before Elmund spread himself on the floor. Most likely that the killer did it and then put Elmund down.'

'And it's very significant,' Martin said.

The others looked at him and saw a very worried expression on his face.

He actually went and sat in Colesvain's chair by the fire

and ran a hand over his face.

'I tried to convince myself that this was all harmless. Elmund's interest in magical texts and sorcerous material. Then the Hermes Trismegistus turned up, and it was just a fascinating parchment. Granted, Elmund got terribly excited, but he was a harmless old man.'

'The was bit is certainly right,' Cwen confirmed.

'This is hardly the time for levity, I think,' Wat said with a sigh. Cwen punched him hard on the arm.

Hermitage gave them a tut, but at least saw that Martin wasn't paying attention.

'Then Elmund is murdered,' Martin went on. 'And the Hermes volume is mysteriously burned. And now this.'

'What does it mean?' Cwen asked.

'That it's all connected,' Martin sighed. 'You are right that the star on the floor is the same symbol as was in the demonic image.'

'It's also the five wounds,' Hermitage said.

'Five wounds?'

'Of our Lord crucified. Hands, feet and the spear. In some of the old texts I've come across, the symbol has a very Christian context.'

'But more often, it doesn't,' Martin said. 'And in this situation, I think Christianity is a long way away.'

'Can I repeat the question,' Cwen said, with clear signs of impatience. 'What does it mean?'

'I believe it means that someone is trying to practice magic. Magic of the most evil intent.'

'Really?' Cwen sounded as if she thought this was complete nonsense. 'Do people do that?'

'Deluded people,' Hermitage said. 'But we know that there are a lot of those in the world. As I believe I have said on several occasions, there is no such thing as magic. But that doesn't stop some people thinking that there is.'

'And they kill librarians for it, do they?' Wat asked.

'In this case, they seem to have done,' Martin confirmed. 'The book of Hermes mysteriously burned, Elmund ritually murdered before it, the five-pointed star on the ground.'

'What were they trying to achieve?' Wat asked. He did seem to be taking this seriously now. He even glanced about the library nervously, as if thinking there might be something lurking in the shadows.

'I don't know,' Martin admitted. 'I'm no expert in this area, although I now suspect Elmund may have been.'

'Really?' Hermitage was surprised, as Elmund had shown no signs of being an expert in anything.

'His superficial interest probably hid a deep knowledge. And he was hardly likely to tell anyone about it.'

'I suppose not.'

'This could have been something Elmund himself was trying.'

'With a cut throat?' Cwen asked.

'I suspect the cut throat was the result of what he was trying.'

'He didn't do it very well, then?'

'So,' Hermitage said very slowly, as his thoughts organised themselves. 'It could be that there is no murder. And no murderer.'

'Someone did that,' Wat nodded towards Elmund in his penultimate resting place.

'Or something,' Martin added.

That gave Hermitage a real new worry.

'But,' he tried to convince himself as much as anyone else. 'It could be that Elmund was carrying out some rite that

The Hermes Parchment

required him to give his own blood and he just gave a bit too much.'

'And the burned book?'

'All part of the ritual. Perhaps he was trying to summon a demon or something. Fire and blood could be required. The fire got all out of hand, and the blood got all out of his body.'

'How come the rest of the book isn't burned?'

Hermitage didn't have an answer to that.

'And the star on the floor?' Cwen asked.

'Drawn by Elmund for the summoning.'

They were all quiet in thought as they considered the possibility. Hermitage thought that it did make some sense. Yes, the book was a problem, but there was probably an explanation for that if he could just think of it. This was simply a case of a foolish old man doing foolish things and coming to a very foolish end.

'And Picot covered in blood?' Cwen asked.

Hermitage shrugged. 'He probably came in here to look for one of his books, found Elmund and tried to revive him. When he found he was too late, he ran from the house in shock.'

'I can believe that,' Martin said. 'Picot running away from real trouble is much more likely.'

'There it is then,' Wat said, with some relief. 'Colesvain's men will find Picot. He'll confirm what happened, and we can all go back to making tapestry and counting books.'

'There is another possibility,' Martin said.

'I rather worried that there might be.'

'Someone else did this. It was still a ritual, but one that required the sacrifice of Elmund.'

'And the burning of the book?'

'Could be a result of what was tried or part of the

ceremony itself. If something was summoned from the book, it could leave the burnt remnants behind.'

'Oh, come on now,' Cwen sounded as if this was all getting completely out of hand. 'You're not seriously suggesting that demons were conjured from a book using a dead man in a star? I don't believe it.'

'I'm suggesting that someone did believe it.'

'How do we find out?' Hermitage asked, knowing that he really didn't want to find out at all.

Martin frowned in deep thought.

'There may be a way.'

'It doesn't involve blood, does it?' Wat grimaced.

'No, of course not. There could be someone we can ask.'

'Someone we can ask?' Hermitage didn't like the sound of people you asked about demons and sacrifices. 'In Lincoln?'

'Outside of the town. It's not someone I know or have ever met, but he has a very powerful reputation.'

'A reputation, oh good,' Hermitage whimpered a bit.

'If rumours are true, he lives in the woods to the east of here.'

'Lives in the woods,' Cwen checked. 'Like a witch.'

'All sorts of people live in woods who are not witches,' Hermitage pointed out. 'It could be a woodsman.'

'A woodsman who knows all about demons?'

'Erm, yes.'

'It is neither a woodsman nor a witch,' Martin said. 'The name bandied about town is The Crowman.'

'The Crowman?' Wat checked. 'Or is it The Crow Man.'

'Just The Crowman. I've heard him referred to by the folk of town as a wise man. They go to him for cures and the like.'

'Ah, so he's the good kind of crowman and not the demonic variety.'

The Hermes Parchment

'I have heard nothing of any ill about him. But he is rumoured to be knowledgeable on all manner of things; including many of the old ways. There are still those who believe they are cursed and need that curse lifting; they go to The Crowman. Some who want spells casting go to The Crowman.'

'And if they want to get rid of crows?' Cwen asked.

Martin ignored her. 'There were even rumours of a small demon playing havoc with the building of the cathedral.'

'Judging from what Godrinius told us, he succeeded.'

'It was an imp, they say. The Crowman was called for.'

'By the church authorities?' Hermitage found that hard to believe.

'No, by the workmen. The masons and carpenters.'

'Superstitious folk.'

'Quite. But they believed that The Crowman got rid of the imp for them.'

'So, who else would you ask about a dead librarian?' Wat said. 'Especially one killed in front of a book of magic with a star drawn on the floor.'

'This is clearly more than a plain murder,' Martin said. 'And I still don't believe that Picot would do the deed. The answer to the mysterious questions surrounding all this may well lay in the library somewhere, in one of the books. But it could take us a lifetime to find it. Asking The Crowman will take less than a day.'

'Right,' Cwen said, clapping her hands together. 'Let's go and see the old wise man in the woods and find out all he knows about demons.'

'Oh, yes,' said Brother Hermitage. 'Let's.'

Caput XVI Wisdom in the Woods

'Isn't Derby that way?' Godrinius asked as Hermitage, Wat, Cwen and Martin passed through the east gate on their way to the old man of the woods. He broke off a very intimate chat he was having with a couple of very dubious-looking fellows.

'Aha, it is indeed,' Wat said. 'Just got a bit of business to do this way first.'

Godrinius frowned. 'Two months,' he said, quite seriously.

'Not a problem at all,' Wat reassured him. 'Two months it is.'

'You've got two monks now, then?' Godrinius asked, gazing at Hermitage and Martin.

'Oh, er no. Only this one is ours.' Wat nodded towards Hermitage. 'The other one's just his friend.'

'His friend eh?'

'Brother, I mean, just his brother. You know, like monks have brothers.'

'Please yourself,' Godrinius gave a little snort and got back to his discussions.

'See,' Wat hissed at Cwen as they walked on along the road out of town. 'I told you we should have gone back to Derby to start the tapestry.

'And what do you mean, I'm your monk?' Hermitage asked, more puzzled than anything else.

'Godrinius wants a pious work,' Wat said.

'Really pious,' Cwen added.

'And we know we can do pious because you're with us, see?'

'Not really.'

'Well, never mind. We can worry about pious tapestry

when we get back to Derby. Which can't be soon enough.' He hurried everyone along the road. 'How far are these woods with The Crowman in them?'

'I don't know, really,' Martin said. 'They're not the sort of woods I visit.'

'Could be miles then?'

'I don't think so. The people of the town seem to consult The Crowman quite regularly, so he's not going to be far away.'

Quite naturally in England, anywhere that wasn't town was woods anyway. Some areas were cleared for timber, but most of the country was woods of one sort or another. They were only a few hundred paces from the east gate of Lincoln before the woods began in earnest.

The road here led down a gentle slope and off into the distance. The fact that it did so in a perfectly straight line said that the Romans had come this way; come this way, built a road on it and then gone that way quite regularly. The surface was pitted and collapsed in most places, so it was no great thoroughfare anymore.

'This is the Wragby road,' Martin said.

'Wragby road?' Hermitage asked.

'The road to Wragby.'

'Hence the name,' Wat said. 'Very helpful.'

'How do we find one Crowman in a wood?' Cwen asked, with yet another punch for Wat's arm.

'We'll find someone to ask.'

'Directions to the wise man of the woods, eh?' Wat checked.

'If he's as busy as is told, I'm sure we will see someone around.'

'There could be a bit of a queue,' Cwen suggested. 'If he's as wise as you say, there might be people lining up for some wisdom.'

'I'm sure the mention of Lord Colesvain will get them out of the way,' Wat said.

'Or get something horrible done to us,' Hermitage suggested. The idea of consulting some old man of mystery who lived in the woods had been bad enough when he was standing in a library. Now that he was in the woods, it was quite disturbing.

He had to be honest and say that he had not actually met many old men of mystery in woods, but the one or two he had come across were positively strange. They always cackled and poked at people, and laughed as if they knew something horrible about you.

And then they said things. Odd things. The sorts of things that only men of mystery in woods said. At the time, they appeared to be complete nonsense. "Beware the beast with two horns that stands upon the way", that sort of thing.

But then you'd start worrying about it, well, Hermitage would. Could the devil be about to appear before him? Was he to be cast off into hell?

Then he'd be walking somewhere and there would be a cow in the way or a goat, and he'd see that it had two horns. It was amazing. Did the old man of the woods know that he was going to bump into a cow or a goat?

Or did the old man of the woods know that everyone bumps into a cow or a goat sooner or later, so the chances of such a useless prophecy coming true were pretty good?

This time they were going to ask specific questions about magic and demons. Perhaps, if this particular old man of the woods had some rude and secret dwelling, Hermitage could wait outside.

The Hermes Parchment

'Ah,' Martin said, to disturb Hermitage's worry. 'Here's a likely fellow.'

Coming along the road towards them was a true born peasant of the land. He was a young lad, of about seventeen or so, and clearly a worker of the land. His clothes were hardy and simple, his shoes still caked in mud from the last time he stood in a field, which was probably only an hour or so ago. He even had a straw in his mouth, which he twiddled from side to side as he walked along.

Doubtless, he was on some errand or other and was taking his time about it, as it had got him out of that field.

'Aha,' Martin called as soon as they were close.

'Ar?' the boy replied.

'Know you where may be found The Crowman?'

Cwen whispered to Hermitage and Wat. 'Why's he talking like that? "Know you where may be found?" Why doesn't he talk properly?'

'That could be the way the common folk talk around here,' Hermitage suggested. 'We know everyone in the country has their own peculiar way of speaking.'

'Yes, but they don't put the words in the wrong order. We'll be talking like one of your old manuscripts next. "knowst thou where mayst be finding of ye Crowman". Nobody really talks like they're out of a book about, what-do-you-call-it, old times?'

'History?' Hermitage suggested.

'That's the one.'

Hermitage couldn't see that this should be a worry just at the moment. As long as the boy understood, that was all they needed.

'Eh?' the boy asked, as he drew to a halt; doubtless welcoming an opportunity to delay the errand that was already delaying his work.

'The Crowman,' Martin repeated.

'What about The Crowman?'

'Do you know where we go?'

'Why didn't you say that? Down there on the left.' The boy beckoned off towards the woods further along the track. 'Have you got an appointment?'

'Appointment?' Hermitage asked. 'What's an appointment?' It was very odd for him never to have heard of a word. He couldn't even think what the Latin root might be.

'No idea,' the boy shrugged. 'But you have to have one. Funny old thing, The Crowman. Not even English, they say. Talks funny enough for that to be right. You have to arrange to see The Crowman, you see. Can't just turn up.'

'Why not? Are there so many people who want to go?'

The boy shook his head. 'Oh yes. And likes things organised, does The Crowman.'

Hermitage was starting to warm to this mysterious figure. He thought he had got the idea of what an appointment might be, but it was odd that a traditional old wise man of the woods operated a system of appointments. If he was that wise, wouldn't he know who was coming anyway?

'We visit at the behest of Lord Colesvain,' Wat said.

'Really?' The boy sniffed as if he'd never heard of the name. 'You can give it a go, I suppose.'

'Well, thank you.'

'But if you haven't got an appointment, you won't get in. And all of you can't go anyway. Only one at a time.'

'We'll enquire of The Crowman once we get there,' Martin said. 'Thank thee.'

'Thank thee?' Cwen snorted a laugh. 'I hope this Crowman doesn't talk like that. We'll never understand what we're

The Hermes Parchment

being told.'

They left the farm lad to go about his business and followed the directions on into the woods.

It was actually quite obvious where The Crowman resided. There was a neat dwelling off to the left-hand side of the road, set in a small clearing with vegetables growing all around and a goat tethered to a post far enough away that it couldn't eat them.

As they drew up, they saw that there was even a sign by the side of the road. A very good representation of a crow was drawn with charcoal on a plank of wood that pointed towards the house.

The place itself was very traditional but quite large. A pit had been dug in the ground, and into this stakes were set to support the roof. This was made of thatch and grass and dropped nearly to the floor. The front wall was wattle and daub, of course, but looked well maintained, and even freshly daubed in some places.

A well-made wooden door sat in the middle of the front, and the whole place must be at least 30 feet square, a huge accommodation for one old man of the woods.

Hermitage was getting confused. This was not fitting the image of a wise old man of the woods, let alone one called The Crowman. Surely the place should be ancient and decrepit and hung about with strange symbols and objects. It didn't give much confidence in the quality of the wisdom if it just looked like a rather nice house.

No one had any comment to offer, so Martin led the way to the front door and pushed it open.

The inside was as dark as it should be. There were no windows, but candles burned around the sides of a much smaller room than they'd been expecting.

Candles were also a surprise. They looked like good ones as well; the sort of thing usually the preserve of nobles or great halls. Being The Crowman must pay well.

'Can I help you?'

Hermitage actually jumped off the floor as he realised that there was someone in the room with them. Off to the left, as his eyes adjusted to the gloom, he saw a rather wizened old man sitting on a three-legged stool. Of even greater shock was the fact that the man had a large book on his lap and a quill in his hand. As far as mysterious old men of the woods went, this one was remarkably well equipped, organised and learned.

'We have come to seek your advice,' Martin said.

'My advice?' the old man sounded surprised at this. 'Why would you want my advice?'

Ah, Hermitage could see that this was a deep and penetrating question. Rather than go straight to the problem in mind, the old man was prompting the visitor to explain his reasons; very clever.

'We are dealing with a series of perplexing events that we think your knowledge may be able to illuminate.'

'My knowledge?'

'Indeed. You are renowned for your wisdom in esoteric matters.'

'Well,' the old man said, now closing the book on his lap. 'That's very kind of you to say, but I think you've got the wrong end of things.'

'You don't know us, of course,' Martin explained. 'And we have never visited you before, but this is a very pressing matter.'

'I'm sure it is, but I don't think I can help.'

'You don't know anything about it yet,' Cwen complained

rather snappily.

The old man gave her a withering gaze. 'And you don't know that I'm not The Crowman.'

The pause was long and embarrassing.

Hermitage thought that this might explain why the house didn't at all look like the dwelling of a wise man. Perhaps The Crowman's home was behind this place, off deeper in the woods somewhere. That would be more like it. Still, it was a bit awkward, barging in and asking for mysterious advice from the wrong old man.

'Oh,' Martin eventually said.

'Not very wise, is it, blurting out your problems before you check who you're talking to?'

'Well, it just seemed that…,'

'I'm an old man sitting in a house in the woods and you just assume that I'm wise, is that it?'

'No, that is, we, erm..,'

'Go up to all old men in the woods and ask for advice, do you? Not all old men are wise, you know. Some of them are very stupid indeed. I could name several within half a mile of here.'

'You are in a house with a sign outside that's got a crow on it,' Cwen pointed out. She obviously thought that the confusion was entirely the old man's fault.

'Do I look like The Crowman?'

'I don't know, do I? I've never met him before.' Cwen was getting a bit cross now, which was never a good sign.

'Exactly. Your first question should have been, excuse me, are you The Crowman? There you are, there's a bit of wisdom for free.'

Martin took a breath. 'We have some questions that we think The Crowman may be able to help with.'

'That's better,' the old man smiled at them all now.

Hermitage got the distinct impression that this old man quite liked being awkward and had got rather good at it.

The book on the lap was opened once more and the old man scanned through the pages. 'I could fit you in next Tuesday,' he said. 'Around noon?'

So this was the home of The Crowman? Hermitage was getting even more confused.

'Next Tuesday?' Cwen shrieked as quietly as she could manage, which wasn't very quiet. 'How can you dispense wisdom next Tuesday?'

'We can do it every day of the week. The Crowman is very wise.'

'I don't see anyone else here.'

'That's because they've all got appointments. They don't come until the time of their appointment.'

'Yes,' Hermitage said. 'This word, appointment, where does it come from?'

'Hermitage,' Wat interrupted. 'I think we'll worry about what words to use after we've got on with the main business of the day?'

'Ah, right.' Hermitage tried very hard to concentrate on demons and murder and not etymology.

'Well, I don't see anyone having an appointment.' Cwen pressed on, looking around the room that just had them in it.

'That's because they're consulting with The Crowman.' The old man nodded towards the back of the house.

Now, Hermitage realised that the place was split into two. This front part was obviously where the old man sat to deal with The Crowman's visitors. The man himself must be in the back half of the house, dispensing his wisdom in private. He now saw that there was a curtain against the back wall, through which he assumed The Crowman must be.

'We'll wait,' Cwen said.

'The next appointment will be here soon,' the old man said. 'Next Tuesday. It's the best I can do.'

'This is rather urgent.' Wat said.

Hermitage recognised Wat's trading voice; the one that could wheedle money out of a man with no money.

'It really would be an enormous help if The Crowman could spare us just a moment of time? Even between the, erm, appointments, would do.'

Cwen's scowl at this loose and soft way of going about things was audible. She would clearly rather knock the old man out of the way and burst in upon The Crowman. 'Perhaps you operate a system of urgent appointments?' she said. 'You know, for when people need a bit of wisdom right now and can't wait a week?'

'I'm sure your need is urgent,' the old man nodded. 'Most people come to The Crowman when it's urgent. Many of them leave it until it's too late.' He gave them all a knowing look making it clear that they were in the latter group.

Wat dropped his voice to a whisper. 'It is a matter involving Lord Colesvain.' He gave the old man his own knowing nod.

'Fascinating,' the old man looked earnest. 'I'm sure that The Crowman will be most interested to hear all about it.'

'Good.'

'Next Tuesday.'

'Let's just go in,' Cwen spoke up loudly. 'I don't think one old man can stop us.'

'I'm positive that he can't,' the old man said, without concern. 'But you'll get no wisdom from The Crowman that way.'

'Look,' Cwen stepped forward and addressed the old man in a very direct manner. It seemed that he was used to this sort of thing though, and didn't flinch in the face of the onslaught.

'I am pretty sure that our business is more important than some farm boy wanting to know when to sow his carrots. Let's just go in. We've got a dead body, mysterious symbols drawn on the floor and a whole book of, what was his name?'

'Hermes Trismegistus,' Hermitage supplied.

'Yes, him. We've got a great big book of Hermes, thingy, burned to ash without anything around it being touched. I think our need for The Crowman is a damn sight more important than anyone else's, and I think he'd want to hear about it now.' She took a deep breath, but her fists were clenched.

Hermitage was confident that she wouldn't actually punch an old man, but she might punch someone.

The old man clearly had a reply ready, but he didn't get a chance to use it. The curtain on the back wall flew aside and they all looked at who appeared.

A youngish woman came out of the backroom, presumably The Crowman's last customer. She did look rather well-to-do, wearing a long dark cloak with a fine black dress underneath. Perhaps she was some noble come to seek the advice of The Crowman. Now that she was out of the way, they might have a chance for a quick word.

'Did you say Hermes Trismegistus?' the woman asked, in a very Norman sort of accent.

Hermitage gaped. He didn't know which surprise to deal with first; that this young woman appeared to know of Hermes, or that she was Norman. 'Erm,' he said, which did little to resolve his problem.

The Hermes Parchment

'I am The Crowman,' the woman said with some impatience.

Well, that simply raised a whole host of new questions. Most of them mysterious. How young women could be wise old men of the woods was just not something he could deal with at the moment.

'You're Norman?' he said, not knowing whether a Crowman who was a woman was any less confusing than one who was Norman.

'How dare you,' The Crowman-person said, clearly insulted. 'I am not Norman, I'm French!'

Caput XVII Wisdom in the Dark

'Come in here,' the woman beckoned that they should follow her through the curtain into the back room. She even looked about as if checking that there was no one else looking on.

'Cancel my appointments,' she told the old man, who grumbled in complaint.

'Ah,' Hermitage said. 'About these appointments?'

'What about them?'

'Where does the word come from?'

That stopped The Crowman in her tracks. 'Really? You come here talking loudly of Hermes Trismegistus and dead bodies, and you want to know about the word, appointment?' She looked very confused.

'If you could tell him?' Wat asked. 'We'll get no peace until he knows.'

The woman shrugged. 'It's a perfectly normal word. Old French, appointer. It just means to arrange things. Is it important?'

'It is to some people,' Cwen sighed. 'Happy now?'

'Yes, thank you.' Hermitage smiled. Old French eh? Now that was something worth exploring further. He knew that words came from all sorts of fascinating places. His own name originated with the ancient Greek eremites, and the blessed Benedict had mentioned anchorites and hermits in his book of instruction which was hundreds of years old. But, if old French could be added to the Latin and Greek and Saxon and Norse, the possibilities were endless.

'Perhaps to the matter in hand, then?' Wat prompted him from his reverie. 'If we've finished with the words? You know, the book and the dead people?'

The Hermes Parchment

'There's only one dead person,' Hermitage said.

'Even so?'

Hermitage nodded that Wat could carry on.

'Can I begin by saying that I am very confused?' Wat was looking at The Crowman as if still expecting someone else to spring out of the walls; someone a bit more crow and a lot more man.

Martin was just gaping while Cwen seemed rather satisfied at this development.

'Sit down,' The Crowman instructed.

They all took simple stools that were scattered about the place, while The Crowman sat in a large chair, hung with dark material.

Hermitage was positively alarmed to see a small table at her side that carried a skull and a collection of very bizarre objects. There were feathers and what looked like small bones of some sort.

'Right.' The Crowman gazed hard at them all. 'What's this about Hermes Trismegistus?'

'Erm,' Wat said. 'What's this about being The Crowman?'

The Crowman looked at Wat with a very penetrating gaze, and even tipped her head over to one side slightly, rather like a crow.

'I mean,' Wat was hesitant now. 'We'd sort of been expecting an old man of the woods, you know the sort of thing. Ragged, ancient, cackling. And you're, erm, not, those things?'

'Why?'

'Why? Well, it's tradition, isn't it? And you're a bit of a surprise, that's all. And as you say, you're erm French?'

'That's right. What's wrong with being French?'

'Nothing. Nothing at all. I'm sure it's lovely. Absolutely

our fault, but I imagine that old men of the woods in this part of the world tend to be a bit more, what can I say, Saxon?'

'You want an old, ragged Saxon man cackling at you? Will you take wisdom from a cackling Saxon but not a French woman? I can get Norgood outside to come and do some cackling if you like?'

'Oh, well, no, it's all right, I'm sure.'

'I am The Crowman, alright?' This was a rather snappy Crowman, Hermitage thought. It could be the darkness and the mysterious nature of the location, but he could swear that the "alright" came out more like "caw right."

'The wisdom of the crow has been granted me, and I dispense it to those who seek.'

'Excellent,' Wat nodded.

'King Philip is a superstitious fool.'

'Is he?' Wat was sounding a bit nervous about being in the dark with The Crowman now.

'King who?' Cwen asked.

'Quite right,' The Crowman agreed. 'King who, indeed.'

'No, I really mean who? I've never heard of him.'

'He's the King of France, isn't he?' The Crowman moved her head towards Cwen in what was an alarmingly crow-like manner.

'And that's not Normandy?'

The Crowman's eyes widened. 'Of course, it's not Normandy, child. The Duke of Normandy is vassal to King Philip.'

'Has anyone told the Duke of Normandy?' Wat whispered.

'Only asking,' Cwen said.

'So, you've come to England with your wisdom.' Wat said this as if it was the most natural thing in the world.

The Hermes Parchment

'Just so.'

'And Crowman? As in man?'

'That is my title. And folk are like you; too simple in their heads.'

'Simple in the head, quite right,' Cwen agreed.

'Like you, they think wisdom only comes from old men of their own kind. They are drawn to The Crowman, and then once they speak to me, they are content.'

'Or they're not allowed out,' Wat hissed.

'Now,' The Crowman positively squawked. 'Hermes the thrice great? What do you know?'

'Thrice great?' Martin had found his voice now, although it sounded a bit fragile.

'Of course.' The Crowman held her arms up in the air and called out, 'Thoth the great, the great, the great.'

Her audience all looked at one another with a common thought; would they be able to leave soon?

'Erm, Thoth?' Hermitage asked. He considered it best to be polite to plainly mad women in dark tents who had skulls and bones on their tables.

'Thoth the god of magic,' The Crowman said as if this should be perfectly obvious to anyone. 'Down the ages, his name has been corrupted and translated. And Hermes is the messenger of the gods.'

'Of course, he is,' Wat said as if it had stupidly slipped his mind for a moment.

'Hermes the god of merchants, trade and commerce, roads and travellers, thieves and tricksters, sport and athletes.'

'All of that, eh?' Wat said. 'Busy fellow.'

The Crowman's arms went up again. 'And Hermes brings us the words and wisdom of Thoth the great, the great..,'

'The great, yes.'

'So.' The Crowman gave Wat a very angry look. 'What do you know?'

'Know? Nothing,' Wat said blankly. 'That's why we've come to the dark tent in the woods. If we knew, we wouldn't have come to find out, would we?'

The Crowman looked a bit confused by this argument. 'You know the name, and you mentioned a book. Come, tell all,' she instructed.

'We had a book,' Hermitage spoke up. 'But it's gone now.'

'Gone?' The Crowman was alarmed by this. 'Gone where?'

'Burned. It burned up completely.'

'Ah, did it?' The Crowman nodded now as if she knew something about books that burned up completely. 'And what was this book?'

'We really don't know. It was a very large book, all in Greek and it had the name Hermes Trismegistus in the front.'

'A large book? Set with jewels?'

Hermitage was surprised and encouraged that she seemed to know of it. 'That's the one. We hadn't read any of it before it was gone.'

'Apart from Poimandres,' Martin put in.

'Poimandres,' The Crowman breathed the word as if she'd just been given a cup of fresh nectar.

'There was a drawing in the middle,' Hermitage said. 'But we didn't understand that either. And then, in the middle of the night, the librarian, Elmund, was murdered. His throat was cut right in front of the book. And the book itself was all burned away.'

'Except the cover,' Martin said. 'That was untouched.'

'Well, it would be,' The Crowman explained, without explaining anything.

The Hermes Parchment

'And there was a star drawn on the floor where Elmund lay.'

'Ha,' The Crowman let out a laugh. 'The poor fools. And where is the book now?'

'Erm.' Hermitage looked at the others to check that he had actually said it was burned. They appeared to be as confused as he was. 'Gone. As I say.'

'No, no,' the Crowman replied as if Hermitage was some sort of idiot. He was used to this response to things he said, so recognised it quite easily. 'There was no ash?' she asked.

'Well, no.'

'Of course not. It is only the substance of the book that has gone.'

Hermitage couldn't help but think that was usually all there was to a book.

'It can be recovered. It would take a lot more than the fire of man to destroy that book. In any case, it probably used the fire to escape.'

'The book used the fire to escape?' Cwen checked.

'It is not unexpected.' The Crowman waved away the whole plethora of questions that swarmed around books escaping by fire. 'Where did you get the book? That's the question. Where was it found.'

'In a box,' Hermitage said, happy to get back to more mundane matters.

'Hidden in the bottom of a large box?' The Crowman asked. She seemed nervous about this question.

'Well, yes.'

'Aha!' The Crowman jumped from her chair and hopped with glee; literally hopped, but with both feet at the same time, like a bird. 'Were there any markings in the box?' she asked when she came to a halt.

'It came from the monastery of Rooksby,' Hermitage said. 'The name was in the box.'

'Although that place is long gone,' Martin added.

'Rooksby! Of course, of course. How could I be so stupid?'

Wat looked like he had a ready answer to that question on his lips.

'So,' Hermitage said, as The Crowman added no more. 'What can you tell us?'

The Crowman considered them all as if only now remembering that they were in the room with her. She returned to her seat, a very serious look on her face, her eyes darting from side to side. As she sat, she beckoned them to draw near; then nearer; then nearer still.

When they were almost sitting in the chair with her, she lowered her head and whispered into the close circle.

'You have discovered the great book of Hermes Trismegistus.'

They all nodded in anticipation. Even Wat seemed enthralled by the surroundings and the atmosphere.

'It has been burned away.' The way The Crowman said "burned away" made it sound much more mysterious and significant. 'And in front of the book, a body! Throat cut and lying in the sacred star.' She sat back in her chair.

The others all rose slightly on their stools.

It was Wat who spoke first 'That's what we told you!'

'And it is the truth.'

'Well, of course, it is. We know that. We were there. What's the point of us tramping all the way out into the woods to see the mysterious wise Crow-thing, if all she does is tell us what we already know?'

'What does it mean?' Hermitage asked, thinking that the woman hadn't been much help so far, but perhaps they were

The Hermes Parchment

asking the wrong questions.

'Ah.' The Crowman nodded as if Hermitage had hit the nail on the head. 'What does it mean?'

'That's right,' Wat said. 'We've told you what happened, and you've very wisely told it right back to us. Do you even know what it means?'

'Of course,' The Crowman seemed a bit offended by Wat's doubt.

'Go on then, old wise Crowman,' Wat intoned, actually managing to sound quite rude.

'I am of The Black Bird,' The Crowman said.

'The blackbird?' Cwen turned up her nose.

'No, not The blackbird, The Black Bird. The convocation of The Black Bird.'

'I see,' Wat said. 'And this helps, does it?'

'I have ancient knowledge,' The Crowman almost sang.

'You've got something, that's for sure,' Wat half muttered. 'Ancient, modern? Any knowledge at all would be quite welcome just at the moment.'

'Wat!' Hermitage reprimanded. 'Let The Crowman tell this in her own way.'

'What? Tell us what we already told her, only in a sing-song voice? That'll make a big difference.'

'The book of Hermes has been passed down through the ages,' The Crowman said, pointedly telling everyone except Wat. 'It was taken from Egypt unto Rome.'

'Unto,' Cwen snorted.

'And from there,' The Crowman now started ignoring Cwen as well, which didn't leave her much of an audience. 'It was passed into the hands of the convocation.'

'I see,' Martin said. 'When was this?'

'In ancient times.' The Crowman said with due solemnity,

and some extra solemnity to add to the moment.

'Earlier than last year, then?' Wat asked.

'It was passed from group to group but became lost.'

'Careless,' Wat said. 'For a convocation of black birds.'

The Crowman continued to ignore him. 'Lost around the time of the Caesar named Julius. We believe he brought the book to Britain, being a member of the convocation. But, when he departed to deal with rebellion, he left it here.'

'Who?' Cwen asked.

'Caesar. Julius Caesar.'

'Who's he, then?'

'Oh, really Cwen.' Hermitage had to speak up. 'Julius Caesar was a Roman.'

'Right.' Cwen nodded. 'Roman. Probably spoke Latin then.' She sounded quite disparaging of people who spoke Latin.

'And Julius Caesar was a blackbird?' Wat was starting to shake his head at all this nonsense.

'Now we can fill in the missing years.' The Crowman looked very satisfied and was talking mainly to herself. 'When Caesar was driven from these shores, he must have left instruction for members of the convocation to secrete the book and protect it from capture by the unworthy. And what better place to be founded for such a purpose, than somewhere called Rooks-by. It would be a clear signal to all from the convocation who came looking.'

'He didn't just take it away with him again?' Wat suggested. 'You go to all the trouble of invading a country, only to leave your book behind when you go home. Must be so frustrating.'

Cwen poked Wat hard in the leg and mouthed, "shut up" quite clearly.

The Hermes Parchment

'And how many years ago was this?' Wat asked seriously, looking to Hermitage for the answer.

'About a thousand.'

There was a silent pause in the room at this.

'Very well hidden, then,' Wat observed.

'It must have been moved about and used though,' Hermitage went on. 'The book was in very good order and the box certainly wasn't a thousand years old. I also doubt if the monastery of Rooksby was established for the purpose.'

The Crowman snorted at his ignorance.

'Julius Caesar having come to England before our Lord was even born,' Hermitage pointed out.

'Hm,' Wat nodded agreement. 'Bit hard to have a Christian monastery when there's no such thing as a Christian.'

'The house of Rooksby was not Christian when it was established. It probably only became so later.'

'After some Christianity became available, probably.' Wat seemed happy to pass his analysis on to the group.

'But the book is found,' The Crowman, well, crowed. 'You must take me to it.'

'We can take you to the cover,' Wat said. 'And we did actually come here to ask about the dead body? The murdered one.'

'Someone has been trying to release the powers of the book,' The Crowman said. 'They have conducted a ritual and failed, miserably.'

'Elmund?' Martin asked.

'Tough ritual if you have to cut your own throat,' Wat said.

'Where is the book?' The Crowman asked.

'In the house of Lord Colesvain,' Hermitage said.

'Aha.' The Crowman sounded as if this explained quite a lot.

'Is that significant?'

'Others have sought my wisdom,' The Crowman sang.

'Did they have any better luck?' Wat asked.

'Others from the household of Lord Colesvain. Now, I see why.'

Hermitage thought it was a bit alarming that someone else in the house knew about the book. But, how could they? He had only just pulled it out of the box. Mind you, the box had been in the house for a while. And all those rude books on top didn't seem quite the thing for a Christian monastery so mysterious that it had been established sometime before Christianity.

'Was, erm, Lord Picot one of them?' he asked, as mildly as he could.

'Aye,' said The Crowman. 'Aye, he was.'

Hermitage swallowed.

'And others,' The Crowman said with heavy significance. 'And others.'

Caput XVIII Wisdom in a Library?

The journey back to the house of Lord Colesvain brought no more information from the mouth of The Crowman. She would not reveal who from the house of Colesvain had been to see her, saying that her meetings were private. When it was pointed out that she'd already told them about Picot, she refused to say any more.

Wat was keen to mention that they hadn't actually got much information from her at all, but the others were more hopeful that something useful would be coming. The more mysterious information was, the slower it came.

Knowing where Lord Picot's interests mainly lay, he didn't like to speculate too hard about what sort of thing he'd been asking. He might have discussed books, but they'd have been a lot more mundane.

The gathering of tradesmen at the east gate had dispersed when they returned, but the local folk who were about gazed at The Crowman with naked awe. They had obviously never seen her outside of her dark demesne. Some looked a little annoyed to see her out and about. If they'd known she did house calls, they needn't have bothered with an appointment.

As they walked past the cathedral building site, the site with no building, they saw one or two of Colesvain's people wandering about. They didn't look like they'd achieved anything or were even bothered about doing so. They had the familiar look of the person relieved of their work and doing their best to avoid going back to it.

'Any luck?' Wat called to a couple of them who were sitting on a large piece of Roman stone, kicking their legs and chatting. 'Finding Lord Picot?' he added.

They immediately leapt up from their stone and started

looking all around it. 'Nothing here,' one of them called over.

'Picot could be sitting in a tavern covered in blood and this lot wouldn't find him.' Wat shook his head.

The house was still deserted when they arrived. The door was unlocked, but nothing seemed to have been disturbed.

The Crowman looked about as if she'd never been in a house before and was quite in awe of the place. 'Take me to the book,' she instructed.

Martin led the way into the library, where The Crowman only had eyes for the large cover of the Hermes book, that still lay on the table. As she drew close, seemingly in some sort of daze, she sidestepped the pool of blood and squatted down to consider the mark of the star on the floor. She then rose and went to the book.

Hesitantly, and with obvious reverence, she slowly laid a hand on the cover and breathed out.

'This is a great moment for the convocation of The Black Bird,' she said. 'Recovery of the great volume of Hermes.'

'Very great indeed,' Wat said. 'Apart from all the missing bits that were on the inside, I imagine.'

'You say this was in a box from Rooksby?' she asked Hermitage.

'That's right. It's over there.'

The Crowman left the book with a wistful glance and went over to examine the box. She ran her fingers over the burned in letters "Rooksby" and sighed. She then moved to a more intense examination of the interior.

'What other books were here?' she asked as she almost climbed into the box to consider its depths.

'Oh, erm,' Hermitage said. 'Just one or two that had probably been put there out of the way of the library. I'm not sure they'd have come from Rooksby as well.'

The Hermes Parchment

The Crowman emerged from the box. 'Why not?'

'They were of an entirely different nature.'

'I'm sure they were, but it is important that I know.'

Hermitage really couldn't bring himself to describe those volumes at all, let alone in the sort of detail that was needed. He saw that some of the pile he'd taken out of the box was still sitting on a table nearby.

'Ah, there they are,' he said in genuine relief, pointing to the collection.

The Crowman went over and picked the first one up, opening the pages, while Hermitage looked the other way. 'I see,' she said, in a very thoughtful way.

'I think that, erm, Lord Picot may have put them in the box. For safekeeping, you know.'

'I doubt that. These are very important works.'

Hermitage wasn't sure what importance could be given to that sort of thing.

'They too are the volumes of the convocation of the Black Bird and have been lost all these years.'

Hermitage started to have some worries about just what sort of convocation this was.

'They show the chakra channels of the body.'

Hermitage knew they showed rather too much about the body, but what The Crowman was rambling on about, he had not a clue.

She could obviously see the confusion in the room. 'Even more ancient wisdom from the east,' she said. 'The great conqueror Alexander was a member of the convocation and he added to our knowledge.'

'Who?' Cwen asked.

'I have come across that name in some of the texts,' Martin said. 'The Cosmographia of Hieronymus, if I'm not mistaken.'

'Was there anyone who wasn't in this convocation?' Wat asked.

'So, all these books came from Rooksby?' Hermitage was quite disappointed about that. The esoteric knowledge from Hermes was fascinating, but was all the other material really necessary?

'Just so.' The Crowman nodded in quiet satisfaction.

'Are we any closer to finding anything out that we don't know already?' Wat asked. 'Or are you going to carefully explain that all of these things are books and that they came out of a box marked "Rooksby"?'

'What I have seen only confirms my suspicions,' The Crowman said seriously. 'The star on the ground, the position of the body, and the book of Hermes. It all indicates a ritual.'

'To what end?' Hermitage asked.

'Without the book, we cannot tell precisely. We would need to know what page was being used and what spell cast. But there would not be many that require the sacrifice of an innocent in the pentagram.'

'I don't think Elmund was very innocent,' Martin said. 'And he did have an unhealthy interest in this sort of thing.' He considered the book and blood once more. 'Could he have brought this upon himself? Was there some ritual that he tried to complete, which resulted in the burning of the book and his own death?'

The Crowman looked at them all very intently. 'That,' she said. 'I do not know.'

'Pretty much as expected,' Wat said.

'The book has been lost for so long, that the details of what it contains are mysteries and legends. It is possible that there is something of that nature contained in the pages, but I cannot say for certain.'

'Is there anyone who could?' Wat asked. 'Someone a bit wiser, perhaps?'

Cwen's punch landed once more.

'Could you start on the other arm soon? This one's wearing out.'

'Shame your mouth hasn't worn out,' she said. 'If it had, I could stop hitting you.'

'In any case,' Martin said. 'The book is burned away.'

'Is it?' The Crowman asked.

Wat opened his mouth but thought better of it.

She came back to the book now and stroked the cover in what seemed like a rather personal manner, for a book. She then closed her eyes and pulled the cover open to reveal the charred remains inside.

She ran her hands over the inside covers, front and back, and then bent forward to look more closely at the blackened stumps of pages.

'Hermes,' she sighed as if recalling a long-lost lover. She now touched the remains of the pages, moving what was left of the front page out of the way. A frown developed on her face, and she flicked at the page ends with her finger.

She then smelled her finger, which looked like a rather revolting thing to do, and rubbed her finger and thumb together.

'Do you have a cloth?' she asked, without looking up.

'A cloth?' Martin asked.

'Something to wipe the book with.'

'Wipe it?' Martin asked as if he had never heard of the concept of wiping something with a cloth.

'Here,' Cwen said. 'Use this.' She snatched Wat's square of

scented silk from his waist and handed it over.

'Oy,' he protested. 'That's not for cleaning old books, you know.'

The Crowman took the material and very gently brushed it against the inside spine of the book, flicking burnt remnants away.

'Ah,' she cried out.

'What is it?' Hermitage asked.

'See for yourself.' She stepped back from the book and indicated that Hermitage should come forward.

He did so and bent to examine the inner spine of the book, where The Crowman had brushed the blackened fragments clear.

'Oh, my,' he said.

Martin now stepped forward and joined Hermitage. 'Well, goodness me.'

'Anyone care to say something a bit more helpful?' Wat asked.

'The book is not burned at all,' Hermitage said.

'It looks surprisingly fire damaged if that's the case.'

'Only the front page has been burned. The title page. We can still see the letters of the name quite clearly. All the other pages have been carefully cut out and taken away. The ends have been smeared with a little ash to make it look as if they've caught fire as well.'

'Which explains the lack of ash,' Martin said. 'And the fact that the covers of the book are not damaged. Whoever did this must have cut all the pages out except the first one. They then held the book open while they burned that and used the ash to make it look as if the rest had gone.'

'How ingenious,' Hermitage noted.

'And did they cut Elmund's throat at the same time, or

afterwards?' Wat asked.

'Who can say?' The Crowman mused.

'Not the wise one from the woods, obviously.'

'One thing we do know is that Elmund did not take the pages from the book,' Cwen said, with a glare at Wat's arm. 'There's someone else involved here. He can't have tried his ritual and got it horribly wrong, died on the floor, and then got up and taken the pages away.'

'True,' Wat agreed.

'Crowman,' Cwen addressed the woman. 'You said that others from this house had come to see you.'

'Many come to see me,' The Crowman replied, in a very superior manner.

'Who?'

The Crowman shook her head slowly. 'I cannot reveal the secrets of the sacred.'

'You mentioned Picot,' Wat said. 'That's one secret of the sacred revealed. We have a librarian with no blood inside him anymore, and someone out there with the pages of the book. You could be taking the secrets of the sacred to your grave if you're not careful.'

The Crowman didn't seem concerned about this. 'All manner of people seek my aid. Servants, peasants, the well-to-do.'

'Servants, eh?' Hermitage said, thinking of those in the kitchen who had expressed a desire to kill their master. Granted, it was Elmund who had died, and it would be hard to cut the wrong person's throat by mistake, but it was all a worry.

'Any of them ask about books of Hermes, and what to do with them?' Wat asked.

'Of course not. I only found out about the book when you

came to me.' She looked at them all through narrowed eyes. 'How do I know that you have not done this?'

'Us?' Hermitage squeaked a bit.

'I have never seen you before. You come to my home with tales of the great missing book, and what do I find? The book is gone, your Elmund is dead, and you claim not to know what happened. It is quite possible that you did all this.'

'Now, really,' Martin protested.

'And why would we traipse all the way out to see you if that was the case?' Wat asked.

'Because you carried out the ritual and it went wrong. Elmund is dead. You had to remove the book so that it would not be taken, and now you seek my knowledge to follow your devious intent.'

'We've been seeking your knowledge all day now, and haven't found it yet,' Wat retorted. 'I'm not convinced you know anything at all. All we've had is a bunch of stories about some mysterious convocation none of us has ever heard of. Pah! And it was us who told you about the Hermes book. You haven't told us anything we didn't know already.'

Hermitage thought this was going a bit far. 'Apart from Julius Caesar and Alexander,' he said.

'Which could all be made up,' Wat said. 'After all, they're not exactly available to confirm her story, are they?'

The Crowman looked as if all this talk was washing over her and there were probably more interesting people to talk to.

Wat sighed heavily. 'There's nothing for it, Hermitage. I think you'll have to report back.'

Hermitage was used to Wat by now and was confident that there would be some sort of explanation for this in a moment. Who he would report to, he had not a clue, and why he would do it backwards was a complete mystery.

'Ah, yes,' Cwen said, who had obviously got to the explanation all on her own.

'Report back, eh?' Hermitage said, as if he was considering this proposal with great care, and not actually waiting to be told what it meant.

'After all,' Cwen went on. 'Colesvain is the king's tenant-in-chief and this concerns his household.'

'And you being the King's Investigator,' Wat said. 'I think the best thing to do is keep King William informed.'

Well, that was odd. Wat had never thought that keeping King William informed of anything was a very good idea in the past; why now, all of a sudden?

'And Le Pedvin,' Cwen added.

'Oh, yes.' Wat nodded. 'Mustn't forget Le Pedvin. You know how annoyed he gets when he doesn't know what's going on.'

Now, Hermitage really was confused. He was sure that Wat had said it was best Le Pedvin never knew what was going on. He tried to keep a knowing look on his face but, as actual knowing had long since departed, it was a bit of a struggle.

He looked to Martin and The Crowman, to see if they were doing any better with this. Martin looked just as confused as he did, but The Crowman had a completely different expression. She was giving Wat a very nasty look. This wasn't the haughty and dismissive gaze she'd been giving him pretty much since they met, this said she was now quite cross.

'And didn't we hear that Le Pedvin was asking where in the country all the Normans are?'

'That's right,' Wat said as if he was fascinated by this piece of information. 'Some sort of check, I imagine. So that he and the king know who's where and how much tax they have to pay, that sort of thing.'

'And get rid of anyone who's not welcome in what is now their country.'

'Could be,' Wat agreed. 'Of course,' he went on as if talking to the room. 'If we knew who in Colesvain's household had been consulting The Crowman, we could follow those possibilities, and probably wouldn't have the time to tell the king at all.'

'Or Le Pedvin.' Cwen nodded.

'Or Le Pedvin.'

'All right,' The Crowman snapped. She really did look at Wat and Cwen as only a mysterious person from the woods could do; it was a look full of promise of horrible things to come.

She continued her glaring as she spoke. 'The servant of the house, some of the kitchen drudges, Lord Picot and Colesvain.'

'Colesvain himself?' Wat asked in surprise.

'He is a Saxon of this land and of the old ways,' The Crowman said. 'Why should he not consult The Crowman?'

'And what were they asking about, this quite large gathering from the house of Colesvain?'

The Crowman looked as if she really did not want to say any more but was being forced. 'I did not answer their questions and sent them all on their way.'

'Without your mysterious advice?' Cwen sounded surprised.

The Crowman now took on a pose of pride in her work. 'I dispense wisdom; I do not encourage the tattle of superstition.'

The Hermes Parchment

'I think I'd have to argue with you about that,' Wat said. 'But go on.'

'It is well known in these parts,' The Crowman announced, 'that The Crowman does not deal in curses.'

'Curses, eh?' Cwen sounded as if this was the most informative thing she had ever heard. 'All of them were asking about curses?'

'All of them.' The Crowman looked rather ashamed with herself for giving this away.

'What a happy household. And who were they wanting to curse?'

'I did not discuss the matter. The Crowman does not deal in curses.'

'I bet there's someone in town who does,' Wat said. 'And now we need to locate all these members of the household and find out which one wanted to put a curse on Elmund.' He glanced over at the corpse still lounging in the fireplace.

The Crowman followed his gaze and jumped back a good two feet at what she saw. 'Good God. What's he doing there?' She shrieked.

'Not much,' Cwen replied.

'Oh, sweet Gods in all their heavens,' The Crowman's voice quivered. 'You're all mad.'

'We're mad?' Wat said. 'I like that. You're the Frenchwoman who lives in the woods with bones and an old Saxon.'

Ah. Now Hermitage had it. Wat had threatened her with telling William and Le Pedvin that she was here. That way she'd been forced to tell them what she knew. For a moment, he thought that it was terribly clever. Until he thought it was a frankly dishonest way to go about any sort of investigation.

The Crowman went slowly over to Elmund's resting place.

'What's he doing in the fireplace?' she asked, with frank disbelief in her voice.

'We haven't quite got round to dealing with him properly,' Martin said.

'Not quite got round to dealing with him properly? You've got a dead body in your fireplace.'

'Well, what with Lord Colesvain getting involved, and the book and everything, we've been a bit distracted.'

The Crowman dipped her head and stepped into the fireplace to stand by Elmund. She said nothing but looked quite sorrowful, which was nice of her.

She even laid her hand on Elmund's head and muttered a few words under her breath.

'A bit distracted eh?' she said. 'A bit too distracted to honour a dead body. You are proposing to "deal with him properly", eventually?'

'Oh, yes.' Martin assured her. 'He obviously can't stay there long term.'

The Crowman shook her head at this sorry state of affairs and emerged from the fireplace.

She looked them all over as if trying to make up her mind what to do with them. She even put her hand to her mouth as she considered the remains of the book, the body in the fireplace and the four people standing before her.

Hermitage was rather worried that she was going to tell them all to stand in the fireplace with Elmund until they learned how to behave themselves.

'Right,' she eventually said. 'Here's what you're going to do.'

Hermitage looked forward to this, it was such a relief to be told what to do instead of having to think of it himself; even if he was being told by a young wise French woman.

The Hermes Parchment

'Nothing,' she said.

Well, that was fine, Hermitage could get on with that straight away.

The Crowman turned for the door before pausing there. She held them all with her gaze pointed a finger at them one by one. 'One, do not touch Elmund.'

Hermitage had been hoping that someone else would do that anyway.

'Two, do not touch the book.'

As there was no book left, Hermitage thought he could manage that.

'Three, stay here. I shall be back soon.' She emphasised the instruction. 'Do not go out. Do you understand?'

'Is that still part of three, or is that number four?' Cwen asked.

The Crowman just pointed her pointy finger some more and left.

Caput XIX Blood and Curses

'Nice woman,' Cwen commented lightly.

'Charming house,' Wat added. 'So, erm,'

'Woody?'

'Woody. Just the word. Bit light on wisdom, though. And now where's she gone? Not much help just walking out like that.'

'Perhaps she sees something here that we have missed,' Hermitage suggested.

Wat looked around at the scene of the disaster. 'Not sure what else there is to see.'

'She was a bit odd with Elmund,' Cwen said.

'She's simply a bit odd,' Wat said. 'Looks like we just have to carry on as best we can. If she's up to something, she's obviously not going to tell us what it is.'

Martin now took to one of the stools in the room and sat with his face in his hands. He emerged to look sorrowfully at them. 'This is all really awful,' he said.

'Any bit in particular?' Cwen asked.

'The whole thing. I cannot believe what is going on. I simply came to Brother Hermitage to get help sorting out a library. Next thing I know is that the librarian is lying face down in a pool of his own blood. That could have been an accident, but oh no. He's lying in front of a long-lost magical text, and now we find that the whole house is trying to curse one another.'

Hermitage didn't like to say that he warned him that something like this might happen. Perhaps Brother Martin would reach that conclusion all on his own.

'And this sort of thing happens all the time, does it?' Martin asked plaintively.

The Hermes Parchment

Ah, he'd reached the conclusion quite quickly.

'Well, not this sort of thing, exactly,' Hermitage said. 'I don't think we've ever had to deal with magic of any sort.'

'And there have never been so many books involved,' Cwen said.

'That's true,' Hermitage agreed, thinking that it was a bit of a bonus.

'But dead people?'

'Yes, dead people, I'm afraid.' Hermitage considered the current situation. 'This one is unique though,' he nodded towards Elmund

'And that's another thing,' Brother Martin wailed. 'We're chatting away while the dead person in question is sitting in the fireplace!'

'That is unusual,' Hermitage nodded. 'I had one on a sundial once.'[8]

'A sundial?'

'They'd taken him off by the time we got there.' Hermitage offered some crumb of comfort.

Martin simply looked bewildered at this. 'And now curses,' he moaned.

'That is a new one,' Cwen said, sounding quite pleased to have something fresh to consider. 'But it does give us something to work with. If we know who was trying to curse whom, and why, it might give an indication of who did for Elmund.'

'It's hardly a curse, is it?' Martin pointed out. 'Having your throat cut. Curses are normally about illness, or your crops dying, that sort of thing.'

'But there was a great big book of magic,' Wat said. 'Could

---

[8] The Case of The Clerical Cadaver covers the very latest thing in timepieces

be that Elmund was the one trying to do the cursing.'

'Who would he want to curse?' Martin asked. 'He wasn't averse to cursing people in person, I don't know why he'd bother with a book.'

'The Hermes book probably had some really good curses in it. You know, powerful stuff.'

'I still can't think of anyone he would really want to get at that way. He spent all his life in here.'

'Ardith?' Hermitage suggested. 'You said that he really didn't like her.'

'Yes, but it's a bit of a step from really not liking someone to trying to curse them from a book of magic and ending up with your throat cut.'

No one had a suitable answer for that.

'And there's another reason Elmund wouldn't curse anyone,' Martin went on.

'Oh yes?'

'He was too lazy. You saw. He spent his entire day sitting around reading books. Why would he even get out of his chair? No one was bothering him.'

'But he did have an interest in this sort of thing, magic and the like. He got very excited by the book. Wanted to take it away, even at the expense of leaving the library for the first time in years.'

'Curses are nonsense anyway,' Martin said. 'We all know that.'

'Superstition,' Hermitage agreed.

'It was a significant book though,' Cwen said. 'You could always take it away and hit someone with it. That'd do some damage.'

'What?' she asked, as they all just looked at her.

'We need to find everyone,' Wat said. 'It's no good talking

The Hermes Parchment

away in the library when the streets of Lincoln are full of people who want to curse one another. We need to find out what they were up to. That way, we may get a clue about what happened to Elmund.'

They all accepted that this was true, but no one seemed too keen on going out into the streets and looking.

'And Picot was the one who ran out of the room with blood all over him,' Cwen reminded them. 'I think that probably makes him the most likely suspect.'

'A man only slightly less lazy than Elmund,' Martin said.

'Come on,' Wat urged them all towards the door, rather like a shepherd driving his flock to their death. 'We know some of the servants are loitering around the cathedral. We can start there. Might even bump into the mysterious Ardith. I wonder who she's cursing?'

'Me probably,' Martin sagged as he left the room. 'For not giving her the books.'

Once out into the street, a thought bothered Hermitage. They turned left and headed back towards the centre of the town, not seeing anyone of interest in the vicinity.

'Ardith was after the books, wasn't she,' he said. 'In fact, she was extremely anxious to get hold of whatever she could.'

'Taking them one at a time, you mean,' Martin said.

'Exactly. Perhaps she was looking for the Hermes book?'

'Why would she be doing that? We didn't even know it was there until you opened the box.'

'But The Crowman knew about it. Not where it was, obviously, but she knew it existed. And Colesvain must now have the largest gathering of books for miles around. Perhaps this Ardith is up to something. After all, we already suspect she is not who she seems to be.'

'She could be another blackbird,' Cwen suggested.

'Could be,' Wat agreed. 'So, she came in, killed Elmund and took the book?'

'Bit of a dramatic way to do it,' Cwen said. 'Why not just hit him with something.'

'Can you stop going on about hitting people with things?' Wat asked. 'It makes me nervous.'

Cwen sniffed at him. 'It's still a lot of trouble to go to. Drawing a star, laying him out, the throat business? There are quicker ways of doing it if all you want is a book.'

'And,' Hermitage followed the story. 'Cutting the pages out might be the only way she could take them. After all, the whole book was far too heavy for one person.'

'Yes,' Wat agreed. 'It has to be something connected to the contents. If I saw a great bejewelled book like that just ready for the taking, I'd cut the pages out as well - and leave them behind. In fact, why not just prise the jewels out and stick them in your pack. Whoever did this is not after the book for money.'

Hermitage was already thinking that the whole situation was as bad as it could be. Having it confirmed that the theft of the book was for mysterious and probably evil purposes was not helping him at all. 'It's still quite a big thing,' he said.

'The book?' Wat asked.

'Of course, I don't know what else we're talking about. Even the pages cut out would be a handful to move. Whoever took them must have been carrying quite a load.'

'The sort of thing people might notice,' Cwen suggested.

'Well, wouldn't you? Someone comes out of Colesvain's house, staggering along with a huge bundle of parchment in their arms?'

'People, that's what we need,' Wat said. 'People we can, what's the word?' He turned to Hermitage.

The Hermes Parchment

'Any word in particular?'

'The nasty-sounding one for asking people questions.'

'Ah, interrogate.'

'That's it. We need some people to interrogate. Preferably roughly.'

'Interrogate?' Martin sounded interested. 'From interrogare, how interesting.'

'Isn't it?' Hermitage agreed. 'I find that so many words and phrases are useful in investigation, that one might almost think the Romans invented the whole topic.'

'I bet they knew how to do it properly,' Wat mused. 'Ah, here's someone.'

Hermitage noticed a perfectly innocent-looking individual, walking up the road. Whoever this was, they had clearly just come up Steep Hill, as they were still panting from the effort. It was a simply dressed man, who bore a massive load of kindling and wood upon his back. Hermitage couldn't help but think that there must be trees on top of the hill; bringing them up from below seemed an awful effort.

'I don't think he's even going to know what we're talking about,' Hermitage suggested. 'The fellow has obviously just climbed up the hill with his load. That must have taken an age. He's certainly not one of Colesvain's household.'

'You never know,' Wat said, apparently considering the wood-carrier with some enthusiasm.

Hermitage thought that actually, he did know in this case, but there was no holding Wat back.

'Ho there, you with the timber,' Wat called.

The man managed to look up from under the load that towered from his back. 'Don't stop me,' he panted.

'Beg pardon?'

'Don't stop me. If I stop, I'll never get going again.'

'Where are you going?'

'Hill Top lodgings,' the man gasped. 'Why they have to have their wood brought up the hill, I do not know.' He took struggling breaths. 'There's perfectly good stuff up here, but oh no, they have to have it from below.'

'Nearly there,' Cwen encouraged.

'Taken me half a day to bring this lot,' the man complained. 'Then I'll have to go and get more.'

'I hope they're paying well,' Wat said.

'That they are.' The man managed to cackle through his wheezing. 'Still, some things just aren't worth the money though, are they?'

From the look on his face, it was clear that Wat didn't understand those words.

'I don't suppose you know anything about Lord Colesvain's household,' Hermitage asked. He could see that they were wasting their time with this poor fellow. If he had spent the entire day bringing his load up from below, he would hardly have anything useful to say about the goings-on in the lord's house.

The man managed to indicate with a slight twist of his head, that they were going to have to follow him to the door of the Hill Top, which was now very close.

With a great sigh of relief, the man twisted to one side, released the rope that was binding the whole load to his back, and let it drop on the street by the door.

'My God,' the man swore. 'That's better.' He was still creased double as if his burden had permanently bent him in half. Very slowly, and with many groaning noises of complaint, he righted himself, rubbing his back as he did so.

'Have you ever thought of getting a small cart?' Cwen asked, with some contempt. 'You know, the sort they use to carry wood? One with wheels, that sort of thing.'

'A cart? What do you think I am, made of money?' He gave Cwen a very dismissive look. 'Cart? Ha!' He twisted his neck and back into their normal shape. 'Now, what was you asking?'

'About Lord Colesvain's household,' Hermitage repeated. 'If you've just come up the hill, I doubt if you know anything useful.'

'The bloody goings-on, you mean?' the wood man asked.

'Bloody goings-on?' Hermitage was surprised. Perhaps there had been some other bloody goings-on, and the house of Colesvain was quite famous for this sort of thing. Martin hadn't mentioned anything.

'Must have been pretty bloody,' the man said. 'Judging from all the blood that was on Lord Picot when he went running down the hill. Some sort of commotion, I reckon.'

'Some sort of commotion?' Hermitage was taken aback by the answer, as well as its casual nature. 'Yes, there has been a bit of a commotion.'

'And you saw Lord Picot running down the hill?' Wat checked.

'Hard to miss him. There's not many folk go running down the hill at all, let alone lordships. Dangerous thing to try. One missed step and it's a broken neck.'

'You know him then?'

'Everyone knows him. Puts himself about, he does.'

Hermitage wasn't too keen on hearing about the putting about. 'And the blood?'

'Dripping it was.'

'Are you sure it was him?' Cwen asked. 'With that load on your back, you were looking at the ground, I should think.'

Hermitage thought that was a very astute observation.

'You can't miss him,' the woodsman replied. 'Especially with him shouting on about the curse and all.'

'Erm, what curse?' Hermitage asked, as calmly as he could.

'I don't know, do I? I only just come up the hill with my load. He's the one running down covered in blood and shouting about curses. And I was a bit busy with this lot at the time.' He gestured at the pile of wood.

'What was he shouting about curses?' Martin asked. 'What were his actual words?'

'It's the curse, it's the curse,' the man reported. He was starting to look questioning about who these people were, and why they wanted to know all this. 'And before you ask, no, I did not stop him for a nice chat about curses and which one in particular concerned him most.'

'He didn't mention anything about a book? Or someone called Elmund?' Hermitage asked.

'No. Funny that, isn't it? Man covered in blood running for his life down a hill doesn't shout out all the details of the people he's met and what books he's read.' The man glowered at them. 'Who are you people, anyway?'

'This is Brother Hermitage,' Wat did the introduction. 'He's the King's Investigator.'

'Is he?' The man didn't seem disturbed by this. 'And that's good, is it?'

'Not really,' Hermitage muttered.

'We'd better get down the hill and look for Picot,' Martin said.

'And don't ask me which way he went,' the wood carrier said. 'I haven't got eyes in the back of me head.'

'Did anyone follow him?' Hermitage asked, thinking that this could be quite important. After all, Colesvain's household was out looking for him. A man covered in blood running down a dangerous hill should be hard to miss.

'Anyone else covered in blood and shouting about curses, you mean?'

'No.' Cwen was now showing her impatience with a rather impudent wood carrier. 'Anyone at all? Just a normal person. Two arms, two legs, you know the sort?'

The man seemed annoyed at the question. 'There was someone, but they wasn't shouting.'

'Were they running?'

'Ar.'

'They were?' Hermitage was intrigued by this. Perhaps Colesvain's people had caught him by now. 'Someone was following Picot?'

'Could be.'

'You said running down the hill was dangerous. Why would they be running if they weren't following Picot?'

'Good point,' the man admitted.

'And I don't suppose you saw who it was because you had your load on your back.'

'That'd be right.'

'At least we know someone was after him,' Hermitage said to the others. 'If we go back to the house, we could find they're all back there.'

'A woman,' the wood man added.

'A woman?'

'I can tell the difference between a woman's and man's legs when they go running by, you know.'

'How long ago was this?' Wat asked. 'Just now?'

'No, it was near the bottom of the hill, some while ago, I'd say.'

'Not The Crowman then,' Wat said. 'She was with us.'

Hermitage scoured his mind for who else was involved in

all this. 'Could be one of Colesvain's drudges,' he said.

Wat dismissed this idea with a snort. 'From what we've seen of Colesvain's people, they stopped running as soon as they were out of sight.'

'Who then?'

'What about this mysterious cathedral woman from the non-existent cathedral, Ardith?'

'Could be,' Martin agreed. 'Although Picot really could have anyone running after him.'

'If it was a woman, they'd be running away from him, normally,' the woodsman said. 'Now, if you don't mind, I've got another load of wood to bring up.'

'We'll come with you,' Wat said. 'We need to find Picot.'

'Oh, that'd be lovely,' the man replied as he spat on the ground.

Caput XX Over the Bridge and Far Away

'He could be miles away by now,' Cwen complained as they made their way down the hill with a rather grumpy wood man. 'If he kept running, as seems likely, he could be halfway to I don't know where.'

'Canwick,' the woodsman said.

'Beg pardon?'

'If he kept running, he'd be halfway to Canwick by now.'

'Ah, I see.'

'That's if he was going to Canwick, of course. Could be Boultham.'

'Could it, really?'

'Oh, yes. Pace he was going, be halfway to either of them by now, I reckon.'

'Well,' Wat said. 'That's very helpful, I think.'

'Is there anything at Canwick or Boultham that would help him?' Hermitage asked. He did think that running from a room with blood all over your hands would be a rather random process, but then he didn't know Picot. Personally, he couldn't imagine choosing a destination very carefully in those circumstances, simply running away would be the priority.

'Help the Colesvains?' The wood man sounded surprised at the suggestion. 'I don't think there's any folk would be helping them.'

'See,' Cwen said with a nod of her head that she had been right all along. 'People hate the Colesvains.'

'So they finish off his librarian? Just to show how cross they are?' Wat was not taking that idea seriously.

'What about the sheriff?' Cwen asked.

'What about him?' The woodsman asked, rather quickly

and nervously.

'Shire Reeve,' Hermitage corrected quietly.

'Colesvain was going to send for him to help find Picot. Surely someone would be out looking down here.'

'Oh, you won't get the sheriff downhill.'

Hermitage really couldn't make any sense of that. Perhaps the sheriff was a very large fellow who wouldn't be able to make it up the hill again if he went down.

'He probably considers it beneath him,' Martin explained.

'Well, erm, it is beneath him?' Cwen said, sounding as puzzled as Hermitage felt. 'It being down the hill and all.'

'Uphill is better.'

'Is it?'

'Oh, yes.'

'In what way, better?'

Martin explained as they walked on. 'Uphill is where the Colesvains live. It's where the sheriff's house is, the castle, the cathedral, the bishop's house, all of that.'

'The important people,' Wat said.

'Exactly. They all tend to stay near one another and let the people down the hill get on with things.'

'And if the important people go down the hill, they may not get a warm welcome,' Cwen said. 'Or get one that's a bit too warm.'

'I have been told that there can be some difficulty,' Martin said, not really giving much away.

'So why would Picot run down the hill?' Cwen asked. 'Get away from the important people?'

'It could just be panic,' Hermitage said. 'After all, he may have simply found Elmund murdered in the library and ran in terror.'

'Or he murdered Elmund in the library and ran downhill

to get away from the sheriff.'

The woodsman had stopped walking now and was looking at them all with a very worried look on his face. 'Murder?' he asked in a trembling voice.

'Oh, yes,' Wat said happily. 'Did we not mention the murder? That's where all the blood came from.' He sounded as if he thought the woodsman would be happy to get this piece of information.

'You get away from me,' the man called as he started to back off.

'We didn't do it,' Hermitage said patiently. 'We're investigating.'

'Not all over me, you're not.'

'It means we're trying to find out who did it.'

'And you think it might be Picot?'

'It's possible,' Hermitage agreed.

'Then you keep away. I don't want anything to do with the Colesvains at all, never mind if they're killing one another.' Looking around himself, clearly searching for a way out, the man saw a small track leading off to the left just at the bottom of the hill.

'My wood is this way,' he called, and simply ran off.

'Interesting,' Cwen observed. 'People really don't like the Colesvains, do they?'

'It must have been rather startling to discover that we're looking into murder,' Hermitage said. 'The poor fellow is a simple woodsman, after all.'

'Not that simple, if he takes wood to the Hill Top,' Wat said. 'What do we do, then? Keep going to Canwick or Boultham? We don't know where Picot's gone, and as Cwen said, he was running.'

They all stopped now that they were down on flat land and

looked about as if Picot would pop out from behind a tree at any moment.

The bridge over the River Witham was in front of them, and there was a fair bit of traffic coming and going. This was probably the only crossing for miles and was naturally a busy spot.

'A clue,' Hermitage said.

'Where?'

'No, that's what we need. A clue.'

'That would be helpful, yes,' Wat agreed with a shake of the head.

'The bridge,' Hermitage said. 'Martin, would Picot have to cross the bridge if he was going to either Canwick or Boultham?'

'Well, yes,' Martin said. 'Canwick is up the hill on the other side and Boultham is further south. The old Roman dyke goes off that way,' he indicated to his right. 'And that blocks all roads. Even though it's so clogged up you could probably walk across.'

'There you are. We simply ask the bridge keeper which way Picot went. There can't have been many people covered in blood being followed by a woman who went this way.'

Wat and Cwen looked a bit surprised that this was actually quite a good idea. They nodded at Hermitage and then towards the bridge, indicating that he could go ahead.

'Ah, yes,' he said. 'Perhaps it would be best if one of you asked?'

'Why us?' Cwen asked.

'Well, I am a monk, and bridge keepers tend to be quite brusque fellows, in my experience.'

'Quite brusque fellows,' Cwen laughed. 'Oh, Hermitage. You're the King's Investigator, for goodness sake. Get up there and demand that he tell you what you want to know in the name of the king.'

'Ooh, I couldn't.' Hermitage felt weak at the very idea.

'Oh, for heaven's sake.' Wat shook his head and grabbed Hermitage by the arm, dragging him towards the bridge.

Martin followed along behind, looking just as trepidatious as Hermitage.

The traffic on the bridge was busy, but things were moving quite quickly, so they simply joined the back of the queue on the northern bank of the river.

There were a couple of other monks in the small crowd, and they exchanged polite nods with Hermitage and Martin. They also gave Wat and Cwen rather disdainful looks.

'What's the toll here, anyway?' Cwen asked.

'I'm not sure, to be honest,' Martin replied. 'I came from the north and the route to you in Derby is to the west. I imagine it's a penny or less.'

'And I shouldn't think Picot had to pay,' Cwen said, 'what with his father being the tenant. This is probably his bridge anyway.'

There was a bit of trouble up ahead of them as they got closer to the bridge. The keeper was clearly in dispute with someone.

As is natural in situations like this, all the other people waiting gathered close so that they could see what was happening; and perhaps get the chance to laugh at someone else's misfortune.

In this case, the misfortune was befalling the two other monks.

'I don't care,' the bridge keeper was saying when they got within earshot.

From what Hermitage could see of the man, he looked the

type not to care. He was a large individual, probably picked for his role because he could stop quite a large cart in its tracks. Two fairly small monks would be no trouble.

'But,' one of the monks was trying to explain. 'Our monastery has an exemption from the toll.'

Hermitage knew that was quite reasonable. The bridge owner would see it as his Christian duty to let monks and priests travel without cost. Alternatively, some church officials might have had a quiet word and made it pretty clear what would happen to the bridge owner in the hereafter if he didn't let its people pass unhindered.

'No,' The bridge keeper replied. 'You might have had an exemption under the Danelaw and then King Harold. But now it's King William and Lord Colesvain, and there aren't any exemptions.'

'We weren't told of any change,' the other monk pointed out.

'Now you have been,' the bridge keeper said, apparently thinking that this cleared everything up nicely.

'But we must pass,' the first monk was a bit fretful now. 'We have travelled far; from York, no less. And we near our home.'

'Of course, you can pass. Pay the toll and off you go.'

'We have no money,' the monk pointed out as if it should be obvious to the most hardened bridge keeper that these were poor monks.

'That's easy, then.' The bridge keeper even smiled.

'Excellent.'

'Yes. You can't cross.'

Hermitage nudged Wat in the ribs and nodded towards the troubled monks.

Wat nodded agreement that they were indeed, troubled.

The Hermes Parchment

The two monks were now casting pleading looks around the gathering of locals, their message being a plain request for aid.

The gathering of locals looked on, as interested in who might offer some aid as the monks.

'You can spare a penny,' Hermitage nagged.

'You can tell him you're the King's Investigator and make him let them over.' Wat only let this suggestion hang in the air for a moment before releasing a heavy sigh and stepping forward.

'How much for two monks, then?' he asked the bridge keeper.

'A penny,' the bridge keeper replied.

With a look towards Hermitage that said he was keeping an account, Wat handed over a coin.

'Thank you, thank you,' the monks bowed and smiled their gratitude. 'We shall say a prayer for you.'

'It'll take more than one,' Cwen muttered.

'If you tell us your name?' the monk asked.

'Wat the Weaver,' Wat said with a grin.

The monks looked spectacularly shocked and crossed themselves vigorously. They looked to be in two minds about whether they wanted to cross the bridge at all now. They'd obviously rather it wasn't with a penny from Wat the Weaver.

'Wat the Weaver, eh?' the bridge keeper nodded with his own smile large on his face; his was a lot less savoury than the monks'. 'What brings you to my bridge? Carrying a large cargo of tapestry, are you?' The man peered around as if hoping to spot a cart full of Wat's works.

He absent-mindedly waved a hand to indicate that the monks could go ahead and cross the bridge. Apparently, they had concluded that Wat's penny was acceptable, as long as they did some sort of penance later, probably.

'Not this time,' Wat said to a disappointed bridge keeper. 'We're actually looking for Lord Picot.'

'Picot?' the bridge man asked. 'Has he bought a tapestry then? Now that wouldn't surprise me. I bet it's something really, really…,'

'No, no,' Wat interrupted. 'Nothing like that. He's gone missing, and Lord Colesvain has sent people out looking. Someone told us they'd seen him come this way.'

'Lord Colesvain sent Wat the Weaver out looking for his son?'

'It's complicated.'

'It would have to be.'

The crowd on the bridge showed some interest in the announcement of Wat the Weaver, but the audience seemed divided. Half of them wanted to get closer, while the other half wanted to get as far away as possible.

'This is Brother Hermitage,' Wat said. 'He's King William's Investigator.'

The crowd around the bridge leapt to action at this name. Pennies were hurriedly thrown at the bridge keeper and the place was clear in no time.

Those passing from north to south obviously passed on the information to those waiting to come up from the other side of the river, all of whom now decided that it was quite nice where they were and they could afford to wait until their passage had cleared; cleared of anyone who had anything to do with King William.

Even the bridge keeper was now looking quite cautious. Interest in the works of Wat the Weaver was obviously defeated by fear of the name of the king.

'So, did you see Picot?' Wat asked.

'Well, yes.'

'And he went south?'

'That's what happens when you cross the bridge from the north.'

'Very helpful. Which way did he go then?'

'Did he make towards Canwick or Boultham?' Martin asked.

'Canwick way, I reckon.' The bridge keeper was frowning. 'Why does the king's man want to know where he's gone?'

'Was he covered in blood?' Cwen asked.

'Might have been,' the bridge keeper was evasive.

'Might have been? It must be a bit unusual. He either was or he wasn't.'

'A bit.'

'A bit covered in blood?'

'And was he followed by a woman?' Hermitage asked.

The bridge keeper nodded.

'I imagine they didn't pay the toll.' Wat assumed.

'It's Lord Picot's bridge, isn't it?' the keeper gave his excuses. 'I can't stop his lordship to pay his own toll.'

'And the woman following?'

'She said she was with him.'

'What did she look like?' Martin asked. 'A middling woman with hair tied tight back and a plain dress.'

'I reckon,' the bridge keeper agreed.

Martin gave a knowing look to the others that this sounded like Ardith.

'And you didn't think Lord Picot covered in blood running over the bridge was unusual?' Cwen enquired.

'I seen him covered in worse.'

'And they went towards Canwick, you're sure?'

'They took the Canwick road.' The bridge keeper looked as if he'd quite like to stop conversing with the king's men now. He could obviously see consequences just over the horizon, and he didn't want to be here when they arrived.

'She hadn't caught up with him?' Cwen asked.

'Well, she couldn't, could she.'

'Why not? Is Picot a fast runner?'

'Ha!' the bridge keeper found that most amusing. 'I'd never seen him run anywhere before today. Didn't know he could. Great lump that he is. No, she was going slow, wasn't she?'

'We don't know, we weren't here,' Wat explained.

'Well, she was.'

'Why?' Cwen asked impatiently after the man failed to deliver an explanation.

'Cos of all that stuff she was carrying.'

'What stuff?'

'What do you call it?'

'I don't know, what do you call it?'

The bridge keeper looked as if he was thinking very hard to get at the concept he was seeking. It clearly had nothing to do with bridges or tolls, so was proving a bit of a challenge. He waved his hands around in the air a bit as if that was going to help.

'The bits.'

'Bits? Bits of what?'

The bridge keeper snapped his fingers, he had it. 'Books.'

'She was carrying books?' Hermitage asked. He could see that that would slow anyone down.

'The bits of books,' the bridge keeper explained. 'The inside bits.'

'Parchment! You mean she was carrying parchment?' Hermitage was quite excited. If this was Ardith, as seemed

The Hermes Parchment

likely, she had armfuls of the Hermes parchment. In which case? He needed a bit of a sit down to work out what this might mean, and this hardly seemed the time.

'That's it. Parchment. Big armfuls of the stuff she had. Probably wanted to light a fire.'

'Light a fire?' Hermitage was appalled.

'It's good for fires,' the bridge keeper said proudly as if he'd had quite a bit of experience burning books.

Hermitage just shook his head in desperate sorrow. 'But she followed him towards Canwick, with the parchment?'

'She did.'

'Where are they going?' Hermitage asked no one in particular. He understood Picot running away, but did he really have a destination in mind? And if Ardith did have the Hermes parchment, had she killed Elmund? There was only one place to go and find out.

'To Canwick,' the bridge keeper confirmed, sounding a bit impatient that he'd already told them this.

'But why?'

'Canna's place, I suppose,' the bridge keeper shrugged.

'Saint Canna?' Hermitage asked, thinking that they were a bit far away from the haunts of the Welsh saint.

'Saint? No, it'd be old Canna, I expect.'

'Old Canna?'

The bridge keeper sighed that these strangers were so ignorant. 'Ancient Canna, From before the Romans?'

They all looked blank. Hermitage couldn't think that anyone from before the Romans would still be around.

'Canna the witch?'

Hermitage suddenly felt cold and swallowed hard. 'Canna the witch?'

'It's where people used to go when they were covered in

blood.' The bridge keeper scratched his head 'Or did they get covered in blood once they'd got there? I forget which.'

Caput XXI Witch Way?

'Now we're getting somewhere,' Cwen said with a rub of her hands as she strode purposefully over the bridge.

Hermitage knew that they were getting somewhere: the other side of the bridge. After that perhaps they could go back to Colesvain's house and see if there had been any developments. After all, if Picot had gone looking for some witch or other, it was hardly their business to get involved.

But then there was Elmund's murder and the fact that Hermitage was the King's Investigator. Perhaps it was his business after all. Besides, there was no such thing as a witch. Church teaching was quite specific about this sort of thing. Of course, the bible mentioned them quite a bit, and they're generally a bad thing, but these were modern times, people shouldn't believe in superstitious nonsense like witches.

In any case, there was no way that this Canna person, whoever they were, had been around since the time of the Romans, that really was ridiculous. This would just be some other, so-called wise person of the woods. And from the description of the bridge keeper, they wouldn't even be as wise as the last one they'd had to deal with.

Hermitage could now see that perhaps Wat had been right. The Crowman hadn't actually told them anything that they didn't already know. Yes, she'd mentioned the ritual and the book, but even that was obvious. No one goes around drawing a star on the library floor and then cutting the librarian's throat in the middle of it if there isn't some sort of ritual going on.

Was that all there was to The Crowman's wisdom then? Simply repeating things back only in a slightly different way? She might be quite clever to make a living that way, but she wasn't very wise.

This Canna seemed to have a bit more history about her, or him. Or maybe it was just a case of one wise person for the top of the hill and another for the bottom. If Canna was of the same ilk as The Crowman, they'd be using the Roman connection to impress people. It was more than likely that they weren't even called Canna. They'd just taken the name to give the locals something to talk about.

Hermitage was very pleased with his reasoning on this matter. Seeing this Canna would be nothing to worry about at all. It would progress the investigation and they could well find Picot. Not only Picot but Ardith and the Hermes parchment. Now that was more of a worry.

If Ardith really had dealt with Elmund in a very permanent and peculiar manner, what else was she capable of? Had she really murdered the old librarian? Did she carry out the ritual with the book? And if she had taken it away, what did she intend to do with it?

He now started a new worry. The house of Canna, whatever it may be, could contain Picot, the witch person and a madwoman who cut peoples' throats. On Hermitage's side, there were only four, and two were monks.

He looked to the way they were going. The land on the south side of the river was flat for some considerable distance. They could see where it started to rise again, but it must be at least a couple of miles away.

Perhaps a cautious approach would be best.

'Perhaps a cautious approach would be best?' he suggested as they left the bridge behind.

'We're miles away, Hermitage.' Cwen said. 'Bit early to start being cautious.'

Hermitage thought that it was never too early to be

cautious.

'I'm surprised the sheriff didn't come down to the bridge to see if Picot had gone this way,' Wat said. 'Or at least send one of his men.'

'Truth be told,' Martin said, 'the sheriff is not a welcome figure down the hill.'

'Or his men?'

'Or his men.'

Wat just raised an eyebrow in question.

'There was some trouble, I'm told,' Martin said. 'Long before my time here, but I gather Lord Colesvain sent the sheriff into the town to collect some overdue taxes.'

'Did he now?' Cwen asked, thoughtfully. 'Just after he'd been made tenant-in-chief?'

'I believe so. One of his first actions.'

'He even wanted us to get tax off Godrinius,' Cwen said.

'And the people down the hill weren't so keen on handing over their tax?' Wat suggested.

'So I gather. They were so un-keen, that they sent the sheriff and all his men back up the hill in a dung cart.'

'Ha!' Cwen laughed.

'From which they had not removed the dung.'

'Surely Colesvain couldn't let something like that go?'

'Absolutely not. So he sent every man he had down the hill.'

'A bit of a battle, then?'

'Apparently not. It seems most of the men were persuaded to stay downhill and not go back at all.'

'Really?'

'Yes. They're quite organised down here. They've declared themselves a haven.'

'A haven?' Hermitage hadn't heard the word used other

than to mean a port of some sort.

'Yes, a haven from taxes, it seems.'

'A tax haven? What a ridiculous idea. How can you have one part of a country paying different taxes from everyone else, let alone one part of a town?'

'You can if you've got more men than the tax collector,' Wat explained.

'Surely, it can't last,' Hermitage said. 'Colesvain will have to collect the taxes sooner or later. He'll just get a greater force.'

'Another reason for the town to hate the Colesvains,' Cwen said.

'And William will want his tax,' Wat said, nodding to himself. 'Very keen on tax is the new king.'

'And a tenant who doesn't deliver?' Cwen suggested.

'Not a very effective tenant,' Wat concluded the thought. 'I wouldn't be surprised to hear of Colesvain sending for some help.'

'To William?'

'No, not to William. That would be an admission of defeat. No, he'll need to get someone else to help him recover his taxes.'

'Meanwhile, giving a nice library to the cathedral keeps William off his back for a while.'

'Not for long, if we know William; which we do.'

Hermitage thought that this was all very interesting, well, no, it wasn't really, and it didn't seem particularly relevant.

'So why would Picot come down the hill?' he asked. 'If the Colesvains are hated down here?'

Martin looked a little awkward as he gave a small cough. 'I think Picot is somewhat more welcome than his father.'

'Really?' Hermitage couldn't see why that would be.

'Oh, I see,' Wat said in a very knowing manner.

The Hermes Parchment

It was a good job one of them had some knowing.

'The young Lord Colesvain is a frequent visitor down the hill, then?' Cwen asked.

'So I am told.'

'Brings his custom and his money and spends it without word getting back to his father about what he's up to.'

'That could be true,' Martin admitted.

'So, if he'd done something truly horrible, for which his father was likely to chop something off, the first place he'd run would be down the hill. A haven from father Colesvain as well as his tax man.'

Martin just shrugged that this was a possible conclusion.

'And once down the hill, he simply keeps going,' Wat said.

'With Ardith on his heels?' Cwen asked.

Hermitage had to express his thought, revolting though it was. 'What if Ardith killed Elmund? Picot walked in on the act, saw what was going on and ran away.'

'Running away,' Martin said thoughtfully. 'Yes, I can see Picot doing that.'

Wat shrugged. 'We might find out when we get to the witch's house.' He gave Hermitage a friendly pat on the back. 'Unless we need an appointment, of course.'

. . .

The house of Canna was more like it.

It was clear that there had been a Roman settlement here. The remains of pavement were scattered about, peeping out from under the soil and the rocks, but Hermitage was gratified to see that a church had been built on the spot. A fine, simple Saxon church squatted on the Roman remains as if keeping them down. Given the Normans' predilection for church building, they'd probably be here before too long to put up something much more substantial.

When they did, Hermitage could only hope that they knocked the house of Canna down in the process.

If ever there was a description of a witch's house to frighten children, it must have been based on this place.

It bore similarities to The Crowman's woodland residence, in that it was simple wattle and daub and was tucked among the trees, seeming to blend in with its surroundings; but not in a nice way. This was the blending in of something very nasty that wanted to jump out at you and do something horrible.

Where The Crowman had her skull and bones to add to the aura of mystery inside, Canna used them as decoration. The outside of this place was hung with the most revolting things covering every spare bit of space. Bones and feathers were obvious, but there were some other things that really didn't bear close examination. They certainly didn't look as if they came from any woodland known to man.

Close examination, which was really to be avoided, revealed that the place was mostly falling down. The roof sagged, the walls bowed, and the door hung at a slant, looking as if it had given up all hope of ever functioning normally again. The rot in the wood made it quite clear that the thing would simply fall apart if anyone tried to move it.

Smoke rose from a hole in the middle of the roof, as well as from several holes that weren't in the middle. And it wasn't even a nice colour of smoke. Whatever was being burned in there should not be put on a fire.

There was no sign of anyone; no Picot, no Ardith and no Canna. Hermitage was quite grateful for this, hoping that perhaps their quarry had not come this way at all. A quick confirmation from a peek inside the hovel, and they could be on their way; Wat and Cwen were probably best at peeking inside a witch's hovel.

'Oh, dear,' Hermitage said. 'No one here then.'

Cwen gave him a disappointed look and stepped up to the hovel, showing not the least sign of worry about the place. She stuck her head through the front opening. 'He's right, no one here. But there has been. And quite recently, judging from the state of the fire.'

'I suppose this Canna person might have gone out into the woods,' Hermitage suggested. 'To gather some more, erm, bones, or something.'

'Or Picot got here, followed by Ardith and they've all gone off together?' Wat said, which was not what Hermitage wanted to think about, let alone hear.

'Why would he? What does Picot want with a witch?'

'If he has just seen a librarian ritually murdered, he probably wants a charm to make sure he's not next.'

'Or, he's come to report to the witch that he successfully killed the librarian,' Cwen suggested with a smile.

'And Ardith?' Hermitage asked.

'There's nothing for it but to look for them,' Wat said. 'Hermitage, you and Martin can go in the church, we'll check around the back, in the woods.'

Hermitage was grateful for that; he'd quite like to look in the church anyway.

Wat and Cwen made their way around either side of the hovel and neither of them screamed in horror, so Hermitage thought it safe to leave them to it.

With nodded agreement, the two monks made their way over to the church. It really had been built on top of the Roman pavement, and the way was solid and clear. It seemed a bit of a disappointment to see a basic Saxon church stuck on top. Yes, it was a fine stone building, narrow, but tall and imposing, but most of the stone had obviously been taken from the ground on which it stood, Other bits had been taken from wherever they could be found and the result was a bit of a mess.

Hermitage was sure that in a few years it would blend in with its surroundings, but he couldn't help but think it looked rather out of place.

Still, a church was a church, and it was a much better place to go looking for murderers than a witch's hovel.

He and Martin stepped up to the large main door and Hermitage heaved on the large iron ring that was set into the middle. The door swung easily, and a draft of cold air swooped out into their faces. It had the familiar scent of a church only used on special occasions as if the air had just been waiting for a chance to get out.

There was no telling who this place had been built for, probably Colesvain's predecessor, judging from the age of the place. It was clearly deserted now; no priest came to welcome them.

Hermitage stepped over the threshold, confident that this place would be as quiet as the grave. Perhaps he could even loiter in here until Wat and Cwen reported back. If Picot and Ardith were long gone, then what else could they do? There was no point wandering the country looking for two people who didn't want to be found.

Once he was within the bounds of the church, he froze and rather wished that he was outside of them again. The space inside was large and dark and clear of any furniture or obstructions. This meant that he had a very clear view of the fact that the floor was strewn with large pages of parchment.

The Hermes Parchment

He didn't need to get close to see that these were the remains of the Hermes book.

Fortunately, their arrival seemed not to have been noticed by the figure who was kneeling on the floor, muttering and cursing as the pages were moved around.

Ardith. So this was where she had come with the book. She was totally engrossed in the display before her, and stood now, to consider the whole of the floor. She had taken all the pages of the book and laid them out in what might be some sort of pattern. Hermitage looked to Martin, who appeared to be just as shocked as he was. They both held their breath.

Hermitage's first inclination was to gently step back across the threshold and fetch Wat and Cwen.

Martin held out a cautionary arm and indicated to Hermitage that they should watch what Ardith was doing.

Apparently unhappy with some feature of the pages, Ardith stepped over several of them to retrieve one from the back. She then brought this over and laid it next to one at the front.

Hermitage was alarmed to see that in the middle of the whole presentation was the page with the face of the demon on it. He rapidly concluded that Ardith had not brought the book here to repair it.

Hermitage was absolutely fascinated by this display of a dismantled book. Obviously, they started life this way; laying the pages on the scriptorium floor would be unheard of, but on a large table, ready for binding, was quite common.

His attention was drawn away by Martin tugging at his sleeve. He looked over and saw that he was being urged to silence. Martin nodded his head towards the back corner of the church and Hermitage followed his gaze.

There, sitting on the floor in the corner was Picot. He was

still covered in blood, but the fact that he was tied up and had a gag in his mouth, made Hermitage think that perhaps he wasn't the one who had killed Elmund.

Hermitage clamped a hand to his mouth to stop the small scream getting out. He did think that he and Martin should be able to manage Ardith, but he'd really rather have Wat and Cwen at his side, or preferably in front.

Martin was clearly of a like mind, and he pulled slowly on Hermitage's arm and inched his way back to the door.

He didn't want to take his eyes off Ardith, in case she did something unexpected; well, more unexpected than taking a book to pieces and laying it out on a church floor, while tying up the son of the local lord. This meant that he walked backwards into the door, rather than through it. The resulting noise caused Ardith to spin on the spot and her eyes widened at the sight of the two monks, as they tried to make a very ineffective escape.

'Aha,' she called out.

Completely distracted, Hermitage couldn't help but think that the shout was just the sort called for on an occasion like this; alarming, yes, but utterly mad.

'Monks,' Ardith announced.

Hermitage couldn't disagree but thought that leaving quite quickly now would be best.

'You'll do,' Ardith cried with a wild whoop. 'Monks will do nicely. Just the thing.'

Before they could scramble their way around the door and out, Ardith was upon them.

Caput XXII The Hermes Parchment

Hermitage still thought that two grown monks should be able to handle Ardith. Obviously, it hadn't worked out that way on this particular occasion, but he was sure that if they went back and started again, the whole situation would turn out very differently.

He comforted himself that they weren't tied up and gagged like Picot, but Ardith did have them trapped in the far corner of the church and was looking very threatening; very threatening and very mad.

A relatively small but purposeful woman just standing there did not constitute much of a trap, but it was working well enough.

They could simply stride forward and brush her aside; they were both much bigger than her. She just didn't look the type to be brushed. She looked the type to do something so comprehensively unnecessary that they'd be feeling the bruises for months; if they ever felt anything at all again.

But she hadn't actually done anything yet, had she? All she'd done was glare at them and rub her hands in quite an alarming manner before herding them into this corner like a couple of sheep. If she laid hands on them, well, that would be the time for action. Probably.

He had to bear in mind that it was now almost certain that Ardith had killed Elmund. He considered that people who cut other peoples' throats and left them in magic stars on the ground should generally be treated with caution. Backing away from such a person until you had nowhere further back to go, was a very wise approach.

Brother Martin had started their encounter with a cry of

"Mistress Ardith! What do you think you're doing?"

This had got the sort of reply that an old Saxon wise man of the woods - who had spent the long years of life perfecting his cackling - would be positively disturbed by.

It was that, quite frightening, noise that had started to drive them into this corner in the first place.

Hermitage thought about simply calling out for help to Wat and Cwen, who must be nearby. Cwen would be just the person to deal with a situation like this. He could even bear her criticism afterwards for not managing Ardith himself.

Hermitage had no idea what she was really planning, but he was sure it wasn't going to be good. The wise words of his father came back to him once again. They were pretty much the only wise words his father had ever given him, so they were never hard to recall.

"If you find yourself in times of trouble, talk. The trouble will either get bored and wander off or hit you quickly, in which case you'll get it over with."

As wisdom went, it wasn't up to much, but anything had to be better than Ardith's increasingly eager look. What she was eager about, did not bear close consideration.

'So, Mistress Ardith,' he tried. 'You have the book, then?' He nodded towards the pages strewn across the floor.

'The book?' Thankfully, the question did seem to distract Ardith from whatever task she had in mind.

'The Hermes parchment, if we can call it such.'

'Aha,' Ardith shrieked a bit, mostly a mad bit.

'But you seem to have, erm, moved it about a bit?'

'Of course,' Ardith almost did a little dance at this question.

Martin and Hermitage exchanged worried looks; they only exchanged them for one another's worried looks so it didn't take them any further forward.

'That was the secret,' Ardith was now terribly excited.

Hermitage didn't really like people getting excited at all. Calm, rational discussion was all that was needed in most circumstances. He had to accept that this situation was pretty unique.

At least Ardith's excitement took her away from them as she skipped over to the pages she had laid out. Hermitage breathed again.

'You see, you see?' She waved her arms towards the laid-out pages. 'They put it together in the wrong order.'

Hermitage and Martin chanced a step away from their corner and peered over at the pages. Martin indicated with a nod of the head that perhaps this was the moment for a run towards the door. Hermitage silently replied that they really couldn't leave Picot to whatever fate it was that Ardith was planning.

Much as he really, really wanted to leave, it seemed clear that Picot was not involved in this. Otherwise, why would Ardith have tied him up? If the young lord really had discovered Ardith in the act of cutting Elmund's throat, it was no surprise the poor boy had run. And he could be next.

Hermitage now reached a worrying conclusion all on his own. Ardith had brought the book down here and was obviously trying to reorganise it. This meant that when it was bound in its covers, it was in the wrong order. The wrong order for what was the big question. He could only conclude that whatever it was Ardith had killed Elmund for, hadn't worked; and now she had Picot.

She was obviously trying to get the book in the right order, then she could have another go. And another go would probably involve another dead body.

'The wrong order, you say?' Hermitage tried.

Martin gave him increasingly urgent looks that leaving now would probably be best.

'Of course,' Ardith replied without looking at them. 'That was part of the secret. Not only was the book hidden at Rooksby, and then secreted in the bottom of the box, the pages were put together out of sequence.'

'I see.' Hermitage didn't see at all, but he didn't like to say that to the killer madwoman. 'And you know about Rooksby and the box, then.'

'Picot told me,' Ardith said. 'Eventually,' she added with a very crooked smile.

There was a small whimper from behind Picot's gag and a look of plain fear in his eyes.

'And you know what order the pages should be in?'

'That's what I'm doing,' Ardith snapped at him. 'Can't you see, I'm doing it?'

'Of course.' Hermitage chanced another pace forward so that he could see the pages more clearly.

'The demon is obviously the middle,' Ardith said. She now seemed engrossed in her task once more, which was a bit of relief from her being engrossed in what she was going to do to them.

Hermitage could see that she had placed the page with the picture of the demon on it in the middle of the floor. It sat right in front of the altar, which seemed entirely inappropriate, but Hermitage didn't like to mention it.

It was clear that Ardith didn't really know what she was doing. She stood and stared at all the pages, obviously hoping that a revelation would come to her.

'And you noticed this when you took the book,' Hermitage said. He tried to sound as if he thought she had been terribly clever.

'That's right,' Ardith agreed, clearly thinking that she'd been terribly clever as well.

'And you had to take the book from the cover because it was too big to carry.'

'Stupid thing,' Ardith shouted at the pages on the floor.

'Pretending to burn it was a devious ploy.'

'I know.' Ardith cackled a bit. 'But you found out!' She turned instantly to anger and threw it at Hermitage.

'No, no,' Hermitage said, holding his hands up. 'Not at all,' he added. 'We went all the way to see The Crowman in the woods.'

'That cow!' Ardith exclaimed.

'No, crow,' Hermitage corrected.

'I mean she is a cow,' Ardith growled. 'I went to her about the book, but she wouldn't tell me anything.' It sounded as if Ardith was keeping a list of grudges that she would attend to once she'd got a couple of demons on her side.

'Really?' Hermitage asked. 'She didn't seem to know anything about it until we saw her.'

'Well, obviously I didn't tell her about the book, you idiot. I asked her some questions that would help, that's all.'

Hermitage thought that the questions must have been so vague that The Crowman wouldn't have had a clue what was going on. He had some sympathy.

'But then I saw it. With my own eyes.'

'The book?'

'Of course, the book.' She gave her attention to the pages once more. 'I watch the library, you know.' She gave a horrible smile.

'I can imagine.' Hermitage's own smile was very weak.

'I watch everyone. All the time.'

'No time for sleep, eh?' Hermitage tried nonchalant.

'Sleep?' Ardith's eyes jumped from side to side, as if she was trying to remember what sleep was. 'Picot is a good boy.' Ardith nodded to the good boy who was bound and gagged in the corner. 'He tells me about the books.'

'That's very good of him.'

'And he'll be useful now.'

'Ah, very good,' Hermitage said, knowing that it wasn't going to be very good at all.

'Once I've got the pages in order,' Ardith spat her irritation that she was not finding the answer she wanted.

Hermitage really didn't know whether he should get to the nub of the matter or whether any sort of discussion of murder might tempt Ardith to try and do another one.

'With Elmund, the pages were in the wrong order then,' Hermitage nodded as if this made perfect sense. Which it probably did to a mad killer.

'That's it.' Ardith seemed grateful that Hermitage was agreeing with her.

'So, once they're in the right order..?'

'We can try again,' Ardith said.

Hermitage was really alarmed that he might have got a bit too close to this woman if she thought he was going to have anything to do with this.

'Properly this time,' Ardith turned her head and gave him an encouraging smile.

The only thing it encouraged him to do was run away, but he held his ground. 'With, erm, Picot?' he asked lightly.

'Perfect,' Ardith agreed. 'He's all ready. Once we've sorted out the pages.'

Hermitage shivered that he was now involved in sorting out the pages as well.

The Hermes Parchment

With Ardith's attention back on the laid-out book, Hermitage wondered if Martin might be able to sneak out and get help. Ardith seemed to consider that Hermitage was now her partner in whatever her ghastly and sinful plan was, perhaps she'd forgotten about Martin.

He turned his head and moved his face and mouth around in a manner that he thought made it clear what Martin should do.

Martin just looked even more worried now.

Hermitage nodded hard towards the door.

Martin indicated that he had got the idea and took a very careful half-step in the right direction.

Ardith didn't notice as she had wandered over to look at one particular page of the book in detail.

'Is this right, do you think?' she asked out loud. She then turned to face Hermitage. Fortunately, she didn't seem to see that Martin was a bit closer to the door than he had been. She beckoned Hermitage to come and join her. 'This page here. What do you think?'

Hermitage could only give a rather horrified look of helplessness at Martin. He hoped that the look said that he would go and occupy Ardith, while Martin went for help; and that Martin had better find some help and bring it here pretty quickly.

'Well,' Hermitage said, as brightly as he could manage. 'Let's have a look, shall we?'

He walked slowly over towards Ardith, making sure not to tread on any of the pages laid out under his feet.

Another noise from Picot's corner caught his attention and he glanced over to see the young lord shaking his head as if warning Hermitage not to get involved. Perhaps Picot had tried to help Ardith with her book sorting, and he got bound and gagged for his trouble.

Seeing that he really didn't have any other choices in this very bizarre situation, he shrugged at Picot and tiptoed towards Ardith.

'See, see?' Ardith was pointing at one page.

Hermitage looked at it and saw a lot of small Greek writing, together with some very obscure drawings of some sort. These were mostly circles and triangles, interlocking and joined by lines. He could see no picture in these, like the demon, but there was something about their pattern that worried him. It felt as if the simple shapes were not supposed to be put together in this manner. They somehow hinted at arrangements that no one had ever thought of before; unnatural arrangements.

'It must be an order of the mystical number,' Ardith said as if her mind was somewhere else.

'Mystical number?' Hermitage asked. He'd come across one or two monks in his time who went on about mystical numbers. They were all very strange fellows who were best avoided. But then they hadn't murdered any librarians, as far as he knew.

'Of course,' Ardith snapped at his ignorance. 'The mystical number, forty-two.'

'Forty-two?' Hermitage asked. He hoped a change of subject might do some good, as he was convinced that Ardith's mind really was somewhere else; somewhere not very nice at all.

'The forty-two judges of the dead,' Ardith huffed impatiently.

'Ah,' Hermitage said, hoping it would achieve something.

'The forty-two judges of ancient Egypt presided over by Thoth.'

The Hermes Parchment

'Thoth the great, the great, the great.'

'Exactly!' Ardith was terribly excited by Hermitage's mention of the name. 'Trismegistus. Thrice master, you see.'

Hermitage just shrugged a bit, which he hoped conveyed the message that he didn't see at all, but hoped it wasn't important.

Ardith turned her attention back to the parchment pages. 'There must be an order of forty-two here somewhere.'

Hermitage stood and looked around at the church architecture, thinking that there might be a forty-two up in the roof somewhere that he could distract Ardith with.

'Once we've found the forty-two, we can get on with the summoning.'

'Oh, the summoning, eh?'

'Exactly.' Ardith now gave Hermitage a very hard glare. 'So start looking or I'll have two sacrifices.'

Hermitage put his hands behind his back and started to wander the isles of parchment, bravely pretending that he had the first idea what he was looking for.

Caput XXIII Help Arrives

Outside of the door, Martin was blissfully unaware of the latest unusual goings-on in the church; apart from the madwoman who had tied up the young lord. It was clear from Hermitage's silent pleading that he needed to find Wat and Cwen and do it quite quickly.

They had gone to check in the woods surrounding the church, and so that's where Martin went. He didn't want to call out, not this close to the church, in case Ardith heard him and realised what was going on. If she appeared at the door and demanded that he returned right now, he was concerned that he would probably do as he was told. She had always been a difficult woman but now seemed positively peculiar.

The woods were unfortunately dense around here. It was obvious that no one was managing them and they had run wild. Most likely this was all church land and no one would be stupid enough to come and help themselves to fuel or food from its property. It was bad enough that the Normans punished everyone who strayed into their precious hunting grounds. A beating or a fine was one thing; the church could send you to hell.

Creeping around the right-hand side of the church, avoiding the brambles and nettles that pressed up to its walls, Martin looked for any sign that Wat and Cwen might have come this way.

Eventually, unable to proceed through the undergrowth, he concluded that they must have taken another route.

The other side of the church was clearer and there was even movement of some of the ground cover as it sprang back from having been trampled. Feeling quite proud of himself at this observation, he pressed on.

Once beyond the end wall of the church, he felt it safe to speak out.

'Master Wat? Mistress Cwen?' he called in a voice barely above a whisper. 'Are you there?'

With no reply, he had to press further into the undergrowth, getting his habit snagged on long trailing brambles. He glanced back at the church that was now some forty feet behind him and chanced raising his voice. 'Wat? Cwen? Where are you?'

He thought he heard a noise off to his left, that might be someone moving about, so he turned in that direction. 'Wat? Cwen?' he asked, suddenly feeling a bit cautious that this might not be them. Who else would be creeping about in the church woods was a question he wasn't going to consider in any detail.

Making sure that his return route was clear, in case he needed to use it in a hurry, he pressed on.

The noise did not move away, so he assumed that whoever this was, was stationary. As he pushed a particularly obstructive bush to one side, voices could be heard.

'It has snagged my leggings,' Wat was full of complaint.

Martin breathed a sigh of relief.

'Oh, dear?' Cwen said, asking why this was a problem and clearly not caring less about the leggings in question.

'The wretched bramble has snagged them. Look at that snag?'

'I can see the snag.'

'It's nearly a hole.'

'It is not nearly a hole, it's just a mark, that's all. For goodness sake, stop worrying about your clothes. We are on the hunt for a killer, you know. I don't think he's going to worry if your leggings have got a snag on them.'

'It's a very big snag.'

'Maybe it'll give the killer somewhere to aim the knife?' Cwen was sounding very bored with the snag. She paused. 'Come to think of it, I've got a small knife somewhere. Maybe I could stab you?'

'Oh, very funny.'

'It won't be if you keep going on about your leggings.'

'If I'd known we were going to have to chase killers into the bramble patch, I'd have worn something else.'

'Bring a change of clothes for killer hunting, did you?'

'Wat, Cwen,' Martin called as he finally got to them.

'Have you seen the size of the snag on my leggings?' Wat asked.

'Erm,' Martin didn't really know what to say. 'Very nasty, yes. But it's about Hermitage.'

'What's he done now?' Cwen asked.

'He's found Ardith.'

'Oh, great,' Wat complained. 'Why did we come in here in the first place if she was in the church?'

'That was your idea,' Cwen pointed out.

'And Lord Picot,' Martin added.

'So, all we've got to do is get out of here without any more damage.' Wat looked at his leggings and at the brambles around him.

Martin looked as if he was quite keen to move the conversation on from leggings and snags. 'And Ardith has tied Lord Picot up in the corner of the church, and is forcing Hermitage to sort out the Hermes parchment.'

That did get a pause in the clothing-centred discussion.

'She's got the book, then?' Cwen asked.

'She has. She was obviously being told about the books by

The Hermes Parchment

Picot, and when she heard of the one with the jewels, she came and got it. The whole burning trick seems to have been her. She thinks the pages are in the wrong order and just need putting right.'

'Putting right for what?'

'I don't know. But if she killed Elmund and has Picot tied up in the corner, I rather think it will be something horrible.'

'And Hermitage is helping her?'

Martin shook his head. 'Only to delay her while I came for help.'

'Didn't bring a knife for these brambles, did you?' Wat asked. He got a slap on the back of his head from Cwen and a very clear direction that he had better start making his way to the church.

They moved back through the woods to regular cries of "oh bloody hell", from Wat every time another bramble got him.

They eventually emerged at the front of the church once more and Wat brushed himself down, examining the damage to his clothes.

'Erm, rescue Hermitage?' Cwen suggested. 'Then do clothes?'

'I wonder if Colesvain would pay for new leggings,' Wat mused. 'After all, it's his book we're after and his librarian who got murdered.'

'Hermitage,' Cwen barked.

'All right, all right,' Wat said as they headed for the church door.

'You there.' A voice called out from the track behind them.

They all turned and saw a whole contingent of men coming towards them. While they weren't actually in uniform, they were dressed very similarly in a consistently aggressive manner; a manner mainly indicated by the swords they carried before them.

There must be at least a dozen of them, and it didn't look as if they were taking their swords out for a bit of exercise.

'Let me guess,' Wat muttered quietly, 'here comes the sheriff.'

The men were all strangers, but the one who had called was pushed aside as Lord Colesvain stepped up from the rear.

'What the devil are you doing here?' Colesvain demanded.

'We've found Lord Picot,' Martin spoke up.

Colesvain didn't say anything but glared at them as if they should be minding their own business. 'And why are you looking for him?'

'Brother Hermitage..,' Martin began.

'The King's own Investigator,' Cwen reminded them all.

'Er, yes. We've all been trying to find out what happened to Elmund. We heard from a woodsman that Picot had been seen running down the hill covered in blood. Then we spoke to the bridge keeper who said he may have come here.'

'Hm.' Colesvain appeared content with their explanation, but still didn't seem very happy that they were here.

'He's in the church,' Martin went on. 'Lord Picot, that is. And Ardith.'

'Ardith?' Colesvain was roused by that name.

'Indeed. She seems to have gone mad. She's got the pages from the library; Lord Picot is tied up in a corner and Brother Hermitage is in there trying to divert her while I came out for help.' He swallowed. 'We think she killed Elmund.'

'What?' Colesvain seemed more puzzled than shocked as if the idea of Ardith doing it had simply never occurred to him.

'That's right.' Wat nodded. 'And now she's got your son

The Hermes Parchment

and the King's Investigator.'

Colesvain simply shook his head, as if he was profoundly disappointed by the way they were making a complete mess of something that was perfectly simple. 'All right,' he sighed. 'We'll take it from here.' He nodded that his armed men should make their way to the church, which they did.

He followed along and pushed through them once more as they gathered at the door.

'You lot wait,' he instructed them. 'Don't want to alarm her if she really has got Picot tied up in there.'

Martin looked rather offended that he was being accused of making this up.

The waiting force did their waiting with swords to hand, while Lord Colesvain pushed the door of the church and entered. He closed it behind him.

Wat looked at Cwen and Martin with some surprise as from inside, they heard the unmistakable sound of a bolt being slid across to lock the door.

'So,' Wat said, as they wandered over and joined the small force. 'You the sheriff's men, then?'

'We are,' one of them growled at him. 'And I'm the sheriff. What's it to you?'

'Oh, nothing, nothing,' Wat smiled. 'Just interested. Bit odd Lord Colesvain locking himself in like that, eh? Just the sort of thing a sheriff would be wanting to know about, I imagine.'

The sheriff gave him a look that said he had never liked people who were interested in things.

'You call me Shire Reeve,' the sheriff insisted.

Wat nodded agreement that a man with a sword was entitled to insist on whatever he wanted.

'Hermitage would like you,' Cwen said.

This got yet another of the sheriff's dismissive looks.

After a few moments of awkward silence, only broken by the occasional cough from one of the sheriff's men, Wat had to speak again.

'Is this right?' he asked eventually.

The sheriff didn't even bother with a reply.

'I mean, all of us out here. We're outside the church, including all your men with the swords, while Lord Colesvain is in there with one madwoman, a monk and a tied-up young lordship.'

'And he locked the door behind him,' Cwen pointed out.

The sheriff didn't seem to have any problem with the arrangement.

'I would have thought it's more normal for the men with the swords to burst through the door. That sort of thing?'

'Lord Colesvain knows what he's doing,' the sheriff dismissed the comment. 'If Lord Picot is in danger, he could be killed before we get to him.'

'He's over in a corner of the church,' Martin said. 'A long way from Ardith and Hermitage. And she seemed to be concentrating on the pages of the book.'

'There you are,' Wat said. 'And Lord Colesvain has been in there a while now. Perhaps he's in danger himself and needs rescuing?'

That did seem to give the sheriff some cause for doubt.

'And it's gone very quiet,' Cwen said. 'For a church with a madwoman in it.'

The sheriff stepped back from the church and appraised it. He seemed to be checking for a window he could look through, just to check that everything was all right, without having to disturb Lord Colesvain. Unfortunately, all the openings were high in the wall, well above the height a man could reach without a very long ladder; a very sensible design to keep attackers out, but less help when you needed to peek in on mad people who were holding prisoners.

He returned to the church door and rubbed his chin in thought.

'All right, stand back.' His men did as they were ordered, Wat, Cwen and Martin stayed where they were.

The sheriff very carefully approached the door and laid his hand on the black iron ring that would lift the latch. He paused here as if expecting Lord Colesvain to open it from the inside at just that moment.

When there was no movement, he very slowly turned the handle and listened hard, just waiting for the instruction to "get out", which he would obey immediately.

When nothing was heard, he turned the handle completely and pushed very timidly at the door. Then he pushed a bit harder. Then he frowned and put his other hand on the door and pushed.

Next, he stood back, looked at the door, turned the handle once more and put his shoulder to the task.

'It's bolted,' he observed, looking rather confused.

'That would be the sound of the bolt we heard,' Wat offered.

'Lord Colesvain must want some privacy while he deals with this woman and rescues his son,' the sheriff concluded.

'Could be,' Cwen agreed. 'Or the madwoman now has the whole family captive and has locked them in.'

The sheriff looked as if he really wasn't equipped to deal with this sort of thing. He considered the door and then his men as if he had not the first idea what to do.

'So,' Wat said, with a rub of the hands. 'What's to do then? Either go back up the hill and hope Lord Colesvain sorts himself and it all turns out all right in the end, or break the door down and find out what the Norman is going on in there.'

'What the Norman?' The sheriff was even more confused now.

'I was trying to think of a rude word to use in front of a monk and "Norman" was the best I could come up with. I think it makes quite a good curse. Get the Norman out of my way, who the Norman do you think you are? That sort of thing.'

Cwen helpfully pushed Wat out of the way so that the sheriff's men could get to the door.

'You know when people say something like "you really are an idiot sometimes"?' she asked.

Wat shrugged.

'In your case, it's all the time.'

With the door before him, the sheriff really had no choice but to try and get through it. First of all, he hammered on it. 'My Lord,' he called out. 'Is all well?'

There was no reply to this. 'My Lord?' he tried once more.

When there was still no answer, he beckoned to his men that they should step forward and attack the door.

Obviously not too sure how they were supposed to actually do this, three of them approached and tried a cautious shove on the door. When nothing moved, they coordinated themselves and got their shoulders together to pile forward.

The first strike on the door did nothing other than rattle it a bit. But at least it did rattle and not simply stand there immobile.

The second thump, which was more like it, led to the sound of cracking timber.

The sheriff called them away again. 'My Lord,' he called

with some urgency.

Still no answer, so he indicated that his men could finish the job.

Satisfied that their approach did seem to be making some progress, the men gathered themselves together. They even stood in a tight line and lowered their left shoulders for the charge.

'One, two, three,' one of them called. On three, they took decisive steps towards the door, which almost inevitably for a situation like this, opened just as they got there. They carried on straight through the open door and into the body of the church, there being no way they could halt their forward progress until they found a door to break down or a wall to run into.

In fact, their legs conspired to trip them long before that happened and they sprawled forward onto the floor, scattering some pages of parchment as they did so.

Wat, Cwen and Martin quickly stepped up to the open door, closely followed by the sheriff.

'Aha,' Lord Colesvain called from the side of the door he had just opened.

He appeared to be unharmed, as was Hermitage. Ardith was still standing amongst her parchment and there was Picot, still tied and gagged in a corner. Whatever Lord Colesvain's rescue attempt was, it hadn't quite finished yet.

'Come in, come in,' Lord Colesvain called with an intensely threatening tone in his voice. He glanced over at Ardith. 'I could do with some witnesses.'

Caput XXIV Magic in the Air

Hermitage's hopes had risen with the first thump on the door, but they hadn't got very far. Lord Colesvain seemed content to take Ardith into quiet conversation, rather than bluster about demanding everyone be released this minute, which he thought would be more helpful.

He did understand that the woman was completely mad and thought that confronting her directly might well have dire consequences. Perhaps the cautious approach was best. It still seemed a bit of an odd way for the king's tenant-in-chief to deal with things. Instant death would be much more normal.

At least the interruption of the men bursting through the door had given him a chance to drag his attention away from the pages of the parchment, which still conspired to give him a very nervous feeling. The more of the things he had looked at, the more he was sure that this was a book full of things that should never have been written down.

He had been fascinated by books all his life and could never usually wait to get his hands on one. Those books had behaved themselves though. They didn't give him the impression that they were hiding something. He was being forced to consider that there might be some magic in this book of Hermes. How else could he explain his forebodings?

'Hermitage,' Cwen's voice called him as a press of people now came into the body of the church. 'Are you all right?'

He smiled weakly and gave her a very careful shrug. Yes, he was all right in the sense that he wasn't wounded in any way. He was still dealing with a madwoman and what he was convinced was a very dangerous book, though. "All right", didn't quite cover the situation.

The Hermes Parchment

A whole troop of men, swords in hand, now gathered in the church, and Hermitage felt some relief at this sight; for once in his life. He was confident that these fellows would be able to deal with Ardith and release Picot. He knew that it was up to him to deal with the book, though.

Lord Colesvain appraised the men and then ordered them to guard the door. He called the sheriff over and had a quiet word in his ear. He might want to deal with Ardith as gently as possible, after all, she was plainly mad.

Hermitage saw Martin at Cwen's side and beckoned that the monk should come and join him.

Martin stepped over, casting a glance left and right in case someone in authority told him to stand still.

'Ah, Brother,' Hermitage sighed quietly. 'Thank the Lord that you are here. And well done for finding all these men.'

'They were coming anyway,' Martin said. 'It seems Lord Colesvain and the sheriff were already on their way.'

'That's excellent. It will be good to get this whole sorry business over with. The sheriff's men can take Ardith and I suppose we have to deal with the book.' Hermitage took a breath. 'Tell me, Brother, when you look at the pages, do you see anything to worry you?'

'Worry me?' Martin clearly thought this was a very odd question in the circumstances.

'Yes. Look at the pages laid out on the floor and tell me if they concern you.'

Martin looked as if he was happy to placate Hermitage, who was in a bit of a state. He looked over the large expanse of floor that was covered in the parchment.

'She seems to have messed them up,' he observed.

'Yes, she's changed them around. She said that they had been bound in the wrong order on purpose. Getting them laid out correctly seemed to be her main priority. Something to do with forty-two.'

'Forty-two what?'

'Judges, apparently.'

'Forty-two judges?' Martin looked and sounded very confused.

'Judges from ancient Egypt. I don't understand a word of it, but it seems important to Ardith.'

Martin looked left and right at all of the pages. 'I can't see that moving them about has achieved anything.'

'You don't see anything, then?'

'What am I looking for?'

'Well, something about the pages disturbs me. I can't read the words, and I can't understand the drawings, but I am just convinced that they are wrong.'

'In the wrong order?'

'No, not wrong as in mistaken, wrong like sin is wrong.'

'Ah.' Martin looked concerned, but it wasn't clear if that was about the book, or about Hermitage.

'Ooh,' Cwen spoke up from the back of the room and she walked slowly over to join Hermitage and Martin.

Hermitage was alarmed to see that she was staring at the pages of parchment as if they were putting on some sort of show.

'They're pretty,' she said in a rather distant voice.

'Pretty?' Hermitage hissed at her. 'What do you mean, pretty?'

'Well, all the shapes. Pretty shapes.'

Hermitage wasn't sure he'd ever actually heard Cwen use the word "pretty" at all. He was positive she'd never said it as if she was in some sort of daze.

'Shapes?' Martin asked.

The Hermes Parchment

'All the shapes, floating above the pages,' Cwen said. 'Why are they there?' She turned her head briefly to give Hermitage a quizzical look.

In that moment, Hermitage could see that something was wrong with Cwen. Her usual expression of drive, determination and almost constant impatience, had given way to a look of serenity. Cwen didn't do serenity. She appeared to be completely relaxed - another very peculiar state for her - and returned her gaze to the parchment as if it was the most wonderful thing she had ever seen.

Wat now joined them and looked at Cwen as at someone who's just said they might have a touch of plague.

'What's wrong with her?' Wat asked Hermitage, as Cwen was clearly in no state to deal with anything.

Hermitage waved Wat to be quiet and spoke softly to Cwen 'You can see shapes?'

'You can see shapes?' Ardith barked across the room and spoke directly to Cwen, ignoring everyone else.

'Oh yes,' Cwen said dreamily. 'Lots of shapes.' She started to walk into the middle of the parchments.

'Where are you going?' Ardith snapped.

'Here,' Cwen said, very slowly pointing towards one page that obviously had her attention. She stopped at the page and carefully considered the image before her feet. 'This one.'

'What about it?' Ardith asked, following Cwen with a very intense look.

Cwen picked up the single page and moved it over towards another one, further to the right. When she arrived there, she looked at the one in her hand and the one on the floor and placed them side by side.

'Bigger shape,' Cwen said, sounding quite pleased with herself.

'Oh, dear,' Hermitage bleated. He looked to Wat and Martin. 'What are these shapes?' he asked Cwen. He knew that he found the pages alone disturbing enough, if Cwen could see shapes, it was going to be something deserving of serious worry.

'The patterns,' Cwen said. She then followed it up with, 'Oh, my.'

'What, what?' Ardith was not getting any happier.

'Well, look.' Cwen beckoned to the floor where the two pages lay.

Ardith obviously couldn't see anything and wasn't at all happy about the fact. 'What are you babbling about?'

'The pages,' Cwen said. 'They fit together like this. They make the shapes.' She held a hand out towards the parchment.

Ardith now pinched her on the arm. 'What do these shapes look like?'

Cwen looked at Ardith and the rest of them and appeared to be simply puzzled that they couldn't see whatever it was that she was seeing.

Hermitage was now positively alarmed. If Cwen could see something beyond the pages themselves, she might be able to tell what order they were supposed to go in. And he had already decided that that was a very bad idea indeed.

He tried to gesture to Wat and Martin that they might need to step in at any moment and do something. What they were going to do, he had not a clue.

Lord Colesvain came over now and watched proceedings with a deep frown on his face.

'If you don't tell me what it is,' Ardith barked, 'I shall tie you all in the corner with Picot.'

'It's not the words,' Cwen said, still talking as if she were in some sort of trance.

'What's not the words?'

'It's the pictures.'

'The pictures? What about the pictures, you stupid girl?'

Ah, now Hermitage knew there was something very wrong indeed. No one called Cwen a stupid girl and got away with it.

'They're not separate, they're one.' Cwen said.

As she said this, Hermitage moved from thinking that putting the book together properly was a very bad idea to knowing for sure that if they did so, it might be the last thing they ever did.

'What the hell is going on?' Wat hissed in Hermitage's ear.

Hermitage couldn't control the tremble in his voice. 'I fear that Cwen sees the true nature of the book. She must have some talent.'

'God, don't tell her that.'

Hermitage tutted. 'A talent that Ardith will use to put the book together.'

'And that's bad, is it?'

Hermitage felt himself starting to quake. 'Wat, you know that I am generally a worrier.'

'I do,' Wat confirmed.

'And that I fret about most things.'

'Very true.'

'My normal demeanour is one of concern, regularly touching upon the heights of fear and trepidation.'

'Quite so.'

'That makes it very difficult for me to get across to you how absolutely terrified I am just at the moment. And it's not about something normally horrible happening, like William sticking a knife in me.'

Wat frowned at Hermitage.

'I fear that if this book gets back together in its proper order, something so horrible will happen that even the most horrible people in the country will comment on how horrible it is.'

'Really?' Wat obviously couldn't see the problem in a few bits of parchment.

'Death,' Hermitage said, feeling more solemn than he ever had before. 'Real death. Not the sort that comes in war or at the end of life. The sort that comes when the soul is lost. Or rather, when it's taken.

'I never believed in magic or any of that nonsense before,' Hermitage went on. 'I still don't. But I don't understand what this book is doing. I am sure that if any more of it is put together, it will do more of whatever it is. And that would be a bad thing for all of us. And I don't just mean the people in here, I mean everyone, everywhere.'

Martin spoke now, and Hermitage was pleased to detect that his Brother sounded as scared as he did. 'Can you see where all the pages should go?'

'No. I think only Cwen can do that. And she has been enthralled by the book. If she truly knew what she was doing, she would stop, but the book has her.'

'Lord Colesvain is here now,' Martin said, offering a crumb of comfort. 'If Ardith is taken, the book can go back to the way it was. No need to put anything together.'

Hermitage nodded. 'He doesn't seem to be doing anything at the moment.' He nodded towards Lord Colesvain, who was just standing there, watching what was going on.

'I am convinced that we should split this book up. Keep its pages apart, preferably in different parts of the country.'

Martin agreed. 'That would be quite possible now that it is

out of its bindings. I don't think I see what you see, but something in me is telling me that we are in mortal danger.'

'This book should never be brought together again.' Hermitage took a pause before his next suggestion, which he knew before he said it, was quite appalling. 'I don't think we should even catalogue it.'

'Not catalogue it?'

Hermitage nodded. 'I cannot bring myself to destroy any book, but if there was one that I had to do, it would be this one. Splitting it up and not cataloguing it will ensure that it is as good as destroyed. Can you imagine being able to find a book without the catalogue?'

'Well, no, obviously. But do we really need to go to such extremes?'

'Just what is it that you think is going to happen?' Wat asked. He nodded towards Cwen who was now walking dreamily amongst the parchment, followed by Ardith. Every now and then she would bend to pick up a particular page and would then move to put it down somewhere else.

No one else in the room could see what the effect of this was, but Cwen seemed quite pleased.

Hermitage had managed to avoid expressing his thought, even as a thought. If drawings of pages could come to life, he dreaded to think what could happen to thoughts.

'The demon,' he whispered.

'The demon?'

'The one in the middle of the book.'

Martin was quite capable of drawing the ridiculous conclusion from this. 'You mean the pages brought together will summon the demon?'

'Not quite.' Hermitage swallowed. 'I believe that the pages are holding the demon in. Like a prison. The legends of

Hermes Trismegistus included the summoning and imprisonment of demons. I know it's nonsense, and I know that I don't really believe it, but I can't help but think that the book is this demon's prison. Putting the pages back in order will open the door.'

'Good Lord.' Martin was taking the prospect very seriously. 'And then what?'

'A demon loose in the world.'

Even Wat had no smart remark for that prospect. Hermitage was disappointed but slightly gratified to see that the weaver now looked as worried as he should do. 'And Cwen?' he asked.

Hermitage shook his head. 'I can only imagine that the one opening the door will be the first to fall.'

Wat swallowed.

They all considered the pages laid before them and breathed deeply.

'Those two pages,' Hermitage pointed nervously at the ones Cwen had first put together.

'Yes?' Martin nodded.

'Can we separate them, do you think?'

'Well, of course.'

'Without Ardith interrupting?'

'I think I can handle Ardith,' Wat said. 'I know you monks don't go in for hitting people, and I wouldn't normally, but in this case, I'm prepared to make an exception. He gave Hermitage a grim look and stepped over to the pages in question. He took the one on the left and lifted it from the floor.

Relief rushed through Hermitage.

'Oy,' the voice of Lord Colesvain boomed around the church. 'What do you think you're doing?'

Wat looked over. 'Oh, just gathering the book, My Lord. Ardith appears to have broken it apart.'

Colesvain stepped over and looked at the pages on the floor. He glared at Wat and ground out his instructions one word at a time. 'Put it back.'

'Put it back?'

'And you,' Lord Colesvain called to the men by the entrance. 'Lock the door.'

The men turned to the door and closed it, sliding the bolts across.

'What's going on?' Hermitage asked.

Lord Colesvain gave him a look that could only be described as evil. 'We've got some work to do, monk. And it looks like your girl is the one to do it.'

It took a few moments for realisation to get firmly bedded in. Hermitage looked at Lord Colesvain and frowned. Then he glanced at Wat and Martin, who he saw were being taken and held by the sheriff's men.

'My goodness. Ardith wasn't trying to take the books from your library.' The truth dropped on him. 'You were trying to give them to her.'

'Well done,' Colesvain congratulated Hermitage on his conclusion.

'Ardith came to me with legends about the book and its powers. She followed its trail from ancient times and was convinced that it was around Lincoln somewhere. But how to find it? It could be anywhere. Then our dear King William wants a gift for his church. So, we can gather books from every church in the county. It had to be here somewhere. And lo and behold, you found it for us.'

'She came to you because you had the authority to find it,' Hermitage said sadly.

'And I have her because she knows what to do with it.' His voice darkened now. 'Or that's what she told me.'

Ardith gave him a glare now.

'But it seems not,' Colesvain said. 'So, she's actually quite useless.'

'Except for the ritual,' Ardith said.

Hermitage didn't like the sound of that at all.

'But it seems that your girl does know what to do with it.' Lord Colesvain said.

'Cwen,' Wat called. 'Her name is Cwen.'

Colesvain waved this detail away as unimportant.

'You can't do it,' Hermitage said. He tried to make this sound as sincere a warning as he had ever given, but he instantly suspected that it would be ignored.

'Oh, yes we can,' Colesvain assured him.

'Lord Colesvain.' Hermitage spoke slowly and tried to sound as authoritative as he could, which was not very much. 'I have only the vaguest idea of what would happen if the book was put together, but I know that it would be very bad. Probably one of the very worst things that could possibly happen. Ever. The sort of thing from which none of us will escape alive.

'This book was put together by Hermes Trismegistus, the thrice great. He seems to have been a keeper of secrets vouched safe to no one in the thousands of years since. I believe he created the book to protect us. If we put it together, that protection will vanish, and a great evil will be released. An evil we have no knowledge of. There may be something in the book to tell us what we might do, but we can't read it.

'To put this book together now would be the most grievous error imaginable. I urge you, I plead with you. Don't do it.'

The Hermes Parchment

Lord Colesvain took a moment to consider Hermitage's argument and looked as if he was giving it due thought.

'Rubbish,' he said. 'Ardith, get over here.'

'What do you hope to accomplish?' Hermitage argued on. 'If this power is released, it will simply destroy us all.'

'Nonsense,' Ardith said, as she joined them, leaving Cwen to happily carry on as if she was picking daisies.

'I assure you that it is not nonsense.'

'Yes, it is. If we open the book, the power will be ours to control. Hermes did it, and he made the book to contain it until it was needed again.'

'He was a wise man thousands of years ago,' Hermitage said. 'He knew things we don't even understand anymore. What on earth makes you think you can follow in his footsteps?'

'Well, I can't, can I?' Ardith was petulant. 'But the girl can. She can see the pages.'

'We'll all be damned,' Hermitage said as if they were his last words.

Ardith tutted. 'The whole point of the book is to control the demon. Once it's released it will do our bidding.'

'This is the King's Investigator you're dealing with,' Wat called from the back of the room. 'I don't think William will be pleased to hear about this. You know how pious he is.'

'Ha ha,' Colesvain laughed and clapped his hands at this. 'That is the most entertaining part of the whole thing. Who would have thought that it would be William's man who would bring us the solution to our problem?'

'To summon a demon?' Wat sounded incredulous.

'Oh, but we have a task for our demon. We're not just inviting it in for a chat.'

'Really?'

'Oh yes,' Colesvain's eyes gleamed with the madness that seemed to be quite common around here. 'We'll have King William's investigator here while we summon a demon, and then instruct that demon to kill King William. Isn't it wonderful?'

Caput XXV Kill Them, Kill Them All!

No one had anything to say to that. Magic books, demons and the murder of the king. How much more peculiar was this day going to get?

'Kill King William?' Hermitage repeated in a daze.

'And all the Normans, if he can manage it,' Colesvain added. 'Mind you, this is a demon, so that shouldn't be a problem.'

Hermitage's overwhelming urge was to tell them that they were all mad. He knew that might make him feel better, but he doubted it would have the desired impact on the mad people.

'Why?' was all he could think of.

'Why?' The word seemed to annoy Lord Colesvain. 'Why? You stupid monk. Why kill the king who's come over here and taken our land? Why kill the king who demands taxes from us at every turn? Why kill the king who constantly threatens to take your lands away and give them to one of his Norman friends?'

Hermitage thought that clarified the question quite nicely.

'The same way you want tax from Godrinius?' Wat asked.

'Shut up. That's completely different. William's said that if I don't get his taxes on time the land will be forfeit. He's already given half the county to his brother, Odo.'

'Ooh, nasty,' Wat said.

'So, he has to go.'

'And there are too many Normans and too few Saxons left alive to do it the normal way,' Wat suggested.

'Exactly.'

'A demon's just what you need.'

'And your friend is going to bring it for us.'

Hermitage folded his arms.

'Or her friends will be dead before the king,' Colesvain added. He nodded to his men who gave their swords a good brandish. 'You can wait for the demon, or we can kill you now. Up to you.'

'This is madness,' Hermitage said. He thought that sounded a bit less personal than calling Lord Colesvain mad.

'Let's just get on with it,' Colesvain ordered.

With true dread in his heart, Hermitage looked over at Cwen. He could see that she was completely unaware of what was going on and was even smiling to herself now as more and more of the book was put together.

He looked at the remaining pages, which were now few in number, and at that moment would have been prepared to sacrifice himself to stop this happening. Perhaps he could rush forward and grab the pages. And then what? He couldn't burn them; he had no flame. He wasn't sure that tearing them up would do anything, even if he could manage it, parchment being quite strong stuff.

Maybe he could grab one and eat part of it? That would stop anyone using it. He suspected that he wouldn't be given the time to start a meal of the parchment. He was positive that Colesvain would not hesitate to order his execution before he could do anything; that was the problem with mad people.

Looking over at the pages, he saw that one seemed to have Cwen's undivided attention.

Colesvain appeared to spot this, and that Hermitage had seen it as well. He stepped up next to Hermitage and drew his own sword. 'Leave her alone,' he instructed.

With a heavy sigh, Hermitage watched as Cwen crossed the floor and picked up the sheet. She brought it back, and carefully placed it on its side, across the top of two others that were lying towards the middle of the floor.

At once, Cwen stepped quickly back and seemed to be gazing with rapt attention at the air about four feet above the floor.

With growing fear, when he didn't know his fear had any more growing to do, Hermitage looked on as Cwen returned to gather other pages and bring them together.

He began to think that if this really did go too far, he might have to do something truly drastic. There was no way he could allow a demon into the world. What would his old abbot say?

He thought that drastic things included grabbing swords from kings' tenants-in-chief and then stabbing them. He had to warn himself that not only would this be the most atrocious sin, but that he simply wasn't capable of doing anything like that. If he tried to grab Colesvain's sword, he'd probably cut himself.

He was reasonably comfortable with the fact that killing Colesvain was justified. Anyone summoning a demon was deserving of such a fate. And he was sure that William would agree. He just knew that in his attempt, the very strong likelihood was that he would be dead, and Colesvain wouldn't.

As Cwen gathered the last of the pages, Hermitage started to notice some disturbance in the air. He couldn't see anything specific; it was as if a heat haze was rising, causing the objects in the room to shimmer. As he was in a freezing cold church, he knew that this explanation was not sufficient.

The shimmering seemed to spread around the church, and he gazed at it with both awe and fear. He could see that the others in the room had noticed this as well and were looking just as worried. Apart from Colesvain and Ardith; they looked very pleased with themselves.

Hermitage was torn. His curiosity wanted to know what was causing this effect, while his common sense was telling him to run like hell.

Eventually, Cwen appeared to put the last page in place. As she did so, she stepped back and gave her blank stare to whatever it was she had created.

Hermitage realised that he had stopped breathing as he looked on, and as moments passed, he began to have doubts. They were comforting doubts. Doubts that said this organisation of the pages was all very well, but it wasn't enough.

'This isn't going to work,' he said, with a confidence that surprised him. 'Putting all the pages together is not sufficient.' He faced the others in the room, happy to turn his back on the now assembled book.

'Hermes was cleverer than this. He must have known that there was a chance the pages would get together in the right order. There are a lot of them, but an accident could see it happen. He protected against that. Even if all the pages are in exactly the right places, the demon will not be released.'

'Well, of course not,' Ardith sniffed. 'We all know that. It needs the final ritual step.'

Hermitage was very disappointed to hear that she seemed to know what she was doing now. He pondered what that last step might be.

'Elmund,' he said, with great sadness.

'Quite,' Ardith still wasn't happy. 'Complete waste of time that was.'

'You killed Elmund in front of the book, but it wasn't in the right order, so nothing happened.'

'I know that now.'

'With the pages in the right order, you need to make another sacrifice.'

'What a clever monk you are.'

Hermitage thought of Cwen and decided at that moment that he would bring the whole scheme crashing down if it came to that. If Colesvain was planning to kill Cwen to summon the demon, Hermitage might as well throw himself into a hopeless fight.

'What do you think we've got Picot for?' Ardith said, nodding to the young man who was still tied in the corner.

'Picot?' Hermitage gasped. 'Lord Colesvain? Picot is your own son.'

'Apparently, that's better,' Colesvain said, showing very little concern.

Ardith now came over to Hermitage and looked at the new layout of the parchment. 'I think we're nearly ready,' she said to Colesvain who nodded.

He actually went over to the tied-up Picot himself and lifted his boy to a standing position.

Not only was the man mad, he was obviously a monster. Hermitage had to think of something. Perhaps he would just kick the pages on the floor back into a mess. If no one else had this wretched "sight" of Cwen's, they wouldn't be able to put them back together. But Wat and Martin were at risk. How would he feel if something truly awful happened?

But wasn't something truly awful about to happen anyway? Lesser of two evils, he told himself. Knowing that summoning a demon into the world must be one of the uppermost evils ever, allowing your friends to be murdered was more immediate, somehow.

Colesvain urged his son forward.

And at that moment the light outside vanished.

There hadn't been much of it anyway, only slim beams creeping in through the openings high in the walls, but now even those were gone.

Hermitage felt his fear run through him and wished that he could follow.

'What's going on?' Colesvain demanded.

'All as expected,' Ardith assured him, although it didn't sound as if she was that sure.

Through the darkened windows, a wind began to blow, and it made an unfortunate howling noise as it pushed past the stonework.

Hermitage was positively quaking now but was glad to notice that everyone else was as well.

The soldier who had had his sword resting on Wat's shoulder was now looking up to the roof with a very pale face. That pale face distorted into one of intense pain as Wat slipped from his grasp, turned and dealt a blow with his knee that most soldiers would consider unfair even in the heat of battle.

The soldier collapsed on the floor in agony, but his companions were too concerned about the goings-on in the church to worry about their fallen comrade.

With everyone's attention distracted, Wat walked away from his prostrate guard and he and Martin went over to join Hermitage.

'What's happening?' Wat asked, over the howl of the wind. 'Is this part of the demon business?'

Hermitage looked at the pages and at Ardith. 'I don't think it is,' he said. 'Ardith looks surprised. This must be something different.'

'Bit of a coincidence then,' Wat observed.

The Hermes Parchment

The wind apparently irritated at being confined to the upper reaches of the building, now began to swirl its way lower and lower into the church. After a few moments, the first parchment began to be disturbed from its position on the floor.

'Stop them,' Ardith called, as one page shifted on the floor and blew out of place.

As the wind dropped lower, it seemed to become stronger, which was odd. Mind you, as Hermitage looked around the inside of this church, he thought that odd was not really a sufficient word for anything anymore.

'The pages,' Ardith now cried. 'Get them.'

None of them moved an inch as one by one, the pages of the Hermes parchment were blown away from their chosen positions.

Colesvain and Ardith ran into the middle of the space and stooped and jumped, trying to grab pages of the book as they flew by. Fortunately, no one else in the room showed any interest in helping out.

Cwen was still dazed but was starting to look a bit puzzled by what was happening.

It was not long before the whole floor was a mess of pages. They were now all in the wrong place, the wrong way up and were such a mess it was hard to tell which was which, let alone get them in order again.

Cwen now stood in the middle of the chaos, and Hermitage felt a weight lift from his soul as he saw that the old Cwen was starting to return. She looked bemused and out of sorts, but her natural anger and irritation were starting to surface.

He looked around the church and saw that the chaos was repeated everywhere.

The sheriff and his men had decided that this really wasn't the sort of thing they should have to deal with, and were simply backing off into the farthest corner they could find. One of them was limping quite heavily and clutching his groin.

Ardith and Colesvain were still trying desperately to recover the pages of the book, but all they succeeded in doing was putting them in even worse order than they'd been in their binding.

Noticing Picot, Hermitage nodded to Wat and he went over to the boy. He untied his hands and removed the gag from his mouth.

The torrent of expletives about his father that immediately tumbled forth, made Hermitage wonder if the gag shouldn't be put back in again. Ignoring Wat, Picot went over to the sheriff's men and was clearly asking to borrow a sword.

Just as quickly as the wind had started, it stopped. The light reappeared through the church window and the place became a simple mess, rather than a hideously ominous scene.

It seemed incredibly mundane when the door of the church creaked open and a figure stood looking in.

'I thought that door was locked?' Wat said.

Hermitage thought it was as well.

Colesvain and Ardith stopped their parchment collection and stood to consider the new arrival.

'Ah,' The Crowman said as she considered the scene before her. 'I think you've got my book.'

Caput XXVI Cometh the Hour

Lord Colesvain seemed completely bewildered by the new arrival. He looked to Ardith, who didn't appear to be any better informed.

'Your book? What do you mean, your book?'

'Well,' The Crowman acknowledged. 'It's probably a bit presumptuous to call it my book as such. Our book might be more accurate. The book protected by the convocation of the Black Bird.'

Colesvain just shook his head as he glanced at the handful of crumpled parchment he was holding. 'A madwoman,' he concluded. 'Sheriff, throw her out.' He turned and went back to gathering the pages.

Hermitage considered the sheriff and his men, none of whom looked particularly keen on approaching The Crowman. In fact, she smiled at them and nodded several acknowledgements to faces she recognised.

'Good to see you again, sheriff,' she said. 'And how is the, erm, trouble?' She mouthed the last word "trouble" rather than say it out loud and nodded at the same time towards the lower half of the sheriff's anatomy.

'Fine, fine,' the sheriff rather snapped back, quite obviously anxious that this was not the moment to start discussing his "trouble".

'And Master Paton,' The Crowman nodded to another of the sheriff's men. 'That awkward business all cleared up now?'

Master Paton didn't even want to reply, and shrank to the back of the group, while his fellows in arms all looked at him.

It became clear very quickly that the sheriff's men were more in thrall to The Crowman than they were to Lord

Colesvain.

'How did you know the book was here?' Hermitage asked. He felt that someone had to deal with The Crowman's arrival, and Lord Colesvain obviously wasn't going to bother.

'Oh, there are methods,' The Crowman said. 'Once I knew that it had been found and had seen the cover and the remains of the pages, it was quite a simple process.' She considered Colesvain and Ardith, still gathering pages and looking at them briefly while they tried to work out which was which. 'I had to return to my house to gather a few things to create a tracing spell, but it was fairly straightforward.' She gave a short shake of her head. 'You didn't stay in Colesvain's house as you were told?'

Hermitage shrugged an apology.

'Pity poor Elmund though. He would have prevented all this.'

'Elmund?' Martin asked. 'Did you know him, then?'

The Crowman sighed and shook her head sadly. 'He was a brother of the convocation.'

'Elmund?' Martin asked. 'We are talking about the same Elmund. The man who spent his entire life in a library?'

'The man who spent his entire life looking for this book.' The Crowman nodded towards the random collection of parchment. 'Even I only found that out when I saw his body. He carried our mark.'

'Mark?'

'A small mark of the Black Bird. It is only there for those who know where to look.'

'And he found the book,' Hermitage noted.

'But then he ran away,' Martin said.

'I imagine he was coming to me,' The Crowman replied. 'Having found the book, he would need to make it safe.'

'And we denied him,' Hermitage felt terrible about that. 'He asked us to help take it away, and we refused.'

'He instructed us to help him without explaining anything,' Martin pointed out. 'If he'd said what was going on, he might have got a bit more cooperation.'

'Would we have believed him?'

Martin reflected on that. 'Probably not,' he admitted.

'And Ardith killed him.' Hermitage stated the horrible fact.

'I don't know for sure,' The Crowman said. 'But I suspect that Ardith was watching out for the book as well.'

'She said that Picot told her it was here.'

'There we have it, then. Ardith knew of the book and had to stop Elmund getting help. She also saw the opportunity to use him for her ritual.'

'So who is she?' Hermitage asked. 'She's obviously not from the cathedral, because there isn't one.'

'Bloody witch,' Picot called from the back of the church. Despite his rage, he had obviously decided that keeping away from danger was probably for the best.

They all turned their heads towards him.

'I was in the library just, erm, checking some books when she came in with Elmund. I hid, just to see what was going on, and then she, well, you know.' Picot made a nice slicing gesture across his throat. 'I got covered in the stuff. What was I supposed to do?'

'Hold her?' Wat suggested.

'She was obviously doing magic.' Picot clearly thought that this was ample reason for not tackling people.

'So you ran.'

'Of course, I did. I didn't want to get cursed. I ran for the witch of Canna, they say she can deal with this sort of thing.'

'You ran from one witch to another?' Wat said. 'Pretty stupid plan, eh?'

'Except, what do I find when I get here, with her hard on my heels?'

'Do tell.'

'She bloody is the witch of Canna.' Picot obviously considered this to be completely unreasonable. 'Dressed up neat she looks like Ardith. She doesn't normally dress like this, you know.'

'Bad luck,' Wat snorted.

'There are those who seek the book for their own purposes,' The Crowman put in.

'Another convocation?' Wat asked.

'Their type would never join together. All they seek is their own personal advancement. And that is why they fail. Down the years, many have sought the book, but none found it, until now.'

'She told Lord Colesvain that it could get rid of King William,' Hermitage said.

'Ha,' The Crowman replied. 'More like get rid of Lord Colesvain if she had got full control.'

Hermitage felt quite bad about finding the wretched thing at all now. How was he to know a book could cause so much trouble? Now that the pages had been disturbed once more, he told himself that the whole thing had been nonsense. Books were not magic; they were very nice, but not magic. There was no such thing.

Some deluded people had convinced themselves that the book had power, and now look what had happened.

'And this Ardith had enough knowledge to know that she could bring about its magic by sacrificing Elmund to its pages.' The Crowman was full of regret for the behaviour of

The Hermes Parchment

idiots.

'Which were in the wrong order,' Hermitage said.

'Exactly.' The Crowman looked at Hermitage as if suspecting him of knowing too much.

Hermitage beckoned to the mess of parchment. 'There was a great wind that blew everything around,' he explained.

'Yes, I know.' The way The Crowman said this made Hermitage not want to ask anymore.

'Someone was putting the pages in the correct order.' She sounded as if she'd found children eating the sweetmeats and wanted them to know that they had all been very naughty.

'I'm afraid that was Cwen,' Hermitage said, his need to be totally open and honest in all things outweighing everything else. Including Wat's heavy sigh and the way he wiped his hand over his face. 'But she didn't seem to know what she was doing.'

'Really?' The Crowman seemed interested.

'What's going on?' Cwen's voice pierced the room. She was still standing in the middle of the space but was looking very angry about it.

'Ah, Cwen, you're recovered,' Hermitage smiled.

'Recovered from what?' she demanded. 'She cast her gaze around the room. 'Someone had better tell me something in a moment, or there is going to be trouble.'

Wat stepped quickly over and gave her a huge and happy hug. Well, it was happy for him, she just looked confused. 'What have you done?' she asked.

'Me?' I haven't done anything. You, on the other hand, have been behaving very strangely.'

Cwen looked as if she was recalling something of this now. 'I could see all sorts of shapes,' she said rather wistfully.

'Yes, you would,' The Crowman explained.

'And they seemed to fit together.'

'Well, they don't want to fit together, but something wants you to fit them together.'

'The demon?' Hermitage whimpered.

'Again, not quite the right word, but it will do.'

'I had the feeling that something very bad would happen if I completed the work,' Cwen said. 'But I couldn't stop myself. It just seemed the right thing to do, as well as being the wrong one.'

'In that, you are correct. But it would have needed another dramatic step.'

'Lord Colesvain was being urged to sacrifice his son.' Hermitage couldn't quite believe the words coming out of his own mouth.

The Crowman now looked very serious. She gave Colesvain a very hard and purposeful stare.

'But he wouldn't have got away with it.' Picot spoke up. He had now moved to join the sheriff's men and was hefting a sword in his hand as if testing it. 'In fact, the day may end up the other way round completely.'

'There must be no death here,' The Crowman instructed in a voice that seemed to come as much from inside Hermitage's head as from outside. 'None. Am I clear?'

Hermitage felt as if this order had such authority behind it that even King William might think twice before stabbing an enemy.

He was pleased to see that Picot lowered the sword, although he didn't seem to understand why he was doing so.

'Now then.' The Crowman appeared to be thinking about exactly what she was going to do next. 'Ah,' she said suddenly. 'I have it. Quite appropriate in the circumstances.'

'You have it? You have what?' Hermitage was getting to

The Hermes Parchment

the point where he desperately needed some explanations. People doing odd things without explanations always made him feel quite sick.

'The way to deal with this situation.' She nodded to Colesvain and Ardith.

'I think the king's tenant-in-chief might be a rather awkward one to deal with?' Wat suggested. 'Perhaps leaving quietly would be best.'

'Oh, no.' The Crowman sounded quite apologetic. 'Steps must be taken. We cannot leave things as they are.'

'We?' Wat didn't sound very keen on that idea.

'Mistress Cwen and I,' The Crowman specified.

'Ah, that's fine then. Do go ahead,' Wat said, which got him another punch from Cwen.

'What can you do?' Hermitage asked, feeling as nervous about any involvement in this as Wat.

'We can help,' The Crowman nodded towards Colesvain and Ardith who had now got all the pages into a heap.

'Help?' Hermitage thought that was a very bad idea indeed. He'd helped with this book the last time and that hadn't gone at all well.

'Just follow me,' she beckoned to Cwen. 'All will be well.'

Hermitage couldn't actually remember the last time all had been well. His invitation to the library in the first place had been a high point, but then it had gone downhill so fast he was in danger of falling off completely.

'My Lord Colesvain,' The Crowman said as she led Cwen back to the middle of the church.

'What do you want?' Colesvain said without looking up.

Ardith had put the pages they had recovered down on the floor and was making a start at trying to sort them out. It was clear that she didn't have the first idea what she was doing.

'Who are you, anyway?' Colesvain demanded. 'You sound like a Norman.' He did look at her face now. 'Just a moment. You're that madwoman from the woods.'

'I am not Norman,' The Crowman snapped. 'Why does everyone assume that I am a Norman?'

'Because you sound like one,' Colesvain bit back.

'I do not sound like a Norman. I sound French because that's what I am. I am from the kingdom of the Francs and not from Normandy at all.'

'Norman, French,' Colesvain shrugged. 'It's all the same to me.'

The Crowman took a deep breath and was obviously swallowing her chosen reply. 'Be that as it may, I think that I can help with the parchment.'

'Why you?'

'I am The Crowman.'

Colesvain gave her a doubtful look. 'Yes, I know that.'

Ardith looked up from her work and snorted.

'The wise one of the woods eh?' Colesvain scoffed.

'Wise and woods is right,' The Crowman confirmed.

'It's the girl,' Ardith seemed to notice that Cwen was there now. 'She can sort out the pages again,' she urged.

'Oh, yes,' Colesvain smiled horribly. 'You know about this book as well, do you?' he asked The Crowman.

'I do. And I believe mistress Cwen and I can quickly get it in the right order.'

Hermitage had a very strong urge to warn her not to do anything of the sort. She had seemed trustworthy but now he had doubts. Could she be after the power of this book herself? Was he being tricked?

Colesvain looked to Ardith, who shrugged that they couldn't do a worse job than she was managing herself.

The Hermes Parchment

'Get on with it then,' Colesvain instructed.

Ardith stepped back from the collection of pages, and The Crowman indicated that Cwen should join her as she knelt on the floor in front of them.

'What are we doing?' Cwen whispered.

The Crowman leaned close to her ear. 'I have some of the sight, but it could be that yours is better. We need to find three pages in particular.'

'Three pages?'

'Yes. If the information has passed down the generations correctly, there should be two pages that present themselves as a pyramid.'

'A what?'

'A pyramid.' The Crowman said with some irritation.

'Yes, I heard you,' Cwen replied, being quite capable of doing her own irritation. 'What's a pyramid?'

'Oh, dear. Erm, it's another old French word.' The Crowman paused for thought.

'A pyramid is like four triangles joined together at their points and sticking up into the air.'

'Oh, yes.' Cwen seemed to recall the page in question.

'Then there's a third that lies across the top of those two.'

'I know the very ones. But, if my memory is working, they were the start of the whole business, do we really want to join them again?'

'This time will be different,' The Crowman assured her. 'You saw them,' she urged. 'See if you can find them again.'

Cwen paused to have a quick scan around, before she started leafing through the parchment, turning each page over and around as required. It wasn't long before she found the first sheet. she laid it out to one side.

'Good,' The Crowman breathed. She seemed very

interested in the page, which gave Hermitage fresh concern as he looked on.

Soon, Cwen had found the second parchment and held it in her hands. 'Last time I did this,' she hissed to The Crowman, 'things started to go badly, quite quickly.' She seemed to sway for a moment and ran a hand across her face as if clearing away a distraction.

'Trust me,' she said, and for reasons best known to herself, Cwen did.

She laid the second page down and seemed to gaze into the air once more. 'That's a pyramid, is it?'

Hermitage had no idea what Cwen was seeing. He would have to ask later.

'That's it,' Ardith crowed. 'I recognise those pages. Carry on,' she instructed. She and Colesvain drew close and peered eagerly at the parchment.

A voice drifted from the back of the room distracting Hermitage from his task.

It was Picot. 'If he tries to kill me, I'll chop his head off. Father or not.' he assured the gathering.

'Cwen,' The Crowman whispered. 'When we find the page that should lay across the top of these two, lay it across the bottom instead.'

'It is one of Hermes's greatest traps. I marvel at it myself. Always assuming it works,' The Crowman added, unhelpfully.

In fact, it was The Crowman who found the page. She held it towards Cwen, who nodded that it was the right one. 'When I lay it down, look away,' she said.

'Lord Colesvain, Mistress Ardith,' The Crowman called. 'This next laying is the key to the whole. Come, see.'

As they drew up to look closely, The Crowman laid the

The Hermes Parchment

page down and stood back at the same time. She pulled on Cwen's arm to make sure she followed.

This time it was Ardith and Lord Colesvain who seemed to be in some sort of daze.

'Don't look,' The Crowman instructed.

Hermitage did as he was told but could see that Colesvain and Ardith were staring intently at the pages in front of them. He could tell from their faces that they now saw something beyond the pages.

There was not a sound in the church. Lord Colesvain and Ardith were silent, doubtless awed by whatever they could see.

And then there was the slightest smell of smoke.

Hermitage chanced a glance back under his own arm and saw that the parchment on the floor appeared to be smouldering slightly. The biggest surprise was that no one was doing anything about it. Colesvain and Ardith simply stood in a daze and watched.

When the smouldering burst into a small flame, Ardith cried out.

In these circumstances, in this situation, Hermitage didn't like to use the expression, but it seemed to be the only one that fitted perfectly; the spell had been broken.

Colesvain and Ardith jumped forward and stamped their feet on the now burning parchment. Unfortunately, all they managed to do was spread the fire further. There was something about these flames that Hermitage found disturbing. It looked as if they knew where they were going.

With each stamp of the foot, a flame leapt to a new sheet of parchment and started to consume that. Any connections between the pages were now gone, and Hermitage knew there was very little chance of them coming back.

The others in the room looked on, not one of them leaping to help with the fire.

Eventually, after a frenzy of stamping and shouting and urgent calls for help, Lord Colesvain and Ardith stood in a thin pile of blackened ash.

Caput XXVII
Getting Away With It's Not What it Used to Be.

'It's a masterstroke,' The Crowman said to Hermitage as they all walked up the hill once more. 'Lay the pages of the book out in the wrong order and it destroys itself.'

Wat, Cwen and Martin looked as if they dearly wanted to ask what on earth had just happened, while at the same time not really wanting to hear.

Lord Colesvain and Ardith were in a heated, but quiet conversation. There was lots of gesticulation, with occasional glances towards Hermitage. He didn't know why they'd be looking at him, but it wasn't comfortable.

The sheriff's men brought up the rear with Picot in their midst. It looked as if they were restraining him from greeting his father in the back with a knife but weren't having to restrain too hard.

Hermitage couldn't help but think that the destruction of the Hermes parchment was awful. He knew the book was a very bad thing, in more ways than he could immediately comprehend, but burning a book? That was the worst thing imaginable.

'Your convocation spent its entire history looking for the book,' he said, feeling some sympathy for The Crowman.

'We did,' The Crowman didn't seem too concerned, which was odd, considering her whole purpose in life had just gone up in flames. 'But it was either to hide it for good or destroy it. Word was passed down that it was a danger. If we could not protect it until the time came when we would know what to do with it, it had to go.'

'I'm sorry I ever found it.'

'Don't be. If you hadn't, it might have been used. Your

finding of it has saved us all.'

'Except Elmund.'

'He would be pleased.'

'And at least we discovered that Ardith killed him.' Hermitage thought that he had some pretty peculiar investigations in his time but finding the killer by magic was simply ridiculous.

...

Back in the library, Hermitage was very disappointed to see that Elmund had not been cleared away by the servants. He still sat slumped in the fireplace, and his blood still stained the floor.

The sheriff joined them all at the scene, still keeping Picot under control, and he scowled hard at the body, which he could see was just the sort of thing he was expected to deal with.

Everyone seemed quite vague and confused to Hermitage's eye. They all carried frowns as if bothered by some nagging voice in their heads.

The focus of this was the cover of the Hermes parchment, which still sat on the desk. It now smelled quite strongly of burnt parchment, as if the pages down in the church were still somehow connected.

'So,' Lord Colesvain said, clapping his hands together as if he had made up his mind how he was going to handle this. 'The book's gone then. That's that. Thank goodness, I say.'

Everyone else simply gaped at him.

Hermitage knew perfectly well that that was not that at all. He couldn't believe that Colesvain was trying to ignore treason, attempted regicide and witchcraft. It was quite a lot for one day. He really wasn't comfortable accusing important people of anything, let alone crimes that would see them cut into bits. At least there was a very practical matter right before their eyes.

'Your librarian sits dead in your fireplace,' he pointed out.

'Yes, yes,' Colesvain tried to dismiss this as if it was the sort of thing that happened all the time.

'Lucky you've got the King's Investigator close by,' Cwen reminded the room.

'Just so,' Wat agreed, for once. 'King William's own personal Investigator.'

Colesvain looked both nervous and angry at that; Hermitage preferred nervous.

'And we must surely deal with Mistress Ardith?' Hermitage said without looking at her.

All the others did look at her.

'I'll handle Mistress Ardith,' Lord Colesvain said in a very threatening tone. 'This is all very serious.'

'Of course, it is,' Wat put in nonchalantly. 'There's also the question of your treason and plot to kill the king with a demon. That sounds pretty serious as well.'

Colesvain turned a very dark shade of red and his fists clenched tightly.

Everyone else in the room behaved as if they were grateful that someone had mentioned this; and that it wasn't them.

'Better be careful what you say, weaver,' Colesvain ground his words out.

'It's not what I said, is it? It's what you said. In the church. Where we all heard you. Including the King's Investigator, who will need to report back to the king.'

'And you were going to sacrifice me,' Picot complained from the side of the sheriff where he wasn't actually being restrained at all anymore.

'We all heard you,' Cwen said. 'And saw you.'

Colesvain's eyes slipped quickly from side to side. Eventually, he smiled. He shook his head rather sadly as if they'd all misunderstood the whole situation.

'That?' he said. 'No, no. That was all a ruse.'

'A ruse?' Wat folded his arms as if he was going to be fascinated to see what this explanation looked like.

'Of course. I am as loyal to the king as the very best man in the land.'

'I think the king's got more trouble than he thinks,' Cwen said.

'You have just witnessed the execution of my marvellous plan to expose a conspiracy against the king's person.'

'With you in the middle of it,' Wat said.

'Not at all. Can you not see that I have successfully revealed Ardith as a witch and the killer of Elmund.' He turned to Ardith with a very serious look. 'You wicked woman,' he said.

Ardith pointed a very pointy finger at him. 'If you think you're going to put this on me, there'll soon be another body in the fireplace.'

'You see,' Colesvain looked shocked and held his arms out towards Ardith. He suddenly seemed to think of something else. 'She put a spell on me.'

'A spell?' Hermitage asked. He looked to The Crowman for advice, who shook her head and smiled as if this was all quite funny.

'Exactly.' Colesvain warmed to his new explanation. 'After I'd told the king that I would give all the books to the library, Ardith obviously cast a spell on me. She hoped to find this magic book. And when she did, the spell was strengthened.

The Hermes Parchment

Now the book is burned, the spell is broken, and I am free once more. Isn't it marvellous?'

'A moment ago you said it was all a ruse,' Wat pointed out.

'A ruse within a spell,' Lord Colesvain said with a deep significance that was incredibly shallow.

'Do you seriously think anyone is going to believe this?' Ardith sneered.

'Foul creature,' Colesvain pointed dramatically. 'Sheriff, take her away.'

The sheriff looked very confused.

'And when you've done that, come straight back here. We need to discuss that manor at Wragby that needs a new lord.'

The sheriff frowned a bit.

'Or, of course, we could talk about the plan for moving the office of the sheriff down the hill. You know, bring some order to the rabble.'

Now the sheriff got it and moved over to take Ardith by the arm.

'You think you're going to get away with this?' Ardith snarled.

'There's nothing to get away with. It's just as I say, you had me under a spell.' Colesvain smiled.

'There's more than one book of magic in the world, you know. And more than one curse that brings horror down upon your head.'

The Crowman took a step forward. 'I shall deal with Mistress Ardith.' This was such a simple and commanding statement of fact, that no one said a word. Apart from Ardith.

'Now, just a minute. This woman has no authority.'

'The authority of the convocation of the Black Bird. One of whose members you have murdered.'

'She's a madwoman from the woods,' Ardith complained. 'You can't hand me over to her. What sort of king's tenant are you if you let the loons from the leaves hand out justice?'

Colesvain seemed only too happy that someone was willingly taking Ardith away. 'As you will, mistress.., whatever your name is.'

'What?' Ardith squeaked.

'Think of it as the victim's family choosing the punishment. Just as tradition demands.'

'She's not even Saxon,' Ardith wasn't giving up. 'She's a bloody Norman.'

'I'm French,' The Crowman insisted loudly, for what seemed like the hundredth time.

'There you are then.' Colesvain seemed to think this was a very good reason to let The Crowman have her way.

'She will come quietly,' The Crowman said. She took another step forward and laid a hand on Ardith's arm. The woman immediately fell quiet and a sort of glazed look came over her eyes.

'What are you going to do to her?' Cwen asked cautiously.

'Do to her?' Nothing,' The Crowman assured them. She gave a short bow to the room and turned to leave.

Colesvain gestured that everyone should stand aside to let her go.

The last person she passed on her way out was Hermitage, and he would swear that he heard her mutter to herself;

'Do to her? Nothing. Do with her? Now that's another question altogether.'

'It's probably for the best.' Colesvain nodded to himself thoughtfully as The Crowman left with her new charge.

'Still got the rest of your problems to deal with,' Wat said.

Colesvain simply gave him a dismissive glance, as if he

really had no business speaking at all.

Wat sucked air in through his teeth, tutted and shook his head slowly from side to side. 'It's all a nasty business. The king's not going to be happy.'

Colesvain's face dropped several levels of insouciance. 'The king need not be concerned,' he said fiercely.

'His tenant-in-chief falling to a magic spell? As we all know, he's a very devout and pious king. He got you donating books to a cathedral that isn't even built yet. Perhaps he'd better think about handing the tenancy on to someone a bit less prone to witchcraft.'

'Like a loyal son,' Picot spoke up.

'Like a loyal son.' Wat pointed at Picot, thanking him for coming up with a very good idea.

Lord Colesvain's teeth were clamped firmly shut and the words had some trouble getting out. 'The king need not be concerned,' he repeated slowly and deliberately.

'Well,' Wat was suddenly bright and cheery. 'That's good to hear. And I'm sure his own investigator will do his bit to reassure the king.'

Hermitage didn't know what that bit was going to be, but reassuring King William about anything did not sound like a good idea.

'Perhaps Lord Picot could write to the investigator what shall we say, every week? Just to let him know that all is well and there's no need for the king's concern to come anywhere near here?'

Hermitage looked from Wat to Cwen to Colesvain and could see that there was something going on. He knew it would be explained to him later.

'I could do that,' Picot agreed, with a rather rude look at his father.

'Ooh,' Cwen spoke up. 'I've got an even better idea.'

'A better idea?' Lord Colesvain sounded as if he wasn't too keen on the first one.

'Absolutely. Brother Hermitage, the King's Investigator, that is, came here to sort out the library, yes?'

Colesvain's reply was inaudible, but Cwen assumed it was yes.

'And the library isn't sorted out yet, is it?' This question was for Martin.

'Erm, no,' Martin replied.

'Hardly surprising,' Cwen said. 'What with us all being distracted by the dead body.' She nodded towards Elmund who was taking very little part in the discussion.

'So, and here's the good bit, Hermitage stays and carries on with the library. That way he's right here to make sure that there's nothing that the king needs to be concerned about.' She held her arms out and smiled at everyone, encouraging their agreement that she had, indeed, had a very good idea.

Hermitage was torn. He was absolutely sure that he did not want to stay in a room with a dead body in it any longer than was absolutely necessary; even if that room was a library. But he didn't want to leave a library either. And this one had so many other attractions. A corpse was enough to take the shine off any room, but the books still called to him; always assuming he didn't find any more magic ones, of course.

He could only assume that Elmund would be removed fairly soon; no one left bodies in the house, even lords who were under magic spells. Once Elmund was out of the way he would be able to think about the books again.

'Good plan,' Wat agreed. 'He could be on the lookout for any more magic as well. You know, in case someone else pops through the window and puts a spell on Lord Colesvain to

The Hermes Parchment

make him try to kill the king again.'

'Oh, yes,' Cwen agreed. 'It's obviously quite common. We all need to do our best to protect Lord Colesvain from witchcraft. He does seem a bit vulnerable.'

Hermitage didn't like the sound of that, and Martin looked a bit concerned as well.

Wat and Cwen were almost giggling though, so he really didn't know what was going on.

Lord Colesvain looked as if he was now made of anger, all the way from his core to just under his skin, and was struggling to keep it in.

'The king will be most grateful that the gift to the library is being sorted out as well,' Wat added. 'It might even be ready by the time there's a cathedral to put it in.'

'And we'll be back in a few weeks,' Cwen said. 'To deliver that tapestry to Lord Colesvain's good friend, Godrinius.'

A small squeak escaped from Lord Colesvain, but he said nothing.

'You don't look too sure, Brother Martin?' Hermitage asked meekly, seeing that Martin appeared fretful.

'Oh, I need the help, there's no doubt. And you are the best for the job, I am sure of that. But,' Martin paused, as if reluctant to say the words that were ready. 'You did warn me.'

'Warn you?'

'That there would be murder and death and bodies. I didn't believe you, but you were correct.' He bowed to Elmund.

'It's all right,' Cwen assured him with a hearty thump on the back. 'We've already got the murder out of the way, it's not likely that there'll be another one.'

Martin gave a weak smile.

'Well, not very likely.'

Finis

Brother Hermitage does not know when to stop.

His misadventures continue in The 1066 From Normandy, which starts below - and there will probably be even more after that.

You have been warned.

The 1066 from Normandy

The Superfluous Chronicles of Brother Hermitage

by

Howard of Warwick

Caput I Visitation

The lone street of Derby was silent in the darkness of a still night as two figures shuffled through its shadows. They had shielded themselves from sight with long cloaks and hoods of dark material, and kept away from the paths, avoiding the risk of even a passing fox reporting their presence.

Their destination was well known in the neighbourhood, and that would be enough for most people to take up lurking. It was also a place of some wealth, and so those who lurked about it in the dark were to be treated with suspicion.

People who went anywhere in the dark these days were usually treated with the sharp end of a Norman sword. The invaders seemed to be very nervous people, considering their strength and military prowess. They clearly thought that everyone was out to get them; people lurking in the dark particularly so. They were right.

No one would stand up to a Norman in broad daylight, but get one on his own in the dark, preferably drunk, and there would be one less to worry about.

But this street was deserted, and the scuttling pair could make their progress without interruption.

Their journey had not been long. Being close by on other business had presented the perfect opportunity to achieve their goal in one night, and it was a very particular goal.

The workshop of Wat the Weaver was home to many attractions for the ordinary man. The more ordinary, and the more the man, the more the attraction.

Tapestry was a magical form, readily accessible for the common folk. Painting was a bit of a specialist activity and was only commissioned by the truly wealthy; the church, mainly. This meant that the images were pious and worthy and not remotely interesting.

Books were a source of more entertaining pictures. The borders and scribbles in margins were very imaginative and presented ordinary, day to day activities in all their detail; the toil of the field and the games of leisure. They also reported the common facts of the wider world, such as that a manticore had the body of a lion, the tail of a scorpion, the face of a man, and could shoot spikes from its mane. But then everyone knew all this, and very few of them had access to a book anyway.

Tapestry, on the other hand, was on display. It showed people going about their routine business and could be seen by anyone who passed by.

People tended to either pass by the tapestries of Wat the Weaver quite quickly or loiter in a very dubious manner. Wat's works displayed normal human activities, but ones that nice people didn't talk about, let alone have pictures of.

All that had changed when Wat invited Brother Hermitage to live in the workshop, but a lot of the common folk still thought of Wat as a fount of the sort of information their mother wouldn't tell them.

The old works of Wat were still out there in the world, mostly hidden under the bed, but that didn't stop people turning up at the workshop expecting to see something on display; well, everything on display, really.

Arriving under the cover of darkness was understandable, but not usually at this time of night. The works of Wat had value, and the less there were of them, the more that value went up. The trade in previously-owned Wat tapestries was booming; a fact that annoyed Wat no end.

The lurking of the visitors had now moved on to skulking.

They crept around the corners of buildings, ducked low under windows and stopped quickly at the slightest noise. They clearly knew the way, but one would go ahead to make sure the next part of their route was clear before the other joined him. Then they swapped roles.

It was understandable that people visiting Wat didn't want to be seen, but these two seemed to be going to extraordinary lengths. It might be a bit odd to see two men travelling at night, but it wasn't unheard of. Keep out of the way of the Normans was the only important instruction. In the dark, it was hard to tell friend from foe until the foe killed you with something. Better just to keep your head down.

Once they reached the end of the town, Wat's workshop being well beyond the last house at the request of the owner of the last house, they paused to take stock.

Their way appeared clear. There were no other folk abroad at this time of night and the darkness was covering their presence most effectively. There was open ground to cover now though. The chance of discovery increased and so the two men were cautious.

They waited and watched, giving the world around them time to make itself known. After a period, which seemed to be mutually and silently agreed, the first one stepped forward, still bent double, and hurried his way over to the low gate that marked the boundary of the workshop's land.

Squatting down by this and waiting yet again, the first man eventually beckoned to the second, who hurried over to join him.

From their position, they surveyed the building ahead of them. A large front door stood firmly shut, and above that, a window from the upper storey room looked down on them like a dark glass eye. To left and right, the building extended, the timbers of its construction standing proud of the wattle and daub infill painted with whitewash.

Further over to the right, other buildings could be seen peeping out from the rear. This was where most of the weaving equipment was and where the works were produced. Wat lent a hand and gave direction, but most of the actual weaving was done by apprentices.

Cwen, a fine young weaver in her own right, also gave instruction; along with criticism and complaint. But, if anyone spotted two people sneaking around the workshop in the middle of the night, it would be Cwen who tackled them; quite literally.

Brother Hermitage would stand there and look aghast, while Wat would offer helpful encouragement from some way off.

There was no movement at all from the workshop though, so the two new arrivals were emboldened to step through the gate, past the vegetable patch and up to the building itself.

Now they appeared to be uncertain for the first time. A whispered discussion concluded that they would go to the left first. Yes, the workshop was to the right, but the apprentices would be there as well; and everyone knew what apprentices got up to in the middle of the night. There was a chance one of them would be up and about and up to no good. Best to avoid any risk of contact.

The upper storey of the building was only one room and everything else was on ground level. Their target was bound to be through one of the windows that they would be able to reach quite easily. The problem was which one. They didn't want to climb in and be apprehended, they needed to know where they were going first.

Round the corner of the building they came to the first

window. This was dark and offered no clue as to what lay inside. The two men sat beneath it, breathing their recent exertion deeply until they were quiet once more.

One man nodded to the other, who slowly turned and rose to a squatting position, from where he could reach the window. Putting his hands on the wall to steady himself, he lifted his head until he could see through the window.

Eyes adjusting to the darkness within he peered hard until he could make out rough shapes. This was not the room he was looking for and so he ducked down again.

He shook his head to his companion, who returned an expression of some impatience. A proper Saxon dwelling would have been one large hall for everyone to eat and live in together. The workshop might have been separate, but that would be it. This bizarre arrangement, obviously preferred by Wat, where people had their own rooms was simply ridiculous. Not since the Romans had there been such extravagance. And it made the task of men in the dark finding what they were looking for, unnecessarily difficult.

Mind you, doing what they planned in a hall full of other people would have been doubly difficult.

With nodded agreement, the two moved on down the building to the next window.

At least this one had no glass in it. It was simply a hole in the side of the building covered with a cloth. The first man followed his process of creeping slowly upwards and lifted a corner of this to one side so that he could peer in. Holding his breath, he stuck his eyes and nose over the edge of the window and strained to see what was beyond.

He ducked down quickly as noises from the room startled him. They were the sounds of someone in their sleep, but it was still a shock. Whoever was in this room was having most vivid dreams, and not happy ones by the sound of it.

The first man shook his head once more and they moved on.

The next window didn't even have a cloth over it. This was just a bare opening and the two men exchanged hopeful looks.

The first man, who seemed to be in charge of window-peeping, now stood to the side of the opening and leaned around so that he could look fully into the room.

With no cloth or glass to obscure his view, he could see more clearly what this room contained. He looked down to his companion and nodded with a horrible smile. The smile he got back was no more pleasant, and the second man stood with a nod, indicating that the first could now get on with it.

Getting on with it involved climbing very carefully and cautiously through the window and into the room beyond. It wasn't a large opening, but this wasn't a large man. He lifted one leg and slid it over the low sill, ducking his head down to slip into the room like a snake of very bad intent.

With a raised hand, the first man indicated that the second should stay put to receive whatever was being taken.

Again pausing so that he could see what he was doing, the first man stepped slowly and quietly forward. In front of him, he saw his goal. A bundle of material was laid out on a low shelf, just ready for the taking. It would need careful handling though, but he had come prepared. Taking a length of material from his belt he stepped up to tie it around his prize.

Quickly, and with obvious experience at this sort of thing, he had the treasure secured and hoisted into his arms. He stepped quickly over to the window and leaned out so that his companion could take the weight.

With their ill-gotten gains out of the house, the two men

quickly retreated into the shadows and made their escape. With any luck, it would be hours before anyone in the workshop was up, let alone discovered that something was missing.

The second man now paused for a moment to haul the load up onto his shoulder and the two of them set off at a fast pace to make sure they were nowhere near Derby when the sun rose.

...

Mornings in the workshop followed their normal routine; mostly chaos with Wat sitting in the middle of it doing nothing to help.

The apprentices had to be roused from their slumber by Hartle, the ancient weaving master, whose shouts and insults were their normal greeting. Bleary-eyed, they stumbled about, doing their very best to fall asleep again wherever they were.

Mrs Grod, Wat's disgusting cook of disgusting food, materialised before daybreak, striding up the path from wherever it was she spent the night. She needed the whole morning to prepare the noon meal for everyone who was going to eat it: which excluded Wat, Cwen, Hartle and Hermitage. A strong young apprentice stomach was required to cope with Mrs Grod's cooking.

The apprentices spent many an entertaining evening speculating on where Mrs Grod went at night. Few of the speculations were either wholesome or actually possible.

Cwen emerged from her own chamber instantly ready for the day and critical of anyone who wasn't. She could only scowl and grumble at Wat, who just sat with his morning beer. The apprentices she could scold and harry, and they soon made their way to the workshop to pick up where they had left off.

Once she and Hartle were satisfied that they were actually doing what they were told, the two of them retreated to find Wat and discuss whether there was any special work that required their attention today.

The oldest loom in the place was showing increasing signs of wear, and Wat's continuous refusal to pay the loom maker for a new one was getting embarrassing. A couple of the apprentices, who seemed more interested than most in loom maintenance and repair, were spending more days fixing the thing than using it.

And it was the biggest one they had. Wat and Cwen had come back from Lincoln with a commission for a very pious and very large tapestry. The client, Godrinius, had started a bit of a trend for pious tapestries amongst the well-to-do Saxons. It was one means of showing King William what a wonderfully devout person you were and how there was no need to take your land and kill your family at all.

The old loom was the only thing capable of producing such works, and there was a very good chance it would collapse completely any day now.

Cwen and Hartle exchanged low whispers as they went to find Wat. Perhaps this was the day that their combined strength might force his fingers into his purse.

Hermitage would join them after his morning devotions, which seemed to go on most of the morning. Many times, he had tried to get Wat to instigate prayers before the day began but seemed to know that his task was hopeless.

Between the three of them, they speculated that giving Wat a choice between buying a new loom or allowing the apprentices half an hour away from work to pray, might kill him.

This time, Hartle carried the latest piece of wood to fall from the loom. The fact that this was mostly dust, held together by woodworm holes, should be evidence that the time to spend was fast approaching.

Agreeing their tactics, Cwen and Hartle made their way to the upper chamber, where they knew Wat would be loitering, enjoying the peace and quiet.

'Well, it's simple, isn't it?' Hartle said aloud.

'Of course,' Cwen agreed.

'We just have to tell them that they can't have their tapestries. Of course, they won't pay, but I'm sure we can manage that.'

'And fortunately, we don't have to tell them, Wat does.'

'Ha, ha. Yes, Good point.'

'Go on, then,' Wat said as they appeared at the top of the stairs. 'What's the latest?'

Hartle held out the piece of wood. 'Heddle peg end,' he announced.

'Every home should have one,' Wat said.

Hartle went over to the window, pushed open the one pane that moved, and flamboyantly crumbled the wood to bits in his hand. 'I imagine you don't want the woodworm moving on to eat the house as well as the loom.'

'A heddle peg's easy enough to replace.'

'And then there's the cloth beam, the shed bar, the crankshaft. Basically, if it isn't cloth or the stone of the heddle weights, the worms have eaten it. You need a new loom.'

'Now,' Cwen added. 'Because if you don't order it now, it won't be here in time to complete the orders.'

'The apprentices can make a loom. Be good for them.'

'They could,' Hartle agreed. 'You've still got to buy the

wood though. And then take the apprentices off the work they're already doing, and wait twice as long for a loom that will be half as good.'

And thus, the discussion continued. Hartle and Cwen made very good arguments for the new loom, and Wat ignored them. As they pointed out, he had no good arguments against them, apart from the fact he didn't want to spend his money.

When Cwen eventually suggested that she and Hartle might put their money together to buy a loom themselves, Wat brightened a little. When they went on to say that this would mean they owned a share of the workshop, he dimmed again.

One of the tapestry orders had come from the Saxon, Thorkill of Warwick. Along with Colesvain of Lincoln, he was the only surviving Saxon noble to retain his estates after the conquest. He had achieved this by being a sycophantic supporter of William and had even started modelling himself on the epitome of the good Norman. This meant that he killed people quite regularly, and a weaver who didn't deliver would be an ideal target.

The prospect of death did focus Wat's attention.

'Hermitage,' he said.

'What about him?' Cwen couldn't see what Hermitage had to do with this.

'He does arguments and the like.'

'He does arguments?'

'You know, working out who's right and wrong.'

'I suppose so. But it's mainly to do with the bible.'

'Yes, but I'm sure he could think about this one.'

'You mean we let Hermitage decide?' Cwen was very surprised at this suggestion. From her experience, Hermitage loved to consider a good argument. He loved to consider them so much that he never came down on one side or the other.

'Can't do any harm?'

Cwen was pretty confident that she could persuade Hermitage to agree with her. With a glance at Hartle, she skipped back down the stairs to interrupt Hermitage's morning prayers.

Hartle sat and took a mug of Wat's beer, doing his best to look very disappointed at this whole situation.

After some time of embarrassed waiting; the embarrassment all being Hartle's, Cwen reappeared.

'Well?' Wat asked.

'Don't know where he is,' Cwen said with a disinterested shrug. 'Perhaps someone's stolen him.'

The 1066 From Normandy is available now.

Printed in Great Britain
by Amazon